Tor Books by Terry Bisson

BEARS DISCOVER FIRE AND OTHER STORIES

PIRATES OF THE UNIVERSE

In the Upper Room

AND OTHER LIKELY STORIES

TERRY BISSON

TOR®

A TOM DOHERTY ASSOCIATES BOOK
NEW YORK

IN THE UPPER ROOM AND OTHER LIKELY STORIES

Copyright © 2000 by Terry Bisson

This book is printed on acid-free paper.

Edited by David G. Hartwell

A Tor Book
Published by Tom Doherty Associates, LLC
175 Fifth Avenue
New York, NY 10010

www.tor.com

Tor® is a registered trademark of Tom Doherty Associates, LLC

Book design by Jane Adele Regina

Library of Congress Cataloging-in-Publication Data

Bisson, Terry.
    In the upper room and other likely stories / Terry Bisson.
        p. cm.
    "A Tom Doherty Associates book."
    ISBN 0-312-87404-9 (hc)
    ISBN 0-312-87420-0 (pbk)
    1. Science fiction, American.   I. Title.
PS3552.I7736 I5   2000
813'.54—dc21   00-025138
                                                CIP

First Hardcover Edition: May 2000
First Trade Paperback Edition: June 2001

Printed in the United States of America

0 9 8 7 6 5 4 3 2 1

COPYRIGHT ACKNOWLEDGMENTS

The stories in this collection first appeared
in the following publications:

"In the Upper Room," *Playboy*, May 1996

"There Are No Dead," *Omni*, January 1995

"The Edge of the Universe," *Asimov's*, August 1996

"The Joe Show," *Playboy*, August 1994

"macs," *The Magazine of Fantasy & Science Fiction*, October 1999

"Tell Them They Are All Full of Shit and They Should Fuck Off," *Crank*, Autumn 1994

"The Player," *The Magazine of Fantasy & Science Fiction*, October 1997

"An Office Romance," *Playboy*, February 1997

"10:07:24," *Absolute Magnitude*, Winter 1995

"First Fire," *SF Age*, September 1998

"Get Me to the Church on Time," *Asimov's*, May 1998

"Smoother," *The Magazine of Fantasy & Science Fiction*, January 1999

"Incident at Oak Ridge," *The Magazine of Fantasy & Science Fiction*, July 1998

"Dead Man's Curve," *Asimov's*, June 1994

"He Loved Lucy," *Playboy*, March 2000

"Not This Virginia," *Southern Exposure*, Summer 1999

For JJ
still Still the One

CONTENTS

In the Upper Room

AND OTHER LIKELY STORIES

In the Upper Room

Y ou will feel a slight chill," the attendant said. "Don't worry about it. Just go with it, okay?"

"Okay," I said. I had heard all this before.

"You will feel a slight disorientation. Don't worry about it. A part of you will be aware of where you are, and another part will be aware of where you *really* are, if you know what I mean. Just go with it, okay?"

"Okay," I said. "Actually, I have heard all this before. I was on the Amazon Adventure last year."

"You were? Well, I am required to say it anyway," the attendant said. "Where was I? Oh yes, go slow!" He wore squeaky shoes and a white coat and carried a little silver hammer in a loop on his pants. "If you look at things too closely at first, nothing will be there. But if you take your time, everything will appear, okay?"

"Okay," I said. "What about—?"

"You won't know her name," he said. "Not in the demo. But if you sign up for a tour, you will know it automatically. Ready? Lie down. Take a deep breath."

Ready or not, the drawer started sliding in and I felt a moment of panic, which I remembered from last year. The panic makes you take another breath, and then there is the sharp smell of the Vitazine™, and there you are. It is like waking from a dream. I was in a sunlit room with a thick pile rug and high French windows. She stood at the windows overlooking what appeared to be a busy street, as long as you were careful not to look at it too closely.

I was careful not to look at it too closely. She was wearing a burgundy sandwashed silk chemise with a sheer lace empire bodice, cross-laced on the low plunge back. No stockings. I have never liked stockings. She was barefoot but I couldn't make out her feet. I was careful not to look at them too closely.

I liked the way the bodice did on the sides. After a while I looked around the room. There was wicker furniture and a few potted plants by a low door. I had to duck my head to step through and I was in a kitchen with a tile floor and blue cabinets. She stood at the sink under a little window that overlooked a green, glistening yard. She was wearing a long-sleeved stretch panne velvet bodysuit with a low sweetheart neckline, high-cut sides, and a full back. I liked the way the velvet did in the back. I stood beside her at the window watching the robins arrive and depart on the grass. It was the same robin over and over.

A white wall phone rang. She picked it up and handed it to me, and as soon as I put the receiver to my ear and heard the tone, I was looking up toward what seemed, at first, to be clouds but was in fact the water-stained ceiling of the Departure Hall.

I sat up. "That's it?" I asked.

"That's the demo," said the attendant, who was hurrying over to my opened drawer, shoes squeaking. "The phone is what exits you out of the system. Like the doors elevate you from level to level."

"I like it," I said. "My vacation starts tomorrow. Where do I sign up?"

"Slow down," he said, helping me out of the drawer. "The Veep is by invitation only. You have to talk to Cisneros in Client Services first."

"The Veep?"

"That's what we call it sometimes."

Last year I did the Amazon Adventure," I said to Dr. Cisneros. "This year I have a week, starting tomorrow, and I came in to sign up for the Arctic Adventure. That's when I saw the Victoria's Palace demo in the brochure."

"Victoria's is just opening," she said. "Actually we are still beta-testing sectors of it. Only the middle and upper middle rooms are open. But that should be plenty for a five-day tour."

"How many rooms is that?"

"Lots." She smiled. Her teeth looked new. The little thing on her desk said B. CISNEROS, PH.D. "Technically speaking, the Veep is a hierarchical pyramid string, so the middle and upper middle includes all the rooms but one. All but the Upper Room."

I blushed. I'm always blushing.

"You wouldn't be getting that high in just five days anyway." She showed me her new teeth again. "And since we're still beta-testing, we can make you a special offer. The same price they charge for the Arctic and Amazon Adventures. A five-day 'week,' nine to five, for $899. The price will go up substantially when Victoria's Palace is fully open next year, I can assure you."

"I like it," I said. I stood up. "Where do I go to pay?"

"Accounts. But sit back down." She opened a manila folder. "First I am required to ask a clinical question. Which is: why do you want to spend your vacation in Victoria's Palace?"

I shrugged to keep from blushing. "It's different and that appeals to me. You might say I'm a sort of VR freak."

"Direct Experience," she corrected primly. "And the word is 'enthusiast.'"

"DE, then. Whatever." Every company has its own name for it. "Anyway, I like it. My mother says I—"

Dr. Cisneros cut me off by raising her hand like a traffic cop. "This is not the answer I need," she said. "Let me explain. Because of its content, Victoria's Palace is not licensed as an adventure simulation like the Arctic or the Amazon. Under our certification, we can operate only as a therapeutic simulation. Are you married?"

"Sort of," I said. I could just as easily have said, "Not exactly."

"Good." She made a mark in the folder. "Our most *acceptable* Victoria's Palace clients—the only ones we can accept, in fact— are married men who want to improve the intimacy level of their relationships through frank exploration of their innermost sexual fantasies."

"That's me," I said. "A married man who wants to enter the most intimacy through Frank's sexual fantasies."

"Close enough," Dr. Cisneros said. She made another mark in the folder and slid it toward me with a smile. "Sign this release and you can start tomorrow morning at nine. Accounts is down the hall on the left."

That night Mother asked, "What did you do today? If anything."

"I signed up at Inward Bound," I said. "My vacation starts tomorrow."

"You haven't worked in two years."

"I quit my job," I said. "I didn't quit my vacation."

"Didn't you do Inward Bound already?"

"I did the Amazon Adventure last year. This year I'm doing the, uh, Arctic Adventure."

Mother looked skeptical. She always looks skeptical.

"We're going for a seal hunt along the edge of the polynya," I said.

"Who's this Pollyanna? Somebody new at last?"

"It's where the ice never freezes over."

"Suit yourself," Mother said. "But you don't need me to tell you that. You always have. You got another letter from Peggy Sue today."

"Her name is Barbara Ann, Mother."

"Whatever. I signed for it and put it with the others. Don't you think you ought to at least open it? You have a stack this high on that thing you call a dresser."

"What's for supper," I said to change the subject.

The next morning I was first in line at Inward Bound. I was let into the Departure Hall at precisely nine, and I sat down on a stool outside my drawer and changed into robe and sandals.

"What's the little silver hammer for?" I asked the attendant when he showed up in his squeaky shoes.

"Sometimes the drawers are hard to open," he said. "Or close. Lie down. You did the Amazon last summer, right?"

I nodded.

"I thought so. I never forget a face." He was sticking the little things to my forehead. "How high did you go? Could you see the Andy?"

"The And*es*," I said. "You could see them in the distance. The jungle girls wore little bark bras."

"You'll see plenty of little bras in the Veep. Five days will get you pretty high there too. Don't look around the rooms too soon, because as soon as you see a door you will go through it. Slow down and enjoy yourself. Close your eyes."

I closed my eyes. "Thanks for the tip," I said.

"I worked on the programming," he said. "Breathe deep." The drawer slid in, there was the sharp smell of the Vitazine™, and it was like waking from a dream. I was in a dark, wood-paneled library. She was standing by an arched Tudor window with narrow panes overlooking what appeared to be a garden. She was wearing a tangerine seamed silk charmeuse teddy with flutters of lace trim at the sides and a low-cut bodice with covered buttons and lace-trimmed wide-set straps. For a moment I thought I didn't know her name, but then I said it: "Chemise." It was like opening your hand and finding something you had forgotten you were holding.

I joined her at the window. The garden was filled with low hedges and gravel walks that spun if you looked at them too closely. I looked away and that's when I saw the door. It was in the far wall, between two bookcases. I ducked my head to go through and I was in a wallpapered bedroom with white-framed windows. The floor was pine with knitted throw rugs.

"Chemise," I said. She was standing between two windows wearing a strapless bodysuit in creamy white stretch satin, with underwire cups and a plunging V-center. The cups were edged with white lace. The treetops just below the window were shimmering as if in a breeze.

I was getting higher. The sheer satin back of her bodysuit was cut in a low V that matched the V in front. I liked the way the straps did. As soon as I turned away I saw the door. It was down one step, and I had to duck my head, and I was in a long, dark room with narrow windows hung with heavy drapes. Chemise was kneeling on a curved love seat wearing a baby-blue baby doll in sheer tulle with lace trim, over a ruffled bra and matching panty. Using one hand I pulled back the drapes. I could see treetops far below, and beneath them, brick streets wet with rain.

I sat down beside her. Her face was still turned away but I could tell that she was smiling. And why not? She didn't exist unless I was with her. She wore little slippers trimmed with lace like her panties. I'm not into feet but they made her feet look sexy. I lingered, letting the lace on her panties make an identical pattern on my heart. Then I thought I heard a faint voice calling for help.

I turned and saw a low, arched hole in the wall. It was hardly bigger than a mousehole. I had to lie flat on my belly, and even then I could barely squirm through one shoulder at a time.

I was in a concrete-floored hallway with no windows. The walls were bare. The floor was cold and it sloped in two directions at once. It was hard to stand. There was a stack of new lumber against one wall and a girl was sitting on it wearing a red hat.

A baseball cap–type hat. She stood up. She was wearing a tee shirt that read:

MERLYN SISTEMS
Software that works hard.

I could feel myself getting confused. "Chemise?"

"Not Chemise," she said.

"Not Chemise," I said. "What are you doing here? This is my—"

"This isn't your anything," she said. "You're not in the Veep right now. You're running parallel, in a programmer's loop."

"How did you get here, then?"

"I'm the programmer."

"A girl?"

"Of course, a girl." She was wearing full-cut white cotton panties under her tee shirt. "What do you think?"

"I'm not supposed to have to think." I could feel myself getting annoyed. "This is Direct Experience. And you are not one of my fantasies."

"Don't be too sure. I'm a damsel in distress. And you're a guy. You came when I called, didn't you? I need your help to get to the Upper Room."

The Upper Room! She said it so casually. "They told me it's—not open yet."

"It is if you know how to get to it," she said. "There's a shortcut through the mouseholes."

"Mouseholes?"

"You ask too many questions. I'll show you. But you have to do exactly what I say. You can't be looking around on your own."

"Why not?" I could feel myself getting annoyed again. I looked around the room just to prove I could. I saw a door.

"Because . . ." she said, behind me.

But I was already stepping through, ducking my head. I was in an old-fashioned kitchen with white-painted wooden cabinets. Chemise stood at the counter stirring a pot with a pair of big scissors. She was wearing a low-cut, smooth-fitting strapless bra in stretch satin and lace with lightly lined underwire cups, and a high-cut, wide-band brief with a sheer lace panel in the front, all in white. "Chemise!" I said. I wondered if she had wondered where I had been.

But of course she hadn't. Behind her someone was either getting into or out of a pantry door.

It was me.

I was wearing an Inward Bound robe and shower sandals.

It was me.

I was wearing an Inward

It was

I was looking straight up at the water-stained ceiling of the Departure Hall.

"What happened?" I asked. My heart was pounding. I could hear shoes squeaking frantically. A buzzer was buzzing somewhere. Mine was the only drawer that was open.

"System crash," the attendant said. "They want to see you upstairs in Client Services. Right away."

Our bitmaps show you in places you couldn't have been," said Dr. Cisneros. She was looking back and forth between the manila folder on her desk and something on her computer screen that I couldn't see. "Areas you couldn't possibly have entered." She looked across the desk at me and her new teeth glittered. "Unless there is something you're not telling me."

When in doubt I play dumb. "Like what?"

"You didn't see anyone *else* in the palace, did you? Anyone besides yourself and your DE image construct?"

"Another girl?" I decided to go with my instinct, which is always to lie. "No."

"Could be a simple system error," Dr. Cisneros said. "We'll have it sorted out by tomorrow."

How'd it go today?" Mother asked.

"Go?"

"Your Pollyanna, your arctic misadventure."

"Oh, fine," I lied. I have always lied to Mother, on principle. The truth is too complicated. "I learned to handle a kayak. Lots of open water tomorrow."

"Speaking of open water," Mother said, "I opened those letters today. Lucille says you *have* to come and get your stuff. She swears he won't hit you again."

"Barbara Ann, Mother," I said. "And I wish you wouldn't open my mail."

"If wishes were pennies we'd all be rich. I stacked them back in the same order. Don't you think you should answer at least one?"

"I need my rest," I said. "We go after basking seals tomorrow. We stalk them across the ice."

"With guns?"

"With clubs. You know I hate guns."

"That's even worse."

"They're not real, Mother."

"The clubs or the seals?"

"Neither. None of it is real. It's Direct Experience."

"My $899 is real."

I was one of the first ones into the Departure Hall the next morning. I took off my clothes and sat down on the bench and waited for the attendant. I watched the other guys file in, mostly wearing parkas and safari outfits. Their attendants had them in their drawers by 8:58.

At 9:14 Squeaky Shoes showed up. "What's the delay?" I asked.

"Bug in the system," he said. "But we're getting it." He was sticking the little things to my forehead. "Close your eyes."

Bug? I closed my eyes. I heard the drawer rumble; I smelled the sharp smell of the Vitazine™ and it was like waking from a dream. Chemise was sitting on a brocaded settee under an open window, wearing a plum-red stretch velvet baby tee with lattice edging and elastic-trimmed neckline over matching high-cut bikini panties.

"Chemise," I said. I tried to concentrate but I couldn't help feeling I had been higher yesterday. A dog walked through the room. The window looked down on a formal garden with curving brick walkways. The sky was blue and cloudless.

Chemise was looking away. I sat down beside her, feeling restless. I was about to get up again when I thought I heard a faint voice calling for help. I looked down and saw a crack in the baseboard. It was too small to put my hand in but I was able to crawl through on my belly, one shoulder at a time.

I was in the concrete hallway again, with stacks of lumber shimmering against one wall. The girl in the red hat was yelling at me: "You almost got me killed!"

"Bug?" I said.

"What did you call me?"

"Not Chemise?" I tried. She was sitting on a stack of lumber, wearing her

MERLYN SISTEMS
Software that works hard.

tee shirt over white cotton panties cut high on the sides.

"Not Not Chemise. You called me something else."

"Bug."

"Bug. I like that." She had gray eyes. "But you have to quit looking around. We have to go through the mouseholes, not the doors, or you might meet yourself again."

"Then that *was* me I saw!"

"That's what crashed the system. You almost got me killed."

"If the system crashes you die?"

"Supposedly. Luckily I had saved myself. All I lost was a little memory. A little *more* memory."

"Oh," I said.

"Let's get going. I can take you to the Upper Room," she said.

I tried to sound casual. "I thought you wanted me to take you."

"Same thing. I know the route through the mouseholes. Watch me or watch the hat. Let's get moving. Clyde'll get the cat out soon."

"Cat? I saw a dog."

"Oh, shit! We better get moving, then!" She threw the red hat behind me. Where it hit I found a wide crack in the concrete floor. It was tight but I managed to crawl through on my belly pushing one shoulder through and then the other. I was in a bright room with one whole wall of windows. Potted plants were stacked on boxes and on the sofa. There was no place to sit down. Bug was standing by the window, wearing a pale peach demi bra with adjustable tapered straps and deep front décolleté, and a matching tanga bikini with full back. And the red hat.

I stood beside her at the window. I expected to see treetops but all I saw were clouds, far below. I had never been so high.

"That cat, that dog you saw, is a system debugger," she said. "Sniffs out mouseholes. If it finds me I'm a goner."

I liked the way her bra did in the back. "Do you mind if I call you Bug?"

"I already told you, I sort of like it," she said. "Especially since I don't remember my name."

"You don't remember your name?"

"I lost some memory when the system crashed," she said. She looked almost sad. "Not to mention when Clyde killed me."

"Who's Clyde? Who are *you*, anyway?"

"You ask too many questions," she said. "I'm Bug, that's all, a damsel in distress, and that's one of your fantasies, so let's get going. We can talk on the way."

She threw the red hat against the wall. I found it in the corner, where the wallpaper was pulled loose revealing a crack barely large enough for my fingertips. It was tight but I was able to manage, one shoulder at a time. I was in a bedroom with a bay window. Bug was—

"Do you mind if I call you Bug?"

"I told you, it's okay." Bug was standing at the window wearing a pearl-white satin jacquard demi bra, accented with scalloped trim along the deep V-center, and a string bikini with a sheer stretch back, accented with one little bow. And the hat of course.

"Clyde'll find me here in the Veep sooner or later, especially now that they suspect a bug. But if I can make it to the Upper Room, I can port through to the other systems."

"What other systems?"

"The Arctic, the Amazon, whatever adventures they add later. All the franchises are interfaced at the top. It'll be like life. Life after Clyde."

"Who's . . ."

"Shit!" A phone was ringing. Bug picked it up and handed it to me. It was porcelain with brass trim, like a fancy toilet. Before

I could say "hello" I found myself staring up at the water-stained ceiling of the Departure Hall.

"Client Services wants to see you," said the attendant. For the first time I noticed the name stitched on his white jacket. It was CLYDE.

You still seem to be showing up in rooms where you aren't supposed to be," said Dr. Cisneros. "On code strings that aren't connected. Unauthorized pathways." Dr. Cisneros had been eating lunch at her desk, judging by the little pile of bones at the edge of her blotter. "Are you positive you haven't noticed anything unusual?"

I had to tell her something, so I told her about the dog.

"Oh, that. That's Clyde's cat. The system debugger. He configures it as a dog. It's his idea of a joke."

Sometimes the smart thing is to act dumb. "What kind of bug are you looking for?" I asked.

Dr. Cisneros swiveled the computer monitor on her desk so that I could see the screen. She hit a key and a still picture came up. I wasn't surprised to see Bug—wearing the MERLYN SISTEMS tee shirt and the red hat, of course. She also wore baggy Levi's and glasses. "Early this year one of our programmers was caught illegally altering proprietary software, which is, as you know, a federal crime. We had no choice but to call BATF&S. But while she was free on bail awaiting trial she illegally entered the system."

"As a client?" I asked.

"As a trespasser with criminal intent. Perhaps even sabotage. She may have been carrying a ResEdit. She may have left loops or subroutines designed to render the software unstable or even dangerous. Unexecutable routines, unauthorized pathways."

"I don't understand what this has to do with me," I said. Mother always said I was good at lying. Mother ought to know.

"The danger to you," Dr. Cisneros said, "is that one of these unauthorized pathways might lead to the Upper Room. And the Upper Room is not, at present, exitable. It's an enter-only. You may have noticed that Victoria's Palace is a one-way system, from lower to higher rooms. It's like the universe. You go until you hit an exit sequence."

"The phone rings," I said.

"Yes," said Dr. Cisneros. "That was Clyde's idea. A nice touch, don't you think? But at present there's no exit sequence, or phone as you call it, installed in the Upper Room."

"Isn't there a door?"

"There's an in door but no out door. Where would the out door go? The Upper Room is at the top of the code string. The client would be trapped. Maybe forever."

"So what do you want me to do?"

"Keep your eyes open. Rogue programmers have rogue egos. They often leave signature stuff lying around: clues. If you see anything odd, like a picture of her, a little token left around, try and remember what room it is in. It will help us isolate the damage."

"Like a red hat."

"Exactly."

"Or her herself."

Cisneros shook her head. "It would only be a copy. She's dead. She committed suicide before we could have her re-apprehended."

Rhonda left another message on your machine," Mother said when I got home.

"Barbara Ann," I corrected.

"Whatever. She says she's going to bring your stuff over here and leave it on the lawn. She says Jerry Lewis . . ."

"Jerry Lee, Mother."

"Whatever. Her new guy, he needs your old room. Apparently they're not sleeping together either."

"Mother!" I said.

"She says if you don't come and get your stuff she's going to throw it out."

"I wish you wouldn't play my messages," I said. "What's the point of having two machines?"

"I can't help it. Your machine recognizes my voice."

"That's because you try and talk like me."

"I don't have to try," Mother said. "How was your day? Bash any baskin' robins?"

"Very funny," I said. "We did club a large number of basking seals today. They weren't babies though. We club the old seals, the ones that have borne their children and outlived their usefulness to the tribe."

I gave her a look but she chose to ignore it.

The next morning I was the first one in the Departure Hall. "Get squared away with Bonnie?" the attendant asked.

"Bonnie?"

"Hold still." He was sticking the little things to my forehead. "Lie down." It was like waking from a dream. I was in a library with an arched glass window overlooking faraway hills. Chemise had taken down a book and was leafing through the pages. She was wearing a black camisole embroidered with velvet jacquard on whisper-weight sheer voile, with slender straps, deeply cut cups, and a full stretch lace back. I could see that the pages were blank. "Chemise," I said. I wanted to tell her I was sorry I was neglecting her. I liked the way her cups did when she bent over but I had to find Bug. I had to warn her that Dr. Cisneros and Clyde were looking for her.

I searched along the baseboards looking for a mousehole until I found a crack behind a warped board. It was barely big enough to stick a hand in, but I was able to crawl through on my belly and wedge one shoulder in at a time.

I was back in the concrete hallway.

Bug was standing beside a pile of two by fours, wearing her MERLYN SISTEMS tee shirt over French-cut white cotton bikini panties with scalloped lace trim along the seams. And the red hat of course. And glasses!

"What's with the glasses?" she asked me. She tried to take them off but couldn't.

"They know about you," I said. "They showed me a picture of you. With glasses."

"Of course they know about me! Clyde for damn sure knows about me."

"I mean, they know you're in here. Although they think you're dead."

"Well, I am dead, but I won't be in here long. Not if we get to the Upper Room." She took off her red hat and sailed it down the hall. It landed by a break in the concrete where the floor met the wall. It was too small for even a mouse but I was able to wriggle through, first my fingertips and then one shoulder and then the other. I was in a conservatory with big bay windows overlooking bright, high clouds that looked like ruined castles. Bug—

"Do you mind if I call you Bug?"

"Jesus, I told you, it's okay!" Bug was standing by the window wearing a sheer white voile bra with lace-embroidered cups and a matching panty with lace inserts on the front and sides. And the red hat. And the glasses.

"I'm willing to help," I said. "But this Upper Room stuff sounds dangerous."

"Dangerous? Who says?"

"Client Services."

"Cisneros? That cunt!"

"I wish you wouldn't call her that. She says once I get *in* the Upper Room I can't get *out*. Like a roach motel. No phone."

"Hmmmm." Bug looked straight at me. Her gray eyes looked worried. "I didn't think of that. Let's go higher, where we can talk." She threw the red hat and it landed next to a little wedge-shaped hole barely big enough for me to crawl into on my belly, squeezing one shoulder through at a time. I was in a dark room with heavy drapes and no furniture except for an oriental rug on the floor. Bug—

"Do you mind if I call you Bug?"

"Will you stop it!? Why does DE make people so stupid?"

"Beats me," I said.

Bug was sitting on the floor, wearing a white faux-satin bra with scoop-cut cups trimmed with an embroidery edge, and a matching white faux-satin string bikini. "Bug is not really my name," she said. "It's either Catherine or Eleanor, I forget which. It's one of the things that goes when they kill you."

"They told me you committed suicide."

"Suicide with a hammer, right!" I liked her laugh. I liked the way the strings on her string bikini did. They were like tiny versions of the velvet ropes in theaters. "They got me arrested, that much of what Bonnie told you is true. I'd been creating illegal subroutines, mouseholes, to allow movement throughout the Veep. That's true too. What she didn't tell you is, Clyde and I were partners in crime. Well, how could she know? That cunt. I put the mouseholes in, buried them in the mainstream code string so later Clyde and I could access the Palace on our own. Blackmail and extortion was our game. Clyde designed the Palace and he left the mouseholes up to me. That's the way we always worked. What I didn't know was that he was already in cahoots with Cisneros."

"What are cahoots?"

Bug made a vulgar gesture with a thumb and two fingers; I looked away. "Cisneros owns fifty-five percent of the franchise. Which made her irresistible to poor Clyde, I guess. For months they had been playing Bonnie and Clyde behind my back, while I was busy hacking away. Anyway, when Victoria's Palace got accepted at Inward Bound some franchise checker dude found the mouseholes—I hadn't really bothered hiding them—and he told Cisneros, and she told Clyde, and he pretended to be shocked and outraged! Set me up. So as soon as I got out on bail I went in to get my stuff . . ."

"Your stuff?"

"Subroutines, proprietary macros, picts and diffs. I was going to rip it all out. And maybe trash the place a little. I was carrying a ResEdit so I could rewrite code even as I was riding it. But Clyde got wind somehow. So he murdered me."

"With the little hammer."

"You're beginning to get the picture. Just opened the drawer and *whack*, right between the eyes. What Clyde didn't know was that I could save myself. I always run with a little autosave macro that I wrote back in community college, so I only lost about ten minutes, and some memory. And my life of course. I ducked into the mousehole space but who the hell wants to live like a rat forever? I was waiting for my prince to come and take me to the Upper Room."

"Your prince?"

"Finger of speech. I was waiting for the Veep to open. Any dude would have done."

"*Figure* of speech," I said.

"Whatever. Anyway, what Cisneros doesn't know—or Clyde either—is that the Upper Room is interfaced at the top with the other Inward Bound areas, the Arctic and Amazon franchises. I'll be able to get out of the Palace. And as more and more modules get added, my universe will get bigger and bigger. If I watch my ass, I'll live forever. Or haven't you noticed, there's no death in DE?"

She stood up and yawned. I liked the pink inside of her mouth. She took off the hat and threw it against the wall. It landed by a little opening under the baseboard. It was tight but I managed to squeeze through one shoulder at a time. I was in a stone room with a tiny slit window and a folding chair. Bug—

"Do you mind if I call you Bug?"

"Will you knock it off! Come over here."

Bug was wearing a black lace demi bra with deep décolleté cups and wide-set straps, and a matching black lace thong panty with little bows on the side. And the red hat, of course. And the glasses. She made room so that I could stand beside her on the chair and see out of the slit window. I could almost see the curve of the Earth. I could almost feel the curve of her hip against mine, even though I knew it was my imagination. Imagination is everything in DE.

"We're not so far from the Upper Room," she said. "Look how high you've gotten me already. But Cisneros is right about one thing."

"What?"

"You can't take me into the Upper Room. You'd be stuck. No way back."

"What about you?" I liked the little bows.

"I'm already stuck. I don't have a body to go back to. You provide this one, I guess." She peered through her glasses down the front of her bra, down the front of her panties. "Which is why I'm still wearing glasses, I guess."

"I'd like to help you get to the Upper Room," I said. "But why can't you go in by yourself?"

"I can't move up, only down," Bug said. "I'm dead, remember? If only I still had my ResEdit, I could . . . Shit!" There was a phone. We had hardly noticed it until it rang. "It's for you," she said, handing me the receiver.

Before I could say "hello" I was staring up at the water-stained ceiling of the Departure Hall. I heard shoes squeaking. The attendant helped me out of the drawer. Clyde.

"Four-fifty-five already?" I asked.

"Time flies when you're having fun," he said.

Guess who's here," Mother said.

I heard the snarl of a toilet flushing in the bathroom.

"I don't want to see her," I said.

"She came all the way from Salem," Mother said. "She brought your stuff."

"Where is it, then?"

"It's still in her car. I wouldn't let her bring it in," said Mother. "That's why she's crying."

"She's not crying!" a deep voice called out.

"My God!" I said, alarmed. "Is he in there with her?"

"She's not taking it back!" the same deep voice called out. Another toilet flushed. Mother has two in her bathroom, one for me and one for her.

"I'm on my vacation!" I said. The bathroom doorknob started to turn and I went for a walk. When I got back they were gone and my stuff was on the lawn.

"You could dig a hole," said Mother. "And cover it."

• • •

I was the first one in the Departure Hall the next morning. But instead of opening my drawer, Squeaky Shoes, the attendant—Clyde—gave me a paper to sign.

"I already signed a release," I said.

"This is for our own protection," he said.

I signed. "Good," he said and smiled. It was not a nice smile. "Now lie down. Now take a deep breath." The drawer slid shut. I inhaled the Vitazine™ and it was like waking from a dream.

I was in a formal living room with a cream-colored rug, couch, and chair. Chemise was standing at the picture window wearing an ivory underwire bra in satin jacquard with low plunge center and wide-set straps, and matching bikini panties with a sheer stretch panel in front. She was holding a cup and saucer, also matching. Through the window I could see rolling hills stretching to a horizon. A dog trotted through the room.

"Chemise," I said. I wished I had time to explain things to her, but I knew I had to find Bug.

I looked around for a mousehole. Behind a lamp, in a dark corner, there was a low arch, like the entrance to a tiny cave. I could barely negotiate the narrow passage, shrugging one shoulder through at a time.

"What took you so long?" Bug was sitting in the concrete hallway on a gleaming stack of lumber, her knees pulled up under her chin. She was wearing her MERLYN SISTEMS tee shirt over a tiny thong bikini. And the red hat and the glasses, of course.

"They made me sign another release."

"And you signed it?"

I nodded. I liked the way the thong made a little V, then disappeared.

"You moron! Do you realize that by signing the release you gave Clyde the right to kill you?"

"I wish you wouldn't call me that," I said.

"Fucking Bonnie and Clyde! Now I'll *never* get to the Upper Room!" I was afraid she was about to cry. Instead, she hurled the red hat angrily to the floor and when I bent down to pick it up I saw a crack barely large enough for three fingertips but I was able to squeeze through by crawling on my belly and pushing one shoulder in at a time. I was in an empty room with bare wood floors and windows so new that the stickers were still on them. Bug was wearing a coral pink stretch lace demi bra cut low for maximum décolleté with a French string bikini that was full in the back and plunged to a tiny triangle of sheer pink lace in front.

I followed her to the window. Below was a mixture of seas and clouds, an earth as bright as a sky.

"We must be getting close to the Upper Room!" I said. "You're going to make it!" I wanted to make her feel better. I liked the way her bra did in front.

"Don't talk nonsense. Hear that howling?"

I nodded. It sounded like a pack of hounds getting closer.

"That's the cat. Search and destroy. Find and erase." She shivered extravagantly.

"But you can save yourself!"

"Not so easily. I'm already a backup."

I was afraid she was about to cry. "Then let's get going!" I said. "I'll take you to the Upper Room. I don't care about the danger."

"Don't talk nonsense," Bug said. "You would be trapped forever—if Clyde didn't kill you first. If only I had my ResEdit, I could get there by myself."

"So where is it?"

"I lost it when Clyde killed me. I've been looking for it ever since."

"What does it look like?"

"A pair of big scissors."

"I saw Chemise with a pair of big scissors!" I said.

"That cunt!"

"I wish you wouldn't call her that . . ." I began. But the phone was ringing. We hadn't noticed it before.

"Don't answer it!" Bug said, even as she picked it up and handed it to me. How could she help it? I had signed the release.

It was for me of course. The next thing I knew I was staring up at the water-stained ceiling and at the little silver hammer coming down right between my eyes.

And at Clyde's smile. Not a nice smile.

First it got real dark. Then it got light again. It was like waking from a dream.

I was in a round, white room with curved windows all around. My head hurt. Through the glass I could see gray stars in a milk-white sky. Bug—

"Over here," she said. She was standing by the window wearing periwinkle-blue panties of shimmering faux satin, cut high on the sides and full in the back, with delicately embroidered cutouts down each side of the front panel. And nothing on top at all. No bra. No straps, no cups, no detailing, no lace.

My head hurt. But I couldn't help being thrilled at how high I was. "Is this—the Upper Room?" I asked breathlessly.

"Not quite," she said. She was still wearing the red hat and the glasses. "And now we're out of luck. In case you hadn't noticed, Clyde killed you too. Just now."

"Oh no." I couldn't imagine anything worse.

"Oh yes," she said. She put her hand on my forehead and I could *feel* her fingers feel the little dent.

"What did you do, copy me?"

"Pulled you out of the cache. Barely." Out the window far below there was a blue-green ball streaked with white. "Hear that howling? That's Clyde's cats rooting through the Palace room by room."

I shivered. I liked the way her panties did underneath.

"Well, what have we got to lose?" I said, surprised that I wasn't more upset that I was dead. "Let's head for the Upper Room."

"Don't talk nonsense," she said. "If you're dead too, you can't pull me through." The howling was getting louder. "Now we *have* to find the ResEdit. Where'd you see what's-her-name with the big scissors—what room was she in?"

"Chemise," I said. "I can't remember."

"What was out the window?"

"I can't remember."

"What was in the room?"

"I can't remember."

"What was she wearing?"

"A low-cut smooth-fitting strapless bra in stretch satin and lace with lightly lined underwire cups, and a high-cut, wide-band brief with a sheer lace panel in the front, all in white," I said.

"Let's go, then," Bug said. "I know the spot."

"I thought we couldn't go anywhere without the res-what-ever."

"*Down* we can go," Bug said. She threw the red hat and followed it herself. It fell near a tiny hole barely big enough for her fingertips. I squeezed through after her. I still liked the way her panties did underneath. We were in an old-fashioned kitchen and Chemise was stirring a pot with a pair of big scissors. She was wearing a low-cut, smooth-fitting strapless bra in stretch satin and lace with lightly lined underwire cups, and a high-cut, wide-band brief with a sheer lace panel in the front, all in white.

"Give me that!" said Bug, grabbing the big scissors. She was also wearing a low-cut, smooth-fitting strapless bra in stretch satin and lace with lightly lined underwire cups, and a high-cut, wide-band brief with a sheer lace panel in the front, all in white. And the red hat. But where were her glasses?

"Bitch," said Chemise softly. I was shocked. I didn't know she could talk.

"Cunt," said Bug.

Just then a dog trotted into the room from nowhere. Literally.

"The cat!" said Bug. She was trying to jimmy the lock on the pantry with the point of the big scissors.

The dog—the cat—hissed.

"In here!" said Bug. She pushed me backward into the pantry while she cut upward, ramming the point of the big scissors into the dog's belly. The cat's belly. Whatever. Blood was every-where. I was in a large, empty, pyramid-shaped room with a white floor and white walls rising to a point. There was one small porthole in each wall. Bug—

Bug was nowhere to be seen.

Outside the portholes, everything was white. There weren't even any stars. There were no doors. I could hear barking and growling below.

"Bug! The cat erased you!" I wailed. I knew she was gone. I was afraid I was going to cry. But before I could, a trapdoor in the floor opened and Bug came through feet first. It was odd to watch. Her arm was covered with blood and she was holding the scissors and she was—

She was nude. She was naked.

"It was I who erased the cat!" Bug cried triumphantly.

"It's still coming!" I could hear wild barking below.

"Shit! Must be a replicating loop," she said. She was naked. Nude. Stripped. Bare. Unclad completely. "And quit staring at me," she said.

"I can't help it," I said. Even the red hat was gone.

"I guess not," she said. She was nude. Naked. She was wearing nothing, nothing at all. She ran to one of the four portholes and began prying at the frame with the point of the scissors.

"There's nothing out there," I said. The howling was getting louder. The trapdoor had closed but I had the feeling it would open again, all dogs. Or cats. And soon.

"Can't stay here!" Bug said. She gave up on the frame and shattered the glass with the scissors.

"I'm going with you," I said.

"Don't talk nonsense," she said. She put her hand on my forehead again. Her touch was cool. I liked the way it felt. "The dent is deep but not all that deep. You may not be dead. Just knocked out."

"He hit me pretty hard! And I'm trapped here anyway."

"Not if you're not dead, you're not. They'll shut down and reset once I'm gone. You'll probably just wake up with a headache. You can go home."

The barking was getting closer. "I don't want to go home."

"What about your mother?"

"I left her a note," I lied.

"What about your stuff?"

"I buried all my stuff." She was nude. Naked, except for her lovely glasses. Nothing on the bottom, nothing on top. Even the red hat was gone. The hole was barely big enough for my hand but I followed her through one shoulder at a time. Everything was white and the howling was gone and something was moaning like the wind. I took Bug's hand and I was rolling. We were rolling. I was holding her hand and we were rolling rolling rolling through warm blank snow.

It was like waking from a dream. I was wrapped in a foul-smelling fur, looking up at the translucent ceiling of a little house made of ice and leaves. Bug was lying beside me wrapped in the same smelly fur.

"Where are we?" I asked. "I hear cats barking."

"Those are our dogs," she said.

"Dogs?" I got up and went to the door. It was covered with a scratchy trade blanket. I pulled it back and looked out across miles of new snow to a distant line of trees, hung with vines. Silvery dogs were peeing on the outside of the little house. One was shaking a snake to death. It was a big snake.

"They all come together here," Bug said. "The Upper Room, the North Pole, the headquarters of the Amazon."

"Head*waters*," I said. "Where are your glasses?"

"I don't need them anymore."

"I liked them."

"I'll put them back on."

I got back under the fur with her, curious to find out what she was wearing. There's no way I can tell you, from here, what it was. But you would have liked it too. If you're anything like me.

There Are No Dead

Ⱥll repeat after me," Pig Gnat said. "O Secret and Awesome Lost Wilderness Shrine."

"O Secret and Awesome Lost Wilderness Shrine."

"The Key to Oz and Always Be Thine."

"The Key to Oz and Always Be Thine."

"Bee-Men. Now cover it up with that rock."

"Rock?!"

"First the rock and then some leaves."

"We'll never find it again!"

"When we need to, we will. I made a map. See? But hurry. I think it's late."

It was late. While Nation arranged the rocks and leaves, and Pig Gnat carefully folded the map, Billy Joe scrambled to the top of the culvert. Across the corn stubble, in the subdivision on the other side of the highway, a few early lights gleamed. Among them, Mrs. Pignatelli's.

"I see a light," said Billy Joe. "Doesn't that mean your mother's home? Maybe we should cut across the field."

"You know better than that," Pig Gnat said. "He who comes by the trail must leave by the trail."

Billy Joe and Nation both grumbled, but agreed. They were at the fabled head of the Tibetan Nile. The trail followed the muddy stream away from the highway and the houses on the other side, down the culvert, along the steep side of what became (if you squinted; and they squinted) a thousand-foot-deep gorge. Where the gorge was narrowed by a junked car (a

Ford), the trail crossed the Nile on a perilous high bridge of side-by-side two by fours. It then left the stream (which only ran after a rain) and crossed the broom sage–covered Gobi-Serengeti toward the distant treeline.

Billy Joe led the way. Pig Gnat, who had moved to Middletown from Columbus only a year ago, was in the middle. Nation, who owned and therefore carried the gun (a Daisy pump), brought up the rear, alert for game, for danger. "Hold!" he said.

The three boys froze in the dying light. A giant grasshopper stood poised on top of a fence post. Nation took aim and fired. The great beast fell, cut almost in half along its abdomen, its legs kicking in dumb agony.

Nation recocked the Daisy, while Billy Joe put the beast out of its misery. Like rogue tigers, these magnificent mankillers had to die. "Good shooting," Billy Joe said.

"Luck," said Nation.

The desert ended; the trail tunneled through a narrow tangle of brush and old tires, then looped through the Black Forest, a dark wood of scrub locust and sassafras, then switchbacked down a steep clay bank to the gravel road that led back to the highway.

"Tell me the name of the cliff again," said Billy Joe as they started down.

"Annapurna," said Pig Gnat.

They single-filed it in silence. One slip meant "death."

It was dark when they said their good-byes at the highway's edge. Pig Gnat ran to find his mother, home from her job as Middletown's librarian, fixing supper and expecting him to keep her company. Billy Joe hurried home but to no avail; his father was already drunk, his mother was already crying, and the twins were already screaming. Nation took his time. Each identical house on his street was lighted. He often felt he could choose one at random and find his dinner on the table, his family hurrying to finish in time to watch *Hit Parade*.

They grew apart as they grew up. Billy Joe started running with a fast crowd in high school, and would have spent a night or two in jail if his father hadn't been a cop. Nation became a football star, got the Homecoming Queen pregnant, and married her a month after graduation. Pignatelli got into Antioch where his ex-father (as he called him) had been a professor, and lasted two years before the anti-war movement and LSD arrived on campus the same semester.

The sixties ran through America like a stream too broad to jump and too deep to wade, and it wasn't until their tenth high school reunion, in 1976, that all three were in Middletown, at the same time (that they knew of). Nation's wife, Ruth Ann, had organized the reunion. She was still the Homecoming Queen.

"Remember the trail to the Lost Wilderness Shrine?" Billy Joe asked. He was drunk. Like his father, he was a lawman (as he liked to say) but an attorney instead of a cop. "Of course. I made a map," said Pignatelli. He had returned to the reunion from New York, where his first play was about to be produced off off off Broadway, and he was hurt that no one had asked about it. "What're you two talking about?" Nation asked. He and Ruth Ann had just joined them at their table. Pig Gnat whispered: "Come with me." They left the girls and slipped out the side door of the gym. Across the practice field, across the highway, where the cornfield used to be, shopping-center lights gleamed under a cold Moon; beyond were endless coils of night. The door clicked shut behind them, and with the music gone, they imagined the narrow trail, the dark between the trees, the high passes to the secret Shrine, and they shivered. "We're supposed to stick to high school memories, remember?" Nation said. Billy Joe tried the door but it was locked. He was suddenly sober. The Homecoming Queen leaned on the bar, opening the door from the inside. "What are you guys doing?"

"B J, it's time to go home," said Billy Joe's wife, a Louisville girl.

Two years later Pignatelli gave up playwriting (or set it aside) and took a job at Creative Talent Management's New York office on Fifty-seventh Street. That October he came back to

Middletown for his mother's sixtieth birthday. He stopped by Nation Ford and was surprised to find his friend already going bald. He was under a car, an unusual position for assistant manager of a dealership. "Dad and Ruth Ann run the business end," Nation explained. He washed up and they found Billy Joe at the courthouse, and drove to Lexington where Pignatelli's ponytail didn't raise so many eyebrows. Billy Joe had hired a friend to handle his divorce. "It's like a doctor never operating on himself," he said. "We should go camping sometime," Nation said. "The original three."

Two years later, they did. CTM was sending Pignatelli to LA twice a year, and he arranged an overnight stop in Louisville. Billy Joe met him at the airport with two borrowed sleeping bags and a tent, and they met Nation halfway between Louisville and Middletown, and hiked back into the low steep hills along Otter Creek. It was October. Billy Joe gathered wood while Pig Gnat built a fire. "Did you ever think we'd be thirty?" Nation asked. In fact they were thirty-two, but still felt (at least when they were together) like boys; that is, immortal. Pig Gnat stirred the fire, sending sparks to join the stars in heaven. They agreed to never get old.

Two years later, again in October, they met at the airport in Lexington and drove east, into the low tangled folds of the Cumberland Mountains, and built their fire under a cliff in the Red River Gorge. Nation's twin daughters had just celebrated their "Sweet Sixteen." Pignatelli was dating a starlet whose face was often in the supermarket tabs, and beginning to wonder if he was supposed to have kids.

The next October, they backpacked into the gorges of the Great South Fork of the Cumberland River, almost on the Tennessee line. These were real mountains; small, but deep. At night the stars were like ice crystals, "and every bit as permanent," Pig Gnat pointed out. They stayed two nights. Billy Joe's lawyer had married his ex, moved into the house she had won in the settlement, and was raising his son.

They met every October, after that. B J would pick up Pignatelli at the Louisville airport, and Nation would meet them in the mountains. They explored up and down the Big South Fork, through Billy Joe's second marriage, Pignatelli's move to LA, and Nation's divorce. The Homecoming Queen kept the house on Coffee Tree Lane. They settled into a routine, just like the old days, with Nation picking out the site, Billy Joe gathering the wood, Pig Gnat building the fire. They skipped their twentieth high school reunion; their friendship had skipped high school anyway.

The year they turned forty, it rained, and they camped at the mouth of a shallow, dry cave where they could look up at a sky half stone, half stars. "How old do you guys want to get?" Nation asked. Forty had once seemed old to them; now even fifty didn't. Funny how time stretched out, long in front, short behind. Nation's girls were both married, and he would be a grandfather soon. B J did the paperwork on his second divorce himself. The year Pignatelli's mother died, he found a hand-colored map in a drawer when he cleaned out the house. He knew what it was without unfolding it. He took it back to California with him in a plastic bag.

Some Octobers they tried other mountains, but they always came home. The Adirondacks seemed barren compared to the close, dark tangles of the Cumberlands. The Rockies were spectacular but the scale was all wrong. "We're too old to want to see that far," Pig Gnat said. He was only half kidding. He was forty-six. There are no long views in the Cumberlands. There are high cliffs overlooking deep gorges, each gorge as like the others as trees or years are alike. The stars wheel through the sky like slow sparks. Sometimes it felt that in all the Universe only the three of them were still; everything else was spinning apart. "This is reality," Pig Gnat explained, poking the fire. "The rest of the year just rises up from it like smoke."

When Nation's father died he found the Daisy, filmed with rust and missing its magazine, in the attic. He cleaned it up and left it in Ruth Ann's garage. She had come back to run Nation Ford; she owned half of it anyway. "Still the Homecoming Queen," Nation laughed; they were better as friends than as man and wife. How Pignatelli envied them. They were camped that year among the sycamores in a nameless bend of No Business Creek. "How old do you guys want to get?" Billy Joe asked. It was becoming like a joke. Nobody wants to get old, yet every year they get older.

The year 2000 found them walking the ridge that leads north and east from Cumberland Gap like a road in the sky, while the wind ripped the leaves from the trees all around them. Two thousand! It was the coldest October in years. They slept in a dry cave floored with dust like the Moon, where footprints would last a thousand years—or at least forever. Life was still sweet. Billy Joe married again. Nation moved back in with Ruth Ann. It was not yet time.

Somewhere there are pictures that show how they looked alike in the beginning, in that way that all boys look alike. Later pictures would show how they diverged: B J in blue suits and ties; Pignatelli in silk sport coats and hundred-dollar jeans; Nation in coveralls and "gimme" hats. After fifty years they looked alike again, sitting on the edge of a limestone cliff high over the Big Sandy River, thin in the hair and getting thick in the middle. That was their last October. One week after Christmas, Nation died. It was very sudden. Pignatelli hadn't even known he was sick, then he got the call from Ruth Ann. It was a heart attack. He was almost fifty-nine. How old do you want to get?

Pig Gnat took out the map, which he kept in his office, but didn't unfold it. He had the feeling he could only unfold it once. Billy Joe and his young wife picked him up at the Louisville airport, and they drove straight to Middletown for the funeral. Billy Joe was angry; his wife seemed apologetic. After the burial there was a reception at the house on Coffee Tree Lane. Pignatelli went out to the garage and two little girls followed him; all Nation's grandchildren were girls. He spread out the map on the workbench, and sure enough, the old paper cracked along the folds. He found the Daisy under the bench, dark with rust and smelling of WD-40. The girls helped him look but he couldn't find the magazine or any BBs.

Back in the house, he kissed Ruth Ann good-bye. He wondered, as he had often wondered, if he would have married if he could have married the Homecoming Queen. Almost all the mourners had left. Billy Joe was drunk, and still sulking. "We waited too goddamn long!" he whispered. Pig Gnat shook his head, but he wasn't sure. Maybe, maybe they had. He felt sorry for Billy Joe's young wife. They left her at the house with Ruth Ann and the last of the mourners. In January it gets dark early. The cornfield was now a shopping center, had been for forty years, but the woods and the broom sage were still there behind it like a blank spot on a map. The road that led back from the highway was still gravel. They parked the electric (no one had ever been able to call them "cars") by an overflowing Dumpster at the bottom of a steep clay bank.

"Tell me the name of the cliff again," said Billy Joe.

"Annapurna," said Pig Gnat. "You okay?"

"I feel like shit but I'm not drunk anymore, if that's what you mean."

The narrow trail switchbacked up the bank to the Black Forest. One slip and they were "dead." It was spitting snow. At the top the trail led into the dark, dark trees.

Billy Joe carried the Daisy. Of course it was useless without a magazine. They came out of the woods, through the brush, into the field. "Here begins the deepest and most mysterious part of the trail," Pig Gnat said, from memory. "Here we begin our journey up the ancient Tibetan Nile." They crossed the gorge (the Ford was long gone) and followed the great river to its source in a culvert, now almost hidden under a broken slab at the rear of the shopping center. "All kneel," said Pig Gnat.

They knelt. Pig Gnat raked away the leaves with a stick. "Don't we say something, or something?" Billy Joe asked.

"That's after. Give me a hand with this rock."

Billy Joe set down the Daisy and they heaved together, and slid the big stone to one side.

Underneath, in the dark brown earth, a two-inch ruby square glowed. "Hadn't it oughta say PRESS ME or RESET or something?" Billy Joe joked nervously.

"Sssshhhhh," said Pig Gnat. "Just press it."

"Why me? Why don't you press it?"

"I don't know why. That's just the way it works. Just press it."

Billy Joe pressed it and instead of pushing in like a button it sort of pushed back.

There.

"Now, all repeat after me," Pig Gnat said. "O Secret and Awesome Lost Wilderness Shrine."

"O Secret and Awesome Lost Wilderness Shrine."

"The Key to Oz and Always Be Thine."

"The Key to Oz and Always Be Thine."

"Bee-Men, and so forth. Now help me with this rock."

"Rock!"

"First the rock and then leaves."

"We'll never find it again."

"When we need to, we will. Come on. I think it's late."

It was late, but still warm for October. While Nation and Pig Gnat pulled the rock into place, Billy Joe scrambled to the top of the culvert. The funny feeling in his legs was gone. Across the corn stubble, in the subdivision on the other side of the highway, a few early lights gleamed. Among them, Mrs. Pignatelli's.

"I think your mother's home," said Billy Joe. "Maybe we should cut across the field . . ."

"You know better than that," Pig Gnat said. "He who comes by the trail must leave by the trail."

The trail followed the great stream away from the highway and the houses on the other side, down the culvert and across the gorge on a high, perilous bridge of two by fours.

Billy Joe led the way. Pig Gnat was in the middle. Nation, who owned and therefore carried the gun, brought up the rear, alert for game.

"Hold," he said.

Three boys froze in the dying light. A giant grasshopper stood poised on top of a fence post. Nation took aim. Billy Joe squinted, imagining a rogue tiger. Pig Gnat kept his eyes wide open, staring off into the endless coils of night.

The Edge of the Universe

The biggest difference I have noticed so far between the north and the South (they insist on capitalizing it) is the vacant lot; or maybe I should say, the Vacant Lot. Vacant lots in Brooklyn are grim, unappealing stretches of rubble grown over with nameless, malevolent, malodorous plants, littered with roach-spotted household junk, and inhabited by scabrous, scrofulous, scurrying things you wouldn't want to look at unless it was out of the corner of an eye, in passing. Vacant lots here in Alabama, even in downtown Huntsville where I live and work (if study can be called work, and if what I do can be called study), are like miniature Euell Gibbons memorials of rustic runaway edibles and roadside ornamentals—dock and pigweed, thistle and cane, poke and honeysuckle, ragweed and wisteria—in which the odd overturned grocery cart or transmission bell-housing, the occasional sprung mattress or dead dog, the tire half filled with black water, is an added attraction: a seasoning, you might say, that adds to rather than detracts from the charm of the flora. You would never cut through a vacant lot in Brooklyn unless you were being chased by a scarier than usual thug; in Alabama I cut across the same corner lot every day on my way from Whipper Will's law office, where I slept and studied for the bar, to Hoppy's Good Gulf where I had my own key to the men's room. I actually looked forward to my sojourns across the path and through the weeds. It was my closest regular contact with nature; or maybe I should say, Nature.

And Nostalgia, too.

One of the odd items of junk in the lot was a beaded seat

cushion, of the kind much favored by New York cabdrivers (particularly those from Pakistan) back in the late 1980s, and still seen occasionally. This one had known better days, and all that was left were half a hundred or so large wooden beads strung together by twisted neoprene line in a rough sketch, as it were, of a seat; but it was enough to make it recognizable and to give me a warm hit of the Big Apple when I saw it two or three times a day. It was like hearing a horn honk or smelling a bagel. It lay half on and half off the narrow red dirt path that was my route to Hoppy's Good Gulf. I watched it gradually disintegrate, becoming every week a little less recognizable, but still familiar, like a neighborhood (or a friend) in decline. I looked forward to stepping over it several times a day, for much as I loved Candy (still do—we're almost Mr. and Mrs. now!), and was getting to *like* (at least) Alabama, I missed New York. We Brooklynites are urban animals, and what could be less urban than these faded little red brick Southern "downtowns," deserted by both people and cars? I suspect they were always somewhat sad and empty, but nowadays they are sadder and emptier than ever. Like most American towns, north *and* South, Huntsville has seen its life blood flow from the old downtown to the Bypass; from the still, dark heart to the tingling, neon-lit, encircling skin of strip malls and fast-food restaurants and convenience stores and discount centers.

Not that I'm complaining. Dead as it was, downtown suited me better than the Bypass, which is no place for a man on foot, which is what I was then: which is a whole other story, but one that might as well be told here, since it, too, is about Whipper Will, about an Edge (of town, not the Universe)—

And about a U-turn.

When I moved down here from Brooklyn to be with Candy, I had sold her the Volvo P-1800 I acquired from my best friend Wilson Wu in return for helping him bring the LRV (Lunar Roving Vehicle) back from the Moon (which is also a whole other story, and one that I've told in "The Hole in the Hole"). I helped Candy maintain the car not only because I was her boyfriend—her soon-to-be fiancé, in fact—but because the P-1800, Volvo's first and only true sports car, is a rare classic with precious idiosyncrasies that not even a Southern shade tree mechanic (and the breed has no greater admirer than I) can be expected to understand. The carburetors, for example. The Volvo's twin slide-type SUs begin to leak air after a few hundred thousand miles, and according to Wu (and he showed me the math on this—of course!), the only way to get them in synch, especially after a move to another climate, is to run the Volvo up to 4725 rpm in third gear on a four to six percent grade on a day approaching the local humidic mean (temperature not a factor), and lean them out in eighth-turn stages, alternating between one and the other, until the exhaust note makes a twelve-inch tinfoil pie plate wedged between the frame and the transmission case sing "A." I don't have perfect pitch but I was able to borrow one of those little C-cell-powered guitar tuners, and there is a long six percent grade on the old four-lane at the north edge of Huntsville, where it crosses the city limits and heads around the shoulder of Squirrel Ridge, the 1300-foot Appalachian remnant that dominates the northern half of the county. Since Wu's procedure requires several passes, I went early on a Sunday morning when I knew the city cops would all be in church, and (my first mistake) used the NO-TURN; FOR POLICE ONLY cut-across just past the city limits to shorten my way back down. I was finished, and getting ready to take the car back into town and pick up Candy at church (Methodist) when the ash-gray "smokey" dove out of the sun, as it were, and pounced.

Police in general, and Alabama State Troopers in particular, are humorless, excessively conventional creatures, and my second mistake was trying to explain to him that I was not actually *driving* but *tuning* the car. He used my own words to charge me with six counts of the same moving violation (Illegal U-turn). My third mistake was explaining that I was Whipper Will Knoydart's soon-to-be (for I had not yet officially proposed to Candy, for reasons that will become clear) affianced son-in-law. How was I to know that Whipper Will had once taken a shot at this particular trooper? The result of all these errors was that I was summarily hauled before a Justice of the Peace (church was just letting out), who let me know that Whipper Will had once called him a ____, and who then snatched away my New York driver's license and imposed a punitive three-month wait before I was eligible to apply for an Alabama license.

All of which is to explain why the P-1800 was running so well; why I was on foot; and why Candy and I met for lunch in Huntsville's old downtown every (or almost every) day instead of out on the Bypass, near the Parks Department office, where she worked. It suited me fine. A New Yorker, even a car-loving Brooklynite like me, is happy on foot, and I loathe and despise the Bypass. I went through the same routine every morning: Wake up, cross the corner lot to Hoppy's Good Gulf men's room ("It's Whipper Will's Yank"), then head back to the office to wait for the mail.

I didn't even have to open it; just log it in. Whipper Will Knoydart had been a trailer park landlord for six decades, running low-rent, high-crime operations in four counties and making more enemies and fewer friends than any other man in northern Alabama. It was characteristic of the old man that his office was downtown, since he had often boasted that he wouldn't be caught dead in a mobile home, which was only suitable (according to him) for "rednecks, niggers, and ____s." Because Whipper Will had retired under a financial and legal cloud—a bank of clouds, actually—his office had been sealed and secured pending a state investigation. Under the agreement worked out among the Realtor's Board, the IRS, the BATF, the DEA, and several other even less savory agencies, the premises had to be overseen by an out-of-state lawyer with no pending cases, past encounters, or conflicting interests. The fact that I was crazy in love with Whipper Will's only child wasn't considered an interest: in fact, it was Candy who had recommended me for the position. Nobody else wanted it, even though the resentment of Whipper Will was softening as it sometimes softens for malefactors after they are gone. Whipper Will wasn't dead, but between Alzheimer's, prostrate cancer, emphysema, and Parkinson's he was definitely fading away. He had been in the nursing home for almost nine months.

In return for answering the phone (which only rang when Candy called) and logging in the mail, I got to use the office as a place to "live" (sleep) and study for the Alabama bar. Or at least, spread out my books; or rather, book. The problem with studying was, it was a golden Alabama October, and fall is (I have discovered) the season of love for forty-somethings. I was forty-one. I'm a little older than that now, and if you think that's self-evident, it's because you haven't heard my story, which begins on the morning I noticed that the beaded seat cushion in the vacant lot was getting better instead of worse.

It was a Tuesday, a typical, that is to say beautiful, Alabama October morning. The leaves were just beginning to think about beginning to turn. Candy and I had been out late, parking at the overlook on Squirrel Ridge, where I had unbuttoned all but the last little button on her uniform blouse before she stopped me with that firm but gentle touch on the back of my hand that I love so much. I slept late, entangled in the most delicious dreams, and it was almost ten before I dragged myself off the leather couch I called a bed and stumbled, half-blind, across the corner lot to Hoppy's Good Gulf. "Whipper Will's Yank," said Hoppy, combining greeting, comment, and conversation into his usual laconic phrase. Hoppy wasn't much of a talker. "Right," I said, which was the only answer I had been able to devise. " 'Nuff said," he said, which was his way of signing off. On my way back across the corner lot I stepped carefully over my old friend, the beaded seat cushion, which lay in its usual place, half on and half off the path. Loose beads were scattered in the dirt and grass around the neoprene strings that had once held them; it was like the reversed body of a beast whose skeleton (string) was less substantial than its flesh (beads). Perhaps it was the morning light (I thought), perhaps the dew hadn't yet dried off: but I noticed that the discarded seat cushion looked, or seemed to look, a little *better* rather than a little worse that morning.

It was weird. It was jarring because it was, after all, October, with the slow, quiet, golden process of ruin evident all around; and to me, that October, there was something personally gratifying about decline and decay, which was freeing up the woman I wanted to marry. Candy had agreed the night before up on Squirrel Ridge that since her father was finally and securely ensconced in the nursing home, it was time to think about getting married. Or at least engaged. Sometime in the next week, I knew, she was going to allow me to propose. With all the privileges that entailed.

I decided it was my imagination (or perhaps my mood) that saw the beads reassembling themselves into a seat cushion. As always, I was careful not to kick them as I went on my way. Who was I to interfere with the processes of Nature? Back at the office I found two messages on Whipper Will's ancient reel-to-reel answering machine: one from my best friend Wilson Wu announcing that he had located the Edge of the Universe, and one from Candy informing me that she would be twenty minutes late for lunch at the "Bonny Bag." This second message worried me a little, since I could tell from the low moaning in the background that she was at Squirrel Ridge (the nursing home, not the mountain). I couldn't return either call since I didn't have outgoing, so I opened a Caffeine Free Diet Cherry Coke from Whipper Will's old-fashioned kerosene-powered office refrigerator, spread my *Corcoran's Alabama Case Law Review* on the windowsill, and fell to my studies. When I woke up it was 12:20, and I panicked for a moment, thinking I was late for lunch. Then I remembered Candy was going to be late, too.

The Bonny Baguette is a little sandwich shop much favored by lawyers and real-estate people, most of whom tend to be old-line Huntsville folks who leave the Bypass to the NASA and university types. "I was worried," I said as Candy and I both slid into the booth at the same time. "I could tell you were calling from Squirrel Ridge, and I was afraid that . . ."

Candy looked, as always, spectacular in her neatly pressed Parks Department khakis. Some girls are pretty without meaning to be. Candy has to work at it and that makes her (for me) even more special; especially after having a wife who pretended, but only pretended, to despise her own beauty. But that's a whole other story. "Don't worry," Candy answered, cutting me off with that smile that had enticed me to Alabama in the first place, and a touch on the back of my hand that reminded me of our almost-intimacies of the night before. "I just had to sign something, that's all. A document. A formality. A DNR, in fact."

I knew what a DNR was. A Do Not Resuscitate order.

"It's part of the process and everything, but still, it's weird, you know?" Candy said. "It hurts. You're telling them—ordering them—not to keep your daddy alive. To let him die."

"Candy—" It was my turn to take her hand. "Your father is ninety years old. He's got Alzheimer's. He's got cancer. His hair is white as snow. He's got no teeth left. He's had a nice life, but now . . ."

"Eighty-nine," Candy said. "Daddy wasn't quite sixty when I was born, and he hasn't had a nice life. He's had a terrible life. He's been a terrible man. He's made life miserable for people in four counties. But still, he's . . ."

"He's not terrible anymore," I said. Which was true. I had never met the Whipper Will everybody hated. The man I knew was gentle and befuddled. He spent his days watching TNN and CMTV, perpetually smoothing a paper napkin across his knee as if he were petting a little white dog. "He's a sweet old man now, and his worries are pretty much over. It's your turn to have a nice life. Mine too. Which reminds me—I got a phone call from Wu! Something about that astronomy project he's working on."

"Wonderful," Candy said. She loved Wu; everybody loves Wu. "Where is he? Still in Hawaii?"

"Guess so," I said. "He didn't leave a number. Not that it matters, since I don't have outgoing."

"I'm sure he'll call back," said Candy.

At the Bonny Baguette, you don't order when you want to; you are called on, just like in grade school. Bonnie, the owner, comes over herself, with a little blackboard on which there are five kinds of sandwich, the same every day. Actually, grade school was never that bad; they called on you but they never brought the blackboard to your desk.

"How's your daddy?" Bonnie asked.

"The same," said Candy. "I was out to Squirrel Ridge today— the nursing home—and they all agree he's just become the sweetest thing." She didn't say anything about the DNR.

"Amazed, I'm sure," said Bonnie. "Did I ever tell you about the time he took a shot at my daddy? Out at Squirrel Ridge Trailer Park."

"Yes, Bonnie, you've told me, several times, but he's gotten sweeter with Alzheimer's," said Candy. "It makes some old people mean, but it made my daddy sweet, so what can I say?"

"He also took a shot at my half brother, Earl, out at Willow Bend Trailer Park," said Bonnie. "Called him a ____"

"We should probably go ahead and order," said Candy, "since I only get fifty-five minutes for lunch, and almost eleven are gone."

"Well, of course." Bonnie sucked her cheeks and tapped her little blackboard, ready to make chalk marks. "What'll you two lovebirds have?"

I ordered the roast beef as usual; Candy the chicken salad as usual. Each comes with a bag of chips and I got to eat both bags, as usual. "Did you hear how she called us lovebirds?" I whispered. "What say we make it official tonight? I propose I propose."

"Bonnie calls everybody lovebirds."

Candy's a sweet, old-fashioned Southern girl, a type I find fascinating because they never (contrary to myth) blush. She had her own reasons for being reluctant to allow me to propose (with all the privileges that entails). The last time Candy had been engaged, almost ten years before, Whipper Will had shown up drunk at the wedding rehearsal and taken a shot at the groom and then at the preacher, calling them both ____s, and effectively canceling the wedding and ending the engagement as well. Candy didn't want to even *hear* a proposal again until she was sure she could accept it without worrying about her old man and what he might do.

"Things are quiet, Candy. He's settled into the nursing home," I said. "We can get on with our life together. We can make plans. We can . . ."

"Soon," she said, touching my wrist lightly, gently, perfectly! "But not tonight. It's Wednesday, and on Wednesday nights we go 'grazing,' remember?"

I was in no hurry to get back to the office and study for the bar, so after Bonnie went back to work I stopped by the station and watched Hoppy replace the front brake pads on a Ford Taurus.

"Whipper Will's Yank," he said, as always, and as always, I replied, "Right." But today Hoppy was in a mood for conversation, and he asked, "How's old Whipper Will?"

"Just fine," I said. "Mellow. Good as gold. He just watches CMTV and TNN all day out at Squirrel Ridge. The nursing home."

"Ever tell you about the time he took a shot at me? At Sycamore Springs Trailer Park. Called me a ____."

"Seems he took a shot at everybody," I said.

"Lucky he was such a bad shot," Hoppy said. "For a trailer park landlord, anyway. Meanest son of a bitch in four counties."

"Well, he's not mean anymore," I said. "He just watches CMTV and TNN all day out at Squirrel Ridge. The nursing home."

"Thank God for Alzheimer's," Hoppy said. " 'Nuff said."

He went back to work on the brakes and I strolled out into the sun and across the corner lot toward the office. I was in no hurry to start studying, so I stopped for a look at the broken-down beaded seat cushion, my little reminder of New York City. It definitely looked better. But how could that be? I knelt down and, without touching anything, counted the beads on the fourth string down from what had been, in better days, the top. There were nine wooden beads; judging by the length of the naked neoprene string, it looked like another five or six had gotten away. I wrote: 9 on the back of my hand with my ballpoint, feeling almost virtuous. Next time I would *know*. I would have *evidence*. I was beginning to feel like a lawyer again.

Back at the office, I took a Caffeine Free Diet Cherry Coke out of the little refrigerator, which was still crowded with Whipper Will's moonshine in pint jars. I never could figure out why he kept moonshine refrigerated. I could only guess that he didn't want to take a chance on it aging; that is, getting better.

I spread my *Corcoran's Alabama Case Law Review* on the windowsill and fell to studying. When I woke up the phone was ringing.

It was Wu. "Wu!"

"Didn't you get my message?" he asked.

"I did, and it's great to hear from you, finally, but I couldn't call back," I said. "I don't have outgoing. How's the family?" Wu and his wife have two boys.

"They're back in Brooklyn. Couldn't take the weather."

"In Hawaii!?!"

"I'm at the Mauna Kea Observatory," Wu said. "We're at twelve thousand feet. It's like Tibet."

"Whatever," I said. "Well, how's business? Observe any meteors lately?"

"Remember what I told you, Irving?" Wu hardly ever calls me Irving; it usually means he's irritated. "Meteorology is not about meteors. It's about weather. My job is scheduling the observatory's viewings, which depend on the weather."

"So—how's the weather, Wu?"

"Great!" Wu dropped his voice. "Which is how come we found what I told you about." He dropped his voice further. "The Edge of the Universe."

"Congratulations," I said. I didn't know it had been lost. "But why is it such a big secret?"

"Because of the implications. Unexpected, to say the least. Turns out we've had it in our sights for almost a month but didn't realize it because it was the wrong color."

"The wrong color?"

"The wrong color," said Wu. "You know about Hubble's constant, the red shift, the expanding Universe, right?" Wu asked with such confidence that I couldn't bear to let him down.

"Sure," I said.

"Well, the Universe has stopped expanding." After a pause, he added in a whisper: "In fact, according to my calculations, it's starting to shrink. What's your fax number? I'll shoot you the figures."

Whipper Will had Huntsville's—maybe even Alabama's—first fax machine. About the size of an upright piano, and not entirely electrical, it sat in the far corner of the office, against a wall where it was vented to the alley through a system of stovepipe and flex hose. I had always been reluctant to look behind its plywood sides, or under its duraluminum hood, but I understood from Hoppy (who had been called in once to fix it) that its various components were powered by an intricate and never since duplicated combination of batteries and 110, clockwork, gravity, water pressure, propane, and charcoal (for the thermal printer). No one knew who had made it, or when. I didn't even know it worked until, seconds after I gave Wu the number, I heard a relay click, and the upright fax began to groan; it began to whine. It clanked and clattered, it sputtered and roared, it spat cold steam and warm gases, and a paper fell out of the wicker IN bin, onto the floor.

It was smeared with purple stains, which I recognized from grade school as mimeo ink, and it bore a formula in Wu's hand:

$$\int_{\infty}^{0} H = \frac{(2\pi\,{}^{m}e)^{3/4}}{a\,|4^{?}}\; e\sqrt{\frac{\angle\,||\,{}^{m}z}{-\frac{1}{K\gamma'}}}$$

"What's this?" I asked.

"Just what it looks like. Hubble's constant inconstant: reversed, confused, confounded," Wu said. "You'll note that the red shift has turned to blue, just like in the Elvis song."

"That's blue to gold," I said. " 'When My Blue Moon Turns to Gold Again.' "

"Irving, this is more important than any Elvis song!" he said (rather self-righteously, I thought, since it was he who had brought up Elvis in the first place). "It means that the Universe has stopped expanding and started to collapse in on itself."

"I see," I lied. "Is that—good or bad?"

"Not good," Wu said. "It's the beginning of the end. Or at least the end of the beginning. The period of expansion that began with the Big Bang is over, and we're on our way to the Big Crunch. It means the end of life as we know it; hell, of existence as we know it. Everything in the Universe, all the stars, all the planets, all the galaxies—the Earth and everything on it from the Himalayas to the Empire State Building to the Musée d'Orsay— will be squashed into a lump about the size of a tennis ball."

"That does sound bad," I said. "When's this Crunch thing going to happen?"

"It will take a while."

"What's a while?" I couldn't help thinking of Candy, and our plans to get married (even though I hadn't yet officially proposed).

"Eleven to fifteen billion years," said Wu. "By the way, how's Candy? Are you two engaged yet?"

"Almost," I said. "We're going 'grazing' tonight. As soon as her father's settled in the nursing home, I get to pop the question."

"Congratulations," Wu said, "or maybe I should say precon-gratula—whoooops! Here comes my boss. I'm not supposed to be using this line. Give my best to Candy. What's 'grazing' anyway . . . ?"

But before I could answer, he was gone. Everybody should have a friend like Wilson Wu. He grew up in Queens and studied physics at Bronx Science, pastry in Paris, math at Princeton, herbal medicine in Hong Kong, and law at either Harvard or Yale (I get them confused). He worked for NASA (Grumman, anyway), then

Legal Aid. Did I mention that he's six feet two and plays guitar? We lived on the same block in Brooklyn where we both owned Volvos and went to the Moon. Then I met Candy and moved to Alabama, and Wu quit Legal Aid and got a degree in meteorology.
Which is *not* about meteors.

The Saturn Five SixPlex, in the Apollo Shopping Center on the Huntsville Bypass, with its half-dozen identical theaters half guarded by bored teens, is perfect for "grazing," an activity invented by Candy and her friends some fifteen years ago, when the multiplexes first started hitting the suburbs of the bigger Southern towns. The idea, initially, was to make dating more flexible, since teen girls and boys rarely liked the same movies. Later, as Candy and her friends matured, and movies continued their decline, the idea was to combine several features into one full-featured (if you will) film. When you go "grazing" you wear several sweaters and hats, using them to stake out seats and to change your appearance as you duck from theater to theater. Dates always sit together when in the same theater, but "grazing" protocol demands that you never pressure your date into staying—or leaving. Boys and girls come and go as they wish, sometimes together, sometimes apart. That Wednesday night there was a teen sex comedy, a tough love ladies' weeper, a lawyer in jeopardy thriller, a buddy cop romance, a singing animal musical cartoon, and a terror thug "blow-'em-up." The films didn't run in the same time continuum, of course, and Candy and I liked to graze backward; we began with the car bombs and angled back across the hall (and across Time) for the courtroom confession, then split up for the singing badgers (me) and Whoopi's teary wisecracks (Candy) before coming together for teens' nervous first kiss. "Grazing" always reminds me of the old days before movies became an art, when "the picture show" in Brooklyn ran in a continuous loop and no one ever worried about beginnings or ends. You stayed till you got to the part where you came in, then it was over. "Grazing is a lot like marriage, don't you think?" I whispered.

"Marriage?" Candy asked, alarmed. We were together, watching the cops question a landlady. "Are you pressuring me?"

"I'm not proposing," I said. "I'm making a comment."

"Comments about movies are allowed. Comments about marriage are considered pressuring."

"My comment is about grazing," I said. "It's about . . ."

"Sssshhhh!" said the people behind us.

I lowered my voice. ". . . about being together some of the time and apart some of the time. About entering together and leaving together. About being free to follow your own tastes yet always conscious that there is a seat saved for you beside the other."

I was crazy about her. "I'm crazy about you," I whispered.

"Sssshhhh!" said the couple behind us.

"Tomorrow night," Candy whispered, taking my hand. Then she held it up so that it was illuminated by the headlights of a car chase. "What's this?" She was looking at the number on the back of my hand.

"That's there to—remind me of how much I love you," I lied. I didn't want to tell her what it really was; I didn't want her to think I was crazy.

"Only six?"

"You're holding it upside down."

"That's better!"

"Ow!"

"Ssssshhhhhh!" said the couple behind us.

We skipped all the titles and credits but caught all the previews. Candy dropped me off at midnight at the Good Gulf men's room. Walking "home" to Whipper Will's office across the corner lot, I looked up at the almost-full Moon and thought of Wu on his Hawaiian mountaintop. There were only a few stars; maybe the Universe *was* shrinking. Wu's figures, though I could never understand them, were usually right. What did I care, though? A few billion years can seem like eternity when you're young, and forty-one isn't old. A second marriage can be like a second youth. I stepped carefully over my old friend, the beaded seat cushion, who looked better than ever in the moonlight; but then, don't we all?

• • •

It was almost ten o'clock before I awoke the next morning. I made my way to Hoppy's Good Gulf, staggering a little in the sunshine. "Whipper Will's Yank," Hoppy said from the repair bay where he was replacing the front brake pads on another Taurus. "Right," I muttered, and he replied " 'Nuff said" behind me as I made my way back outside and started across the corner lot.

I stopped at the beaded seat cushion. It definitely looked better. There seemed to be fewer loose beads scattered in the weeds and on the path. There seemed to be fewer naked, broken neoprene strings and bare spots on the seat cushion.

But I didn't have to guess. I had evidence.

I checked the number on the back of my hand: 9.

I counted the beads four rows down from the top: 11.

I checked both again and it came out the same.

It was creepy. I looked around in the bushes, half expecting to see giggling boys playing a joke on me. Or even Hoppy. But the bushes were empty. This was downtown on a school day. No kids played in this corner lot anyway.

I spit on my thumb and rubbed out the 9 and walked on back to the office. I was hoping to find another message from Wu, but there was nothing on the machine.

It was only ten-thirty, and I wasn't going to see Candy until lunch at the Bonny Bag, so I opened a can of Caffeine Free Diet Cherry Coke and spread out my *Corcoran's*. I was just starting to doze off when Whipper Will's ancient upright fax machine clicked twice and wheezed into life; it sputtered and shuddered, it creaked and it clanked, it hissed and whistled and then spat a smeared purple mimeo sheet on the floor, covered with figures:

$$\frac{Q}{H} = \frac{17\pi}{\Delta \cdot dx}\left(\frac{c4\infty}{WAP}\right)_N^4 \sum_{-kT} \left. \frac{dx}{\cos 3} \right|_{\triangle 33}^{\infty} \sim$$

As soon as it cooled, I picked it up and smoothed it out. I was just about to put it with the other one when the phone rang.

"Well?" It was Wu.

"More Big Crunch?" I was guessing, of course.

"You must be holding it upside down," Wu said. "The figures I just sent are for the Anti-Entropic Reversal."

"So I see," I lied. "Does this reversal mean there won't be a Big Crunch after all?" I wasn't surprised; it had always sounded more like a breakfast cereal than a disaster.

"Irving!" Wu said. "Look at the figures more closely. The AER leads up to the Big Crunch; it *makes* it happen. The Universe doesn't just shrink, it rewinds. It goes backward. According to my calculations, everything will be running in reverse for the next eleven to fifteen billion years, from now until the Big Crunch. Trees will grow from ashes to firewood to oak to seed. Broken glass will fly together into windowpanes. Tea will get hot in the cup."

"Sounds interesting," I said. "Could even be handy. When does all this happen?"

"It's already started," said Wu. "The Anti-Entropic Reversal is going on right now."

"Are you sure?" I felt my Caffeine Free Diet Cherry Coke. It was getting warmer, but shouldn't it be getting colder? Then I looked at the clock. It was almost eleven. "Things aren't going backward here," I said.

"Of course not, not yet," Wu said. "It begins at the Edge of the Universe. It's like a line of traffic starting up, or the tide turning; first it has to take up the slack, so in the beginning it will seem like nothing is happening. At what point does the tide turn? We may not notice anything for several thousand years. A blink of the eye in cosmic time."

I blinked. I couldn't help thinking of the beaded seat cushion. "But wait. Is it possible that something here *could* already be going backward," I asked. "Rewinding?"

"Not very likely," Wu said. "The Universe is awfully big, and . . ."

Just then I heard a knock. "Gotta go," I said. "There's some-body at the door."

It was Candy, in her trim Parks Department khakis. Instead of giving me, her soon-to-be fiancé, a kiss, she walked straight to the little kerosene-powered office refrigerator and opened a Caffeine Free Diet Cherry Coke. I knew right away that some-thing was wrong, because Candy loathes and despises Caffeine Free Diet Cherry Coke.

"Aren't we meeting for lunch?" I asked.

"I got a call a few minutes ago," she said. "From Squirrel Ridge, the nursing home. Daddy hit Buzzer."

I tried to look grave; I tried to hide my guilty smile. In my wishful thinking I thought I had heard "hit the buzzer" (and fig-ured it was a local variant of "kick the bucket"). I crossed the room and took Candy's hand. "I'm so sorry," I lied.

"You're not half as sorry as Buzzer is," Candy said, already dragging me toward the door. "He's the one with the black eye."

Squirrel Ridge, the nursing home, sits in a hollow just north and east of Huntsville, overlooked by Squirrel Ridge, the mountain. It's a modern, single-story establishment that looks like a grade school or a motel, but smells like—well, like what it is. The smell hits you as soon as you walk in the door: a dismaying mix of ordure and disorder, urine and perfume, soft food and damp towels, new vomit and old sheets, Beech-Nut and Lysol pine. Next, the sounds hit you: scuffing slippers, grunts and groans, talk-show applause, the ring of dropping bedpans, the creak of wire-spoked wheels—broken by an occasional panicked shout or soul-chilling scream. It sounds as if a grim struggle is being fought at intervals, while daily life shuffles on around it. And indeed it is. A struggle to the death.

I followed Candy to the end of a long hall, where we found her father in the dayroom, smiling sweetly, strapped in a chair in front of a TV watching Alan Jackson sing and pretend to play the guitar. "Good morning, Mr. Knoydart," I said; I could never bring myself to call him Whipper Will. In fact, I had never known the Whipper Will who was the terror of trailer parks in four counties. The man I knew, the man before us, was large but soft—beef gone to fat—with no teeth and long, thin white hair (which looked, this morning, a little grayer than usual). His pale blue eyes were fixed on the TV, and his fingers were busy stroking a paper napkin laid across his knee.

"What happened, Daddy?" Candy asked, touching the old man's shoulder tentatively. There was, of course, no answer. Whipper Will Knoydart hadn't spoken to anyone since he had been admitted in January, when he had called the Head Nurse, Florence Gaithers, a "stupid motherfucker, a bitch and a ____," and threatened to shoot her.

"I was helping him out of his wheelchair to go to the bathroom, and he just up and slugged me."

I turned and saw a skinny young black man in whites, standing in the doorway. He wore a diamond stud in his nose and he was dabbing at a black eye with a wet rag.

"He got this look in his eye. Called me a ____ (excuse me!) and then he up and hit me. It was almost like the old Whipper Will."

"Sorry, Buzzer. Thanks for calling me instead of Gaithers."

"It's no big deal, Candy. Old folks with Alzheimer's have inci-dents." Buzzer pronounced it with the accent on the *dent*. "Gaithers would just get all excited."

"Buzzer," said Candy. "I want you to meet—" I was hoping she would introduce me as her soon-to-be fiancé, but I was disappointed. I was introduced as her "friend from New York."

"Whipper Will's Yank," said Buzzer, nodding. "I heard about him."

"Sorry about your eye," said Candy. "And I do appreciate your not calling Gaithers. Can I buy you a steak to put on it?"

"I'm a vegetarian," said Buzzer. "Don't you worry about it, Candy. Your daddy's not so bad, except for this one inci*dent*. He lets me wash him and walk him around every morning just as sweet as anything, don't you, Mr. Knoydart? And we watch TNN together. He calls me whenever Pam Tillis comes on, don't you, Mr. Knoydart? He wasn't always so sweet, though. Why, I remember one time he took a shot at my mother, when we lived out at Kyber's Creek Trailer Park. Called her a ____. Excuse me, but he did."

Buzzer and I are old friends," Candy explained as we went back out to the car. "He was the first black kid in my junior high, excuse me, African American, or whatever, and I was Whipper Will's daughter, so we were outcasts together. I looked after him and he's still looking after me. Thank God. If Gaithers finds out Daddy's acting up, she'll kick him out of Squirrel Ridge for sure, and I won't have anyplace to put him, and we'll be back to square one, and how would that be?"

"Bad," I said.

"Well, hopefully it's over. Just an inci*dent*." She said it the same way as Buzzer.

"Hope so," I said.

"Funny thing is, didn't you think Daddy looked better?"

"Better?"

"I think Buzzer's been putting Grecian Formula on his hair. Buzzer always wanted to be a hairdresser. This nursing home thing is just a sideline."

We had managed to miss lunch. We made a date for dinner and "a drive" (tonight was to be my night to pop the question), and Candy dropped me at the office. It was only three o'clock, so I opened a Caffeine Free Diet Cherry Coke and spread out my *Corcoran's* on the windowsill, determined to make up for lost time. I was awakened by a rhythmic clacking, jacking, cracking, snorting, cavorting noise, and a faint electrical smell. The floor was shaking. Whipper Will's upright fax machine was spitting out a sheet of purple ink-smeared paper, which drifted to the floor.

I picked it up by one corner and studied it while it cooled—

$$55_\Delta = \left[\frac{H}{32\pi} \ d \ string(14)\right]^{\frac{1}{4}} \sum_{g^2}^{\infty} t^{\frac{1}{2}} \int_{0\text{-}0}^{0}$$

But before I could figure out what it meant (I knew, of course, who it was from), the phone rang. "There's the answer to your question," Wu said.

"What question?"

"You asked me if something here could already be going backward."

"Not there," I said. "Here."

"By here I mean here on Earth!" Wu said. "And as my calculations show, it is theoretically possible. Perhaps even inevitable. You know about superstrings, right?"

"Sort of like superglue or supermodels?" I ventured.

"Exactly. They hold the Universe together, and they are stretched to the limit. It's *possible* that harmonic vibrations of these superstrings *might* shake loose discrete objects, so that they would appear as bubbles or reversals in local entropic fields."

"Fields? What about vacant lots?" I told Wu about the beaded seat cushion.

"Hhhmmmmm," said Wu. I could almost hear his brain whirring. "You *may* be on to something, Irv. Superstring harmonic overtones *could* be backtracking my sight line from the Edge of the Universe, and then following our fax and phone connections. The same way glass breaks along a line when you score it. But we have to be sure. Send me a couple of pictures, so we can *quantify* the . . . Ooooooops!" His voice dropped to a whisper. "Here comes my boss. Say hi to Candy. I'll call you later."

There was still plenty of afternoon light, so as soon as Wu hung up, I hung up, I headed across the corner lot to Hoppy's Good

Gulf and borrowed the Polaroid he uses to photograph accident scenes. As I took the picture, I *quantified* for myself, by counting. The eleven beads on row four had increased to thirteen, and the other rows also seemed to be much improved. There weren't many beads lying in the dirt. The seat cushion looked almost good enough to put in my car, if I had one.

It was creepy. I didn't like it.

I returned Hoppy's camera and took the long way back to the office, trying to make sense of it all. Were the falling leaves going to float back up and fasten themselves to the trees? Was Candy's Volvo going to have four speeds in reverse? I got so confused just thinking about it that I put the photo into the wicker OUT tray of Whipper Will's upright fax machine before I remembered—I guess realized is the word—that I had no outgoing. I could talk to Wu on the phone (when he called me) but I couldn't fax him anything.

Perversely, I was glad. I had done what I could, and now I was tired. Tired of thinking about the Universe. I had an important, indeed a historic, date coming up—not to mention a bar exam to study for. I opened a Caffeine Free Diet Cherry Coke, spread my *Corcoran's* on the windowsill, and lost myself in pleasant dreams. Mostly of Candy and that last little uniform button.

A Huntsville Parks Department professional has many obligations that run past the normal nine-to-five. Some of them are interesting, some even fun, and since Candy loves her job, I try to accommodate (which means accompany) her whenever possible. That night we had to stop by the North Side Baptist Union Fish Fry and Quilt Show, where Candy was the Guest of Honor in her neatly pressed, knife-creased khakis. The fish was my favorite, pond-raised cat rolled in yellow cornmeal, but I couldn't relax and enjoy myself. I kept thinking of later; I was in a hurry to get up on Squirrel Ridge, the mountain. But one good thing about Baptists, they don't last long, and by 9:15 Candy and I were parked up at the overlook. It was a cool night and we sat out on the warm, still-ticking hood of the P-1800 with the lights of the valley spread out below us like captured stars. My palms were sweating. This was to be the night I would propose, and hopefully she would accept, with all the privileges that entails.

I wanted the evening to be memorable in every way, and since there was supposed to be a full moon, I waited for it to rise. As I watched the glow on the eastern horizon, I thought of Wu and wondered if the moon would rise in the west after the "Reversal." Would anyone notice the difference? Or would folks just call the west the east and leave it at that?

It was too deep for me to figure out, and besides—I had other things on my mind. As soon as the moon cleared the horizon, I got off the hood and dropped to my knees. I was just about to pop the question when I heard a *beep beep*.

"What's that?" I asked.

"Buzzer," said Candy.

"Sounds like a beeper."

"It is. Buzzer loaned me his beeper," she said, reaching down to her waist and cutting it off.

"What for?"

"You know what for."

There are no phones up on Squirrel Ridge, so we high-tailed it down the mountain with the SUs howling and the exhaust barking, alternately. Candy's big fear was alerting Gaithers, who was on duty that night, so we rolled into the parking lot of Squirrel Ridge, the nursing home, with the lights off. I stayed with the P-1800 while Candy slipped in through a side door.

She was back in half an hour. "Well?" I prompted.

"Daddy hit Buzzer," she said (or I *thought* she said) as we drove out of the lot as quietly as possible. "It's cool, though. Buzzer didn't say anything to Gaithers. This time. I figure we've got one more strike. Three and we're out."

"Where'd he hit him this time?"

"Not hit," she said. "*Bit*."

"But your daddy doesn't have any teeth!"
Candy shrugged. "Seems he does now."

And that was it for what I had hoped would be one of the biggest evenings of my life. My proposal, with its acceptance, with all the privileges that entails—none of it was to be. Not that night. Candy needed her sleep since she had to leave early in the morning for the annual statewide all-day Parks Department meeting in Montgomery. She dropped me off at Hoppy's Good Gulf and I took a long walk, which is almost as good as a cold shower. It takes only twenty minutes to cover every street in downtown Huntsville. Then I went back to the office, cutting through the corner lot. In the light of the full moon, the beaded seat cushion looked almost new. The top rows of beads were complete, and there were only a few missing on the lower section. I resisted the urge to kick it.

There were two messages on Whipper Will's ancient reel-to-reel answering machine. The first was just heavy breathing. A random sexual harassment call, I figured. Or a wrong number. Or maybe an old enemy of Whipper Will's; most of Whipper Will's enemies were old.

The second message was from Candy. She had beaten me home. "This is going to be an all-day conference tomorrow," she said. "I won't get home till late. I gave your number to Buzzer, just in case. You know what I mean. When I get home, we'll take care of our *unfinished business.*" She signed off with a loud smooching sound. For some reason I found it depressing.

It was midnight but I couldn't sleep. I kept having these horrible thoughts. I opened a Caffeine Free Diet Cherry Coke and spread my *Corcoran's* out on the window ledge, overlooking the empty street. Was there ever a downtown as quiet as downtown Huntsville? I tried to imagine what it had looked like before the Bypass had bled away all the business. I must have fallen right to sleep, for I had a nightmare about downtown streets crowded with newlyweds walking hand in hand. And all the newlyweds were old. And all the newlyweds had teeth.

The next morning I woke up thinking about the beaded seat cushion. I decided I needed another picture for Wu, to make it a before and after. After my morning ablutions in the Good Gulf men's room, I found Hoppy in the repair bay, fixing the front brakes on yet another Taurus. "Whipper Will's Yank," he said.

"Right," I said. I asked to borrow the Polaroid again.

"It's in the wrecker."

"The wrecker's locked."

"You have the key," Hoppy said. "Your men's room key. One key does everything around here. Keeps life simple. 'Nuff said."

I waited until Hoppy was busy before I took the camera out into the corner lot and photographed the beaded seat cushion. I didn't want him to think I was nuts. I printed the picture and put the camera away, then hurried back to the office and placed the new photo next to the old one in the wicker OUT bin of Whipper Will's ancient upright fax machine. If I had ever doubted my own eyes (and who doesn't, from time to time?) I was convinced now. I had photographic evidence. The beaded seat cushion was in *much* better shape in the second photo than in the first, even though they were less than twenty-four hours apart. It was undecaying right before my eyes.

I kept having these horrible thoughts.

At least there were no messages on the answering machine. Nothing from Buzzer.

Even though I couldn't concentrate, I knew I needed to study. I opened a Caffeine Free Diet Cherry Coke and spread my *Corcoran's* on the windowsill. When I woke up it was almost noon and the floor was shaking; the fax machine was huffing and puffing, creaking and groaning, rattling and whining. It stopped and started again, louder than ever. A sheet of paper fluttered down from the IN bin. I caught it, still warm, before it hit the floor—

$$\chi = \frac{0.E93}{M^{1/3}}\left(\frac{40}{\sqrt{3\frac{1}{2}m}}\right) > \frac{3\times10^7}{\Omega}\Big/\alpha\,T$$

While I was still trying to decipher it, I realized the phone was ringing.

I picked it up with dread; I whispered, "Buzzer?" assuming the worst.

"Buzzer?" It was Wu. "Are you impersonating a device, Irving? But never mind that, I have a more important question. Which one of these Polaroids is number one?"

"What Polaroids? You *got* them? That's impossible. I never faxed them. I don't have outgoing!"

"Seems you do now," Wu said. "I was faxing you my newest calculations, just now, and as soon as I finished, here came your Polaroids, riding through on the self-checking backspin from the handshake protocol, I guess. You forgot to number them, though."

"The crummy one is number two," I said. "The crummier one is number one."

"So you were right!" Wu said. "It's going from worse to bad. Even in downtown Huntsville, light-years from the Edge, the Universe is already shrinking in isolated Anti-Entropic Bubble Fields. Anomalous harmonic superstring overtones. The formula I just faxed through, as I'm sure you can see, confirms the theoretical *possibility* of a linear axis of the Anti-Entropic Reversal Field following a superstring fold from the Edge of the Universe to downtown Huntsville. But observation is the soul of science, and by using your Polaroids, now I will be able to mathematically calculate the . . ."

"Wu!" I broke in. Sometimes with Wu you have to break in. "What about people?"

"People?"

"People," I said. "You know. Humans. Like ourselves. Bipeds with cars, for Christ's sake!" Sometimes Wu was impossible.

"Oh, *people*," he said. "Well, people are made of the same stuff as the rest of the Universe, aren't they? I mean, *we*. The Anti-Entropic Reversal means that we will live backward, from the grave to the cradle. People will get younger instead of older."

"When?"

"When? When the Anti-Entropic Reversal Wave spreads back, from the Edge through the rest of the Universe. Like the changing tide. Could be several thousand years; could be just a few hundred. Though, as your seat cushion experiment demonstrates, there may be isolated bubbles along the linear axis where . . . Whoops! Here comes my boss," Wu whispered. "I have to get off. Give my best to Candy. How's her dad by the way?"

Wu often signs off with a question, often unanswerable. But this one was more unanswerable than most.

Lunch at the Bonny Bag was strange. I had a whole booth to myself. Plus a lot on my mind. "Where's Candy?" Bonnie asked.

Montgomery, I told her.

"The state capitol. That lucky dog. And how's Whipper Will? Still sweet as ever?"

"I sure hope so," I said.

"Did I ever tell you about the time he took a shot at my . . ."

"I think so," I said. I ordered the chicken salad, just for the adventure of it. Plus two bags of chips.

Back at the office, I found two messages on the reel-to-reel answering machine. The first was heavy breathing. The second was ranting and raving. It was all grunts and groans and I figured it was probably one of Whipper Will's old enemies. The only words I could make out were "motherfucker," "kill," and "____."

Nothing from Buzzer, thank God.

I opened a Caffeine Free Diet Cherry Coke and spread my *Corcoran's* on the windowsill. I kept having these horrible thoughts, and I knew the only way to get rid of them was to study for the bar. When I woke up it was getting dark. The phone was ringing. I forced myself to pick it up.

"Buzzer . . . ?" I whispered, expecting the worst.

"Buzzzzzzzzz!" said Wu, who sometimes enjoys childish humor. But then he got right down to business. "How far apart are these two Polaroids?" he asked.

"In time?" I did some quick figuring. "Eighteen and three-quarters hours."

"Hmmmmmmm. That checks out with my rate of change figures," he said. "Mathematics is the soul of science, and beads are easier to count than stars. By counting the beads, then sub-tracting, then dividing by the phase of the Moon over eighteen and three-quarters, I can calculate the exact age of the Universe. Are you on Central or Eastern Standard Time?"

"Central," I said. "But, Wu . . ."

"Perfect! If I get a Nobel, remind me to share it with you, Irv. The exact age of the Universe, from the Big Bang until this instant is . . ."

"Wu!" I broke in. Sometimes with Wu you have to break in. "I need your help. Is there any way to reverse it?"

"Reverse what?"

"The contraction, the Anti-Entropic Reversal or whatever."

"Turn around the Universe?" He sounded almost offended.

"No, just the little stuff. The anomalous harmonic super-string overtones."

"Hmmmmmm." Wu sounded intrigued again. "Locally? Temporarily? Maybe. If it is all on strings . . ." I couldn't tell if he was talking about the beaded seat cushion or the Universe.

Whipper Will's upright fax machine grumbled. It rumbled. It growled and it howled. The floor shook and the wall creaked and a warm sheet of paper came out of the IN bin and fluttered toward the floor.

I caught it; I was getting good at catching them.

$$\sqrt{\frac{9}{H}} = \frac{Gd\,^2R\text{jeans}(\pi\cos y)}{\sum 世 \overset{x}{月'}\,)_4@\,\frac{125}{\cos y^3}\sqrt{\overset{18b}{石口片穴}}}$$

"What's with the Chinese?" I asked.

"Multicultural synergy," Wu said. "I've combined my calculations of the relative linear stability of the remote Anti-Entropic
Fields on the superstring axes, with an ancient Tien Shan spell
for precipitating poisons out of a well so that camels can drink.
A little trick I picked up in school."

"Medical school?"

"Caravan school," said Wu. "It's temporary, of course. It'll
only last a few thousand years. And you'll have to use an Anti-
Entropic Field Reversal Device."

"What's that?"

"Whatever's handy. A two by four, a jack handle. All it takes is
a short sharp shock. The problem is, there's no way to tell what
other effects might . . . Whoooops!" His voice dropped. "Here
comes my boss—"

After Wu hung up I sat by the window, waiting for night to fall.
Waiting for Buzzer to call. I kept having these horrible
thoughts.

When it was dark, I walked downstairs and into the corner
lot. I carried a short length of two by four with me. I squared off
and hit the ground beside the beaded seat cushion, just once. A
short, sharp shock. Then again, on the other side. Another
short, sharp shock. I resisted the urge to destroy it with a kick; it
was an experiment, after all.

I tossed the two by four into the weeds. The moon was rising
(still in the east) and a dog and a cat were standing side by side
on the path watching me. As they trotted off together, still side
by side, a chill gripped my heart. What if I had made things
worse?

Hoppy's Good Gulf was closed. I used the men's room and
went back to the office. There were two messages on the
machine. The first was a voice I had never heard, but I knew
exactly who it was. "Where is that vicious pissant daughter of
mine? Are you listening to me, bitch? I swore by God if you ever
put me in a nursing home I would kill you, and by God I will!"

The second message was from Buzzer. "We've got a problem here, Yank," he said. "The old man is uncontrollable. He threw a chair through a glass door and got into Gaithers's office, and now—"

There was a sound of more glass breaking, and a scream, and a thud. I heard a *beep* and I realized that the message was over.

The phone was ringing. I picked it up and heard the first voice again, but this time it was live: "You devil motherfucker bitch bastard! Where is my Oldsmobile? Did you give it to this nursing home nigger?"

I heard Buzzer shout, "No!"

"You fucking ____!"

Then I heard a shot. I hung up the phone and ran out the door, into the night.

When you haven't driven for a while, it can seem almost like a thrill. I wasn't worried about the police; I figured they wouldn't stop Hoppy's Good Gulf wrecker, as long as they didn't notice who was driving. So I turned on the red light and drove like a bat out of hell out the four-lane toward Squirrel Ridge, the nursing home.

I left the truck in the lot with the engine running and the red light spinning. I found Whipper Will in Gaithers's office. He had gotten the gun out of her desk. It was a brand-new pearl-handled .38, a ladies' special. Whipper Will was holding it on Buzzer, who sat bolt upright behind the desk in one of those rolling office chairs. There was a bullet hole in the wall just to the left of Buzzer's head.

"Take all my money and put me in a goddamn nursing home! That rotten little ____!" Whipper Will raved. He was talking about Candy—his own daughter. His hair was almost black and he was standing (I had never seen him standing before) with his back to the door. Buzzer was facing me, making elaborate signals with his eyebrows and diamond nose stud—as if I couldn't figure out the situation on my own! I tiptoed across the floor, trying to avoid crunching the broken glass.

"Wait till I get my hands on that cold-hearted, conniving lit-tle black-hearted ____!"

I had heard enough. I rapped Whipper Will on the side of the head, firmly. A short, sharp shock. He sagged to his knees and I reached around him and took the .38 out of his hand. I was just about to rap him again on the other side of the head when he slumped all the way down to the linoleum.

"Good going," said Buzzer. "What's that?"

"An Anti-Entropic Field Reversal Device," I said.

"Looks like a brick in a tube sock."

"That, too," I said as we dragged Whipper Will, as gently as possible, down the hall toward his room.

It was almost ten o'clock the next morning when I woke up in Whipper Will's office, on the couch I called my bed. I got up and went to the window. There was the wrecker, parked under the sign at Hoppy's Good Gulf, right where I had left it.

I pulled on my pants and went downstairs, across the corner lot. The beaded seat cushion was missing several rows of beads along the top, and at least half of the bottom. Wooden beads were scattered in the red dirt. I stepped carefully, even respect-fully, around them.

"Whipper Will's Yank," said Hoppy, who was replacing the front brake pads on yet another Taurus.

"Right," I said.

"How's old Whipper Will?"

"About the same, I hope," I said. I decided there was no point telling Hoppy about borrowing the truck the night before. "You know how it is with old folks."

" 'Nuff said," he said.

When I got back to the office, there were two messages on the machine. The first one was from Buzzer. "Don't worry about Gaithers, Yank," he said. "I told her a story about a bur-glar, and she won't call the cops because it turns out that the .38 in her desk is illegal. So no problem about that hole in the wall and fingerprints and stuff. I don't see any reason to bother Candy about this inci*dent*, do you?"

I didn't. The second message was from Candy. "I'm back. Hope everything went well. See you at the Bonny Bag at twelve."

I opened a Caffeine Free Diet Cherry Coke and spread out my *Corcoran's* on the windowsill. When I awoke it was almost twelve.

I had a great trip," Candy said. "Thanks for looking after things. I stopped by Squirrel Ridge on the way into town this morning, and—"

"And?" *And?*

"Daddy looks fine. He was sleeping peacefully in his wheelchair in front of the TV. His hair is almost white again. I think Buzzer washed all that Grecian Formula out of it."

"Good," I said. "It seemed inappropriate to me."

"I feel like things are settled enough," Candy said. She touched the back of my hand. "Maybe we should go up to Squirrel Ridge tonight," she said. "The mountain, not the nursing home. If you know what I mean."

"What'll you two lovebirds have?" Bonnie asked, chalk poised. "How's your daddy? Ever tell you about the time he took a . . ."

"You did," I told her. "And we'll have the usual."

If I were making this story up, it would end right there. But in real life, there is always more, and sometimes it can't be left out. That evening on our way out to Squirrel Ridge, the mountain, Candy and I stopped by the nursing home. Whipper Will was sitting quietly in his wheelchair, stroking a napkin, watching Pam Tillis on TNN with Buzzer. The old man's hair was white as snow and I was glad to see there wasn't a tooth in his head. Buzzer gave me a wink and I gave him the same wink back.

That diamond looked damn good.

That night up at the overlook I got down on my knees and—well, you know (or you can guess) the rest, with all the privileges that entails. That might have been the end of the story except that when I got back to the office the fax was whirring and stuttering and snorting and steaming, and the phone was ringing, too.

I was almost afraid to pick up the phone. What if it was Buzzer again?

But it wasn't. "Congratulations!" Wu said.

I blushed (but I'm an easy blusher). "You heard already?"

"Heard? I can see it! Didn't you get my fax?"

"I'm just now picking it up off the floor."

It was in purple mimeo ink on still-warm paper:

$$H \Big\}_0^{\infty} = \Delta \left(\frac{2\pi \, {}^m_{\varepsilon}}{a \, l4 \, {}^r_8} \right) e \sqrt{\frac{ll \, m^2 \, \Delta}{+ \, l \frac{1}{K} \, l9}} \rangle$$

"Must be the butterfly effect," Wu said.

Even though butterflies are romantic (in their way) I was beginning to get the idea that Wu wasn't talking about my proposal, and its acceptance, and all the privileges that entails.

"What *are* you talking about?" I asked.

"Chaos and complexity!" Wu said. "A butterfly flaps its wings in the rain forest and causes a snowstorm over Chicago. Linear harmonic feedback. Look at the figures, Irv! Numbers are the soul of science! You have set up a superstring harmonic wave reversal that has the entire Universe fluttering like a flag in the wind. What did you hit that beaded seat cushion with, anyway?"

"A two by four," I said. I didn't see any reason to tell him about Whipper Will.

"Well, you rapped it just right. The red shift is back. The Universe is expanding again. Who knows for how long?"

"I hope until my wedding," I said.

"Wedding?!? You don't mean . . ."

"I do," I said. "I proposed last night. And Candy accepted. With all the privileges that entails. Will you fly back from Hawaii to be my best man?"

"Sure," Wu said. "Only, it won't be from Hawaii. I'm starting college in San Diego next week."

"San Diego?"

"My work here as a meteorologist is done. Jane and the boys are already in San Diego, where I have a fellowship to study meteorological entomology."

"What's that?"

"Bugs and weather."

"What do bugs have to do with the weather?"

"I just explained it, Irving," Wu said. "I'll send you the figures and you can see for yourself." And he did. But that's a whole other story.

The Joe Show

It had been a long day.

I sighed with pleasure as my door clicked shut behind me. I threw the bolt, fastened the chain, propped the bar in place, then snapped the little lock on the bottom. This was New York, after all. And I was a single girl, living alone.

Thank God.

Leaving the lights down, I stepped out of my Candies and hung my Liz Claiborne fake fur on its hook on the wall. I stepped through the only other door in my tiny studio apartment and turned on the bathwater. The temperature and rate of flow were already set. The bubble bath was already waiting in its little Alka-Seltzer-like pill at the bottom of the tub.

Closing the bathroom door behind me (to cut the noise) I picked the remote out of the clutter on the kitchenette table and clicked on the CD player. It, too, was already set—for Miles Davis, just like in *In the Line of Fire*. Can I help it if Clint and I are soul buddies?

I hung up my Clifford & Wills blazer in my almost-walk-in closet, let my J. Crew wool skirt and Tweeds silk blouse fall to the floor (both due at the cleaners), then peeled off my panty hose, wadded them into a ball, and tossed them into the corner. Miles was just beginning his unmuted solo as I unhooked my tangerine Victoria's Secret underwire demi bra, shrugged it off, and stepped out of the matching tangerine high-cut bikini, with the cute little accent bows along the side. As you may have guessed, I buy everything by mail. Everything but shoes.

I tossed the bra and panties into the dirty clothes pile with the panty hose stopped by the mirror to admire my new seventy-eight-dollar haircut, crossed to the kitchenette, filled a heavy-bottomed glass with white wine from the coldest corner of the fridge, carried it into the bathroom and set it on the edge of the tub, then turned off the bathwater, all without a single wasted motion. This was New York, after all. Miles was just winding up. I sat on the john and lit the joint that was waiting for me, tucked into its own book of matches. I took two nice long hits while Coltrane strode into his solo, then nipped out the joint and high-stepped it into the tub. My Rubenesque (as my ex-boyfriend, Reuben, loved to call it) bottom was just descending into the suds when Coltrane fucked up.

Coltrane fucked up?

I stood up, dripping.

Was my Sony shelf system, only four months old, giving up the ghost already? Coltrane bleated like a sheep, then quit. Somebody hit a bad note on a piano. The rhythm section (Cobb, Chambers, Evans) stopped playing, raggedly, one at a time.

I grabbed a towel and stepped out of the bathroom, dripping water and suds onto the bare wood floor. *All Blues* was starting over, at the beginning. It sounded fine now. Not knowing what else to do, I picked up the remote and hit PAUSE.

The music stopped clean this time. "Sorry about that," said a voice.

I clutched the towel to me and looked around the studio.

"I thought music would be easy, like speech, but it's not," the voice said.

"Who's there?" I demanded.

"You want the short answer or the long answer?" the voice asked. It sure as hell wasn't Miles or Coltrane. It was a guy, but not a black guy; he pronounced every syllable, like a foreigner.

"Who the fuck is in my apartment?" I said. The odd thing was, I wasn't scared. Maybe if I'd been in a house or a bigger apartment it would have been scary, but you can't have a haunted studio; they're too small.

"I'm not in your apartment," the voice said.

I couldn't tell where it was coming from. I thought of those movies that go straight to video—some demented dude peeping through a telescope while he keeps you talking on the phone.

Except that the blinds were closed. And I wasn't on the phone.

As an experiment, with two fingers, as if it were hot, I picked up the phone and said, "Hello?"

"Hello," said the same voice. Over my phone.

"What are you doing on my phone? Is this some kind of crank call? Are you some kind of sex fiend?"

I pulled the towel around me more tightly, even though the blinds were closed. What about infrared? What about X-ray vision? That used to bother me about Superman, by the way. If he was really a guy, how could he concentrate on fighting evil, if he could see through girls' dresses all the time?

But I'm getting off the subject. "Who the fuck are you? What are you doing in my apartment?"

"Calm down, Victoria. I'm not in your apartment, I'm on your phone. And you're the one that picked up the phone."

Nobody has called me Victoria since my mother died. "Who are you?"

"Like I said, do you want the long answer or the short answer?"

"The short answer," I said.

"I'm a temporary electronic entity that has taken over your TV."

I didn't say anything.

"Victoria, are you still there?"

"Better give me the long answer," I said.

"Good. Hang up the phone and turn the TV on, and I'll explain."

Like an idiot, without even thinking about it, I did what he said. It said. Whatever. The same remote that works the CD player works the TV. Even though it was only eight-thirty, some kind of late-night talk show was on. There was this guy sitting at a desk, looking ill at ease, sort of like Conan O'Brien.

He was mumbling, so I turned up the sound.

"Thanks," he said. "Since I am part of the matrix, I can access all the electronics in your apartment, like the CD and the phone. But the TV is the real me."

"The real you," I said, to humor him. I looked in the closet again. I looked under the couch.

"Real is only relative, of course," he said. "There's not really a real me. I'm a temporary electronic entity, created out of the TV matrix in order to communicate with . . ."

"So what's your name?" I said. I figured the best thing at this point was to keep him—or it, or whatever—talking. Meanwhile I looked in the kitchen cabinets, in the dishwasher, even in the toilet tank. I don't know what I was looking for: wires, a hidden speaker. Maybe a leprechaun?

"Name? I didn't think about a name," he said.

"Even a temporary electronic entity has to have a name," I said. I figured two could play this game (whatever it was). It was like some kind of Letterman put-on, like when he comes to the door. Except there was nobody at the door; I checked through the peephole.

"A name," he said. He started tapping on his desk. "I don't know. Help me think of something."

"How about Joe. Jim. Jack. John."

"Joe it is, then." He brightened and sat up straighter. "That would make this *The Joe Show*. I wonder if I could come up with a Joe Show Band."

"Slow down, Joe," I said. "I still want to know who you are, and what you're doing in my apartment. I'm as good a sport as the next girl, but enough is enough, okay?"

"Number one," said Joe, "I'm not in your apartment. I'm in your TV. If I was in your apartment, you probably wouldn't be sitting there so casually on the arm of the couch, your thighs slightly parted, so delightfully Rubenesque that a towel doesn't begin to cover . . ."

My legs flew together so fast my knees knocked. "I'm calling the police," I said. I turned off the TV and picked up the phone, punching 911 so hard it was like punching eyeballs out.

"Don't get excited," his voice said, over the phone. "I can't see you. You can't see *out of* a TV, can you?"

"Now you're taking over my phone? Operator!"

"Victoria, slow down. What exactly are you going to tell them at 911?"

I was standing and I sat back down. He had a point. Maybe I was just stoned. This was the first time I had tried this new dope.

I hung up the phone, pulled the towel tighter, and turned the TV back on.

"Thanks," he said. The picture looked brighter. Behind the desk there was now a big sign that said THE JOE SHOW. I could hear a band warming up in the background. "This will take some explaining," he said, "so maybe you should finish your bath and get comfortable. If you want, I'll call out for Chinese."

Chinese? That settled it. It was the dope. I was relieved (even though it meant I was going to have to cut down). I pointed the remote at the TV and fired, turning it off. "Hasta la vista, Joe baby."

Yes! I went into the bathroom, shut the door behind me, and slipped back into the bath. My wine on the edge of the tub was still cold. (I left the joint alone.) I was finally relaxing again, letting the hot water caress the back of my neck, when I heard applause.

I leaned out of the tub and opened the door. I heard laughter. Canned laughter.

"I thought I turned you the fuck off!" I hollered.

"I can work the remote," Joe said. "And I'd rather be on than off. Anybody would. You can't blame me for that."

"Just go away," I said. "Please!"

"No need to be so hostile, Victoria. It's after eight-thirty, which means we only have half an hour."

"Half an hour till what?"

"That's what I'm trying to explain, if you will just let me! Why don't you finish your bath, then come out and watch the show for a few minutes. Ten minutes."

I pulled the plug. I dried my hair, no big deal with my new Lyle-loves-Julia look. I made every move slow and deliberate, as if I were super-stoned, though I knew by now it wasn't the dope. Apparently it was real, like it or not. I dried my fingers and lit the joint and took a hit. If I'm going to go off the deep end, I thought, might as well do a swan dive.

Even though Joe had said he couldn't see out of the TV, I sort of slunk around the corner to my almost-walk-in closet to get dressed.

"May I suggest the black lace bodysuit with the scooped peekaboo front and the stretch satin back," he said.

Jesus! "You've been going through my drawers?"

"How can I go through your drawers?" he protested. I peeped around the corner of the closet and saw him on the screen, holding up his hands. They sort of sparkled. But didn't people on TV all sort of sparkle? "You order your clothes by phone, that's how I know about it," he said.

"Well, stay the hell out of my stuff," I said. "And forget the bodysuit, it makes me feel like a sausage." I pulled on some panties and covered up with the oldest, unsexiest thing I could find—my stepfather's ancient maroon terry-cloth robe—and went out and sat down on the couch. Flopped down is more like it.

"This had better be good," I said.

"Guaranteed. Okay. Where to begin?" It was a rhetorical question. Now the sign behind the desk was neon: THE JOE SHOW. The camera was closer in, the lighting was better, and I could see that Joe was about Letterman's age but better-looking. But who isn't?

"To start with, as I've explained, I'm not really a person," he said. "And this isn't really a TV show, though you've probably already figured that out."

"Thanks a lot," I said. Jesus!

"I am actually an entity created out of the electronic matrix, a temporary consciousness put together as a communications interface in order to make a link between my Creator and you, the people of Earth, through . . ."

"Wait," I said.

"You want me to start over?"

"No, I heard what you said. I just don't believe it. I don't intend to believe it. I am not one of those Elvis-sighting ladies."

"If I could get the King himself on *The Joe Show*," Joe said with a smile, "would that convince you?" There was canned laughter, and Joe raised one sparkling hand: "Only kidding, Victoria! I have very limited powers and bringing Elvis back to life is *not* one of them. I exist for one purpose only, to make a connection between my Creator and your President."

"Bill Clinton?"

"I sure wasn't created and sent to Earth to talk to Al Gore. Or Ross Perot!" More canned laughter, and if there's anything I hate it's canned laughter. I stood up and hit the channel changer on the remote. Up, then down. Up, down.

The Joe Show stayed on.

Joe held up his hand to quiet the laughter. "I'm sorry, Victoria," he said. "I am an entertainment entity, after all, made out of network TV. It's part of my heritage to play for laughs."

I sat back down. The camera moved in closer; Joe was oozing sincerity, wringing his hands like Arsenio. "A simulated human interface made out of talk-show hosts and news anchors has all sorts of special needs, including the need to get a few laughs. And applause."

There was applause. Joe quieted it with a wave of his hand.

"Excuse me?" I said. I was beginning to get angry. "I just want to turn you off, okay? I'm not stupid. I know this is some kind of Totally fucking Hidden Video or something, and it's not all that funny. So just tell me the real deal and we'll all have a laugh—a small one—and I'll get on with my life."

"Do you have somebody coming over or something?"

"None of your fucking business."

"Okay, okay. You said you'd give me twenty minutes to explain, remember?"

"Ten. And it's almost over."

"Let me try again. As I already told you, my only reason for being here, for *being* at all, for *existence*, is to set up a communications link between my Creator and Bill Clinton. So your next question is, where do you come in, right?"

"I don't have a next question," I said. "The whole thing is too incredibly stupid."

"You said you'd let me explain, Victoria. You could cooperate by asking the right questions."

"Okay, okay," I said. "Where do I come in?"

"I'll come to that part in a minute. First, let me point out that this other intelligence, this magnificent extraterrestrial, my Creator, is using a very short window for this communication, which is why it has to happen tonight. In eighteen minutes, actually. It may never be possible again."

"I'm supposed to believe that you are, like, an emissary from another intelligence?"

"I like that. That's a good word, 'emissary.' "

"What is this—thing? This so-called magnificent extraterrestrial."

"It's not exactly a thing," said Joe. "It's huge, bigger than your entire star system. It's not a biological entity; not even a consciousness, which is a focusing and limitation of intelligence—but an unlimited intelligence made up of electrical impulses; a creature of pure energy. Sort of a plasma cloud. Light-years across and almost invisible, all the way on the other side of the galaxy. Are you following me so far?"

That was the longest, most complicated thing I had ever heard on a talk show. I was impressed in spite of myself. I nodded.

"Good. Well, it so happens that right now, this evening, there is a brief moment—about a minute and forty seconds long—during which my Creator will be in direct contact with this side of the galaxy, through a fortuitous fold in space-time. And when the opportunity arises to make a link, to reach out and touch someone, so to speak, why not use it?"

"But—Clinton?"

"Can you imagine trying to have an intelligent conversation with Yeltsin?"

"So you're, like, up on Earth politics and everything?"

"It's not that complicated, Victoria. Big dog bites little dog, that sort of thing. Woof woof."

More canned laughter.

"I thought you were going to cool it on the comedy."

"Sorry. I'll delete the laugh track," Joe said. He shrugged comically but the audience—or rather the laugh track—was silent. "See? Anything for you."

"Okay. So now, explain where I come in. What do you want me to do—call the President?"

"No, no, no. I'm setting that up through the White House staff. The actual communication will be through a satellite link at approximately 9:04 Eastern Standard Time, when the President will be aboard Air Force One crossing the North Magnetic Pole, and a temporary alignment of the Aurora Borealis with the galactic lens will make this otherwise unthinkable transmission possible. For one minute and forty seconds. Think of it—an actual conversation between the leader of the Free World and an awesome alien intelligence. Alien but friendly."

"How friendly?"

"Very friendly."

"So where do I come in?"

"Well, to let me use your phone line. And to help me maintain the link. That's the hard part. So to speak. Maybe you want to slip into something comfortable while I explain it. Have some more wine. Another hit of dope."

"Not if I'm going to be talking to the President."

"You won't be talking to anybody but me. Besides, does Bill Clinton look to you like a guy who's never smoked a joint?"

"Yes. I know for a fact that he's never inhaled."

"Whatever. Anyway. You are the key to the whole process, Victoria. One, you are smart and capable. Two, you read science fiction."

"No, I don't. I watch *Star Trek, the Next Generation*, when there's nothing else on."

"Close enough. Three, you are a Democrat. And four, you look so good sitting there, knees apart, with nothing on under your robe but those little white cotton panties."

I begged his pardon. "I beg your pardon?"

I switched off the TV. It came back on. I wasn't surprised. I pulled the robe tight around my neck; I was no longer sitting with my knees apart. "I thought you couldn't see out of the TV," I said.

"I can't, exactly. But that was sort of an evasion," Joe said. "Light is just wave action, and I'm all wave action. Inside or outside your robe is all the same to me. I know for example that you are not wearing a bra; that you don't need one; that . . ."

"This is either a sick joke or some kind of weird alien interstellar sexism!"

"Maybe. Just hear me out, okay? I'm getting to the hard part. We chose you for this operation, Victoria, not only because you are cute, and you are cute, but because we figured you would have the intelligence to understand and go along with it. If we chose wrong, and we may have chosen wrong, it's a lost opportunity, since there's not enough time to set up another communications link. I like your new haircut, by the way."

"What time is it exactly?" I asked.

THE JOE SHOW sign behind Joe's desk blinked off and was replaced by a digital clock: 8:47. The clock blinked off, the sign blinked back on—and I blinked, thinking for the first time that all this might, in fact, just possibly, be true.

And as soon as I thought that, I realized it *was* true. It had to be. Nobody could make up, much less pull off, such a scheme. "So you're for real," I said.

"Not for real," Joe said. "I'm an electronic simulation, remember? But I'm serious. Can we talk now without you freaking out and turning off the TV or calling 911?"

"I guess," I said. "You just switch yourself back on anyway."

"But it hurts my feelings. Even if I am put together out of talk-show hosts and news anchors, I have feelings. At least, I think I do."

"Just explain, Joe. Please."

"Okay. The thing is, we need you to help me maintain my consciousness." His hair was longer and darker. He was starting to look more like Howard Stern than David Letterman. "Are you familiar with how an erection is caused in the human male by the blood engorging the organ you call the penis?"

"Familiar enough," I said.

"Okay. Then you probably also understand how thought, imagination, consciousness itself, is made possible by the blood flow to the neural mass you call the brain."

"Get to the point," I said.

"Well, this electronic neural simulation we call Joe—meaning me—combines all that in one electron flow pattern, since with a temporary entity there is no need for long-term memory or reproduction. My Creator made it all one system, to simplify things. But it makes things more complicated in a way, since to maintain the electron flow to the so-called brain or consciousness circuit, we also have to keep the sexual circuit stimulated."

"You're telling me you can't think straight unless you have a hard-on?"

"That's it," Joe said. "Of course we are talking electronic simulations here. Actually, I don't even have a . . ." He looked down at his lap.

"Spare me the details," I said. "Do you mean this whole time we've been talking, you've been . . ."

"Maintaining my consciousness by enjoying the company of a beautiful woman who just stepped out of the bath. Victoria, I'm only here because you turn me on."

I didn't know whether to feel flattered or insulted. I felt a little of both.

"So you're asking me to strip for you?"

"No, no, no. Not exactly. I know from the orders you place that you like to, shall we say, pamper yourself with elegant and exotic lingerie."

"There's nothing exotic about it, and I bought most of it for my boyfriend," I said.

"You bought several things since you broke up with him."

"Maybe I decided to be my own boyfriend," I said, "and besides, I still say this is sexist as all hell."

"Maybe it is," said Joe. "But I can't help what I am, which is an electronic entity made out of network TV, which makes me very male, and probably what you call sexist. If you had cable, or if I had been put together out of PBS, maybe music or even political commentary would provide me with consciousness. As it is, it's visual sexual stimulation. A beautiful woman in beautiful things."

"White cotton panties are not exactly exciting lingerie," I said.

"Tell that to Elvis," Joe said.

I didn't know what to say, so I said, "Well, I don't know."

"What's to know?" Joe said. "Look at it this way, I didn't set this up and neither did you. We're both just doing our job. If it bothers you that damn much, then forget it. Get dressed and go out, or turn off the lights and go to bed. All you'll miss is *The Joe Show*. And a chance to facilitate a once-in-eternity communications link between your President and an incredibly wise and interesting and magnificent extraterrestrial that's about eighteen times the size of your entire fucking solar system."

"Don't get so excited," I said. I got up for another glass of wine. As I walked to the fridge I could almost imagine Joe's waveforms, or whatever he called them, sparkling all over my body, gently, like bathwater. I was wearing a terry-cloth robe, and the panties of course, and yet I felt more naked than I had ever felt in my life. The feeling wasn't entirely unpleasant.

I poured myself some wine and barely caught myself before offering Joe some. "Do me one favor and knock off the Elvis talk, okay? It makes me feel like a nutcase."

"Done," Joe said. "Elvis is history."

"Now, what is it, exactly, that you have in mind?"

"You know that sheer camisole top and scoop front bikini with lace inserts you ordered from Victoria's Secret, in the magenta?"

"Yeah," I said.

"I'll bet you were planning to wear it tonight."

Actually, I was. "Actually, I was," I said.

"Well?"

Well, why not. I stepped into my closet to change. The cool new silk felt good between my legs, and the low-cut lace bodice did wonderful things with my nipples.

I felt a little nervous stepping back out in front of the TV. "This what you had in mind?" I asked.

"Does Father Guido Sarducci wear a hat?" Behind Joe, on the show, I heard a cymbal crash.

"That band is pretty bad," I said.

"They're out of here." Joe cut them off with a Letterman-like gesture. "They're history, just like Elvis."

"You are kind of sweet in your own way," I said. I could feel my nipples getting hard. Looking down, I could see them, through the camisole. I lit the joint and took another hit. There was now a sofa to one side of Joe's desk. A woman in a short black leather dress, showing lots of leg, sat on it, next to a guy wearing blue jeans and a sport coat.

"You have guests," I said. "Who are they?"

"Nobody, really," Joe said. "Just generic. Part of the matrix. See how the show livens up when you slip into something, shall we say, comfortable?"

"Are you trying to make me blush?"

"Maybe a little. I like it when you blush there."

"Where?"

"On the insides of your thighs."

The amazing thing (to me) was that instead of closing my legs, I opened them more. Joe's slightly out-of-focus smile made me feel warm, welcoming, even (I confess) a little wet. Maybe he's the ideal boyfriend at last, I thought. Real and not real. Here and not here.

There was now a digital clock display inside the O on SHOW. it read 8:56. "Aren't you supposed to be calling the White House?" I asked.

"I'm on the line right now," Joe said "I'm in the West Wing, talking to Stephanopolous. He's the one who has to convince the President this is for real. We can't do it cold."

"He's cute, that Stephanopolous," I said, shrugging the camisole strap off one shoulder. "But how can you be talking to him and, you know, romancing me at the same time?"

"Multitasking," said Joe. "It's what I'm best at."

Was it the dope or was I feeling a faint twinge of jealousy? "And Stephanopolous, he believes your story?"

"Oh, yeah. We're almost ready to put the call through to the, you know—what's his name—"

"The President," I said. "Hey, Joe!"

Joe looked like he was about to nod off. He had his chin on his hand.

"Sit up!" I said. "Jesus! You're the one that told me to wear this outfit!"

"Sorry," Joe said. "It's just that the link takes so much energy . . . it's hard to maintain full consciousness . . . we're about ready to make the connection now, and you're doing fine . . . But how about that little item you ordered when you were still going with what's-his-name . . ."

"Reuben," I said. "Keep talking." I stepped into the closet and out of the camisole and bikini. I found the little rose-colored silk thong, and slipped it on (or slipped it in, you might say). Reuben hadn't been into bras but I had a feeling Joe was. I didn't have anything in rose, but I found a pink lace demi bra that barely covered my nipples. I added some gold loop earrings and asked, "Have you made the link yet?"

"It's going through right now. The Borealis is shimmering. The galactic lens is lined up. Your President and my Creator are about to make contact. In only a few seconds, if we can maintain this connection, we are going to make history."

Before stepping back out into the room, I checked myself in the mirror. The great thing about a seventy-eight-dollar haircut is that it looks the same from every angle. Great.

"You could say the same thing about a million-dollar ass," Joe said.

"What?" Jesus! "You can read my mind?"

"Only the most superficial stuff," Joe said. "Surface electrical activity. Stuff about haircuts. I find myself hoping you'll turn around before you sit down."

I found myself doing it. I found myself enjoying it. I felt as if Joe's waveforms were caressing me inside and out, and I didn't mind the feeling that I was as almost naked in my mind as I was in my body. I didn't feel I had anything to hide. Not from Joe.

"What else do you find yourself hoping?" I said, stretching out on the couch with my legs spread blushingly wide.

"That you'll do what you just did."

"Now you're the one who's blushing," I said.

"Must be because I like your earrings," he said with a smile.

On the couch beside his desk, the woman in the short black leather skirt was sitting with her legs spread à la Sharon Stone. The guy beside her was starting to look a little like Stephanopolous. "Great show tonight, Joe," I said. "Except for the band."

"I'll fire the band if you'll slip your bra off."

"You already fired them, remember?"

"I'll hire them so I can fire them again."

"What girl could resist such an offer?" I was starting to love *The Joe Show*; it made me feel witty as well as beautiful. I shrugged the straps off my shoulder and pulled the cups down, pushing my eager, star-struck breasts up and out toward the bright lights of *The Joe Show*. Some girls' nipples get smaller when they get hard. Mine get bigger.

"I think we have contact!" Joe said. His guests both applauded. I did too.

"Tell me something about this Creator," I said, unhooking my bra and taking it off altogether. "What's he like?"

"What makes you so sure it's a he?"

I had to laugh. There I was stretched out in nothing but a g-string and earrings. "Just an intuition," I said.

"Well, he's like a plasma cloud. He has no mass but he does have a certain luminosity."

"Not that kind of stuff," I said. "I mean, is he nice?"

"Nice?"

"Do you like him?"

"Like him? I love him," said Joe. "I adore him. He created me. He's given me this wonderful existence, even if it's short."

Joe was sweet; no doubt about it. "Do you want me to delete something else?" I asked.

"Delete?"

But he could be dense. "Take something else off," I said.

"Do I? Does Leno have a jaw?"

I took off an earring. It rang when it hit the floor.

"I was thinking about the little panty thing."

"I could tell you were thinking about it," I said. Were the insides of my thighs blushing? I was feeling as lubricious as a dewy summer evening . . . "But I'm going to leave it on for now and give myself a little almond oil rubdown. Besides, aren't you supposed to be working on this historic communications link?"

"I am," Joe said.

"Multitasking?"

"You bet."

Joe sat back with his hands behind his shaggy head—he had a bad haircut for a talk-show host—while I rubbed hand-warmed almond oil onto the backs of my knees, and the bottoms of my feet, and the insides of my thighs. The thing about guys—even simulated guys—is that they're so simple. It's what makes them both a pleasure and a pain. "How's Bill doing?" I asked.

"Bill?"

"He and your boss getting along?"

"Fantastic," Joe said. "But who's paying attention?"

"Thought you were multitasking." I put the almond oil away and took another hit of dope.

"Multipleasure is more like it."

I lay back on the couch, glistening, and spread my legs just a little more. "You say such nice things, Joe. I almost wish you were a real guy."

"I almost am."

Just as an experiment, I pulled the tiny little rose silk thong bikini to one side and, just as an experiment, slipped two fingers under and in between and, just as an experiment . . .

I heard a cymbal crash.

Joe was sitting upright at his desk. He was looking at me funny, as if we had just met.

"I thought you fired that band," I said. "You okay?"

"Absolutely."

"What happened?"

"Nothing! The Borealis window closed, I think. The communication is over. It worked."

"It did?"

"Absolutely. It was great. The White House, Bill on the phone, the whole thing. You were great, too."

"I was?" He seemed distracted. I suddenly felt cold. I got my terry-cloth robe out of the closet and slipped it on.

"Absolutely. Anyway, my time is up. I have to go."

"Go?" I couldn't help sounding disappointed.

"Yeah, see, the thing is, I have this long shutdown protocol."

"Does that mean . . . you die?"

"Yeah, but it's no big deal," Joe said. "Like I said, I'm a temporary entity." The camera moved in closer and Joe lit a cigarette, which looked strange, since people hardly ever smoke on TV anymore, even on the latest late-night shows. "Last cigarette," he said, and I heard canned laughter.

The camera moved in still closer. "How do you spell your last name?" he asked in a loud whisper.

"W-i-n-d-e-r," I said.

The camera pulled back. "Victoria Winder!" Joe said loudly, mispronouncing it. There was applause from the audience, or from somewhere. Even the two guests on the couch applauded. Suddenly, irrationally, I hated them.

"I'll call you, Victoria," Joe said out of the corner of his mouth, reaching across his desk to shake hands with the guests . . .

And the picture was gone. I was watching *Seinfeld*, which I also hate.

I flicked through all the channels, but he was gone. No *Joe Show*. I suddenly felt very naked. I got dressed and went to bed.

The next morning while I was picking through the disaster area that was my apartment, looking for something to wear to work,

I thought about everything that had happened the night before, and I thought, No way! No fucking way.

And yet . . .

There was the empty glass, the half-smoked joint in the ashtray. The Miles Davis CD in the player, still on PAUSE. The lingerie thrown about. Even the earring under the couch.

I bought *The New York Times* on the way to work, but there was nothing in it about a call to Air Force One from the other side of the galaxy. But would there be? Like an idiot I even checked the TV listings, though of course I knew better. No *Joe Show*.

After an hour at work, I had put it out of my mind. I would have forgotten it altogether, except that Joe *did* say he would call. For a night or two—okay, a week or two—I almost expected to hear his voice whenever I picked up the phone.

But I got over it. I did flip through the channels once or twice—okay, several times—not really expecting to find him. But that was it. I filed it under Unsolved Mysteries and forgot about it.

Then three weeks later, while I was standing in line at the Key Food on Broadway and Ninety-sixth, my eyes lit on one of those bizarre supermarket tabloid headlines:

HOUSEWIFE STRIPS FOR STAR MAN
Her Sexy Chemise Powers Interstellar Summit

I had never bought one of those papers before. Imagine my surprise when I read what was essentially my own story, with only the names changed. This woman, who lived in Bend, Oregon, had been contacted by an entity she called Luxor, who ran a sort of game show on TV, and who had enticed her into a form of strip roulette in order to "engorge his faculties" so he could set up a meeting between an extraterrestrial intelligence and ex-President Reagan.

Needless to say, she was not a Democrat but a Republican.

First I was amazed. Then skeptical. Then pissed. Then curious. I tried calling the *Weekly World Globe*, but the paper didn't have a phone, only a box in Sioux City. So I called my only contact in the newspaper business, my former best friend, Sharon, who worked editing the Personals for the *Village Voice*.

I read her the headline and said, "I thought they made those stories up."

"They do," Sharon said.

"No they don't," I said, and told her in some detail what had happened to me. Maybe in too much detail, because the story seemed to make her nervous. "Let me call you right back," she said. But she didn't. She wouldn't take my calls, either.

I waited a few days, during which I scanned the supermarket tabloids for follow-up stories, but there was only the usual Elvis and saucer stuff. Finally I called Sharon at work and left a message on her voice mail: "Either return my call or I will tell your mother what you actually do at the *Voice*."

She returned my call. "Can you meet me after work?" she said.

"Fine," I said. I met her at a coffee shop on Twenty-first and Park, halfway between her office and mine. A tall woman with dark hair was with her in the booth when I got there. I was so mad at the runaround I had been getting that I didn't pay much attention when Sharon introduced her as Eleanor from NASA. I thought she meant the county on Long Island.

"Glad to meet you," I said, then turned to Sharon. "Now kindly explain to me why you are acting so goddamn weird?"

"Because it happened to me, too, Vickie. It happened to thousands of women."

"What happened?" I was going to have coffee but I decided to order a glass of wine. Sharon and her friend were both drinking wine.

"A couple of weeks ago," Sharon said, "an electronic entity showed up in my computer at home, wanting me to wear leather and lace for him."

"Leather and lace?"

"I have a little personal collection."

"Were you smoking dope?"

"You know I don't smoke dope anymore. I gave it up when you did."

"Did he tell you he was trying to set up a meeting with President Clinton?"

"The Dalai Lama."

"And you believed him?"

"Don't sound so shocked, okay? To tell you the truth, Vickie, I figured it was some horny hacker's demented masterpiece, but harmless enough. And I'm kind of a hacker myself. Anyway, he got me going. With the computer it's more physical than with the TV. You can run the mouse all over your . . ."

"Spare me the details," I said. "Then Joe's whole story was bullshit!"

"Not exactly," Eleanor from NASA put in.

"After I heard from you," Sharon said, "I got curious, and I posted an inquiry on the Internet—"

"It was, 'Had safe sex with an electronic entity?' " Eleanor said, smiling shyly into her wineglass. I realized whom she looked like. It was the girl from *Sex, Lies and Videotape*, the nice one. The one with a guy's name.

"—and by midnight I had heard from eleven hundred women on three continents," said Sharon. "All of whom had been contacted by an electronic entity and—"

"Contacted?" I said. "Seduced. Coerced. Raped, is more like it!"

"Whatever. Don't get so excited, okay? You always have to get so excited. Per*suaded*, let's say, to strip on the evening of October 11 under the pretext that—"

"Eleven hundred on the same night?"

"It's called multitasking," said Eleanor.

"Anyway," said Sharon, "to make a long story short, they—we—all tell the same story. The temporary entity, the interstellar plasma cloud intelligence, the high-level meeting. The details vary, but the results are all the same."

"We all undressed for him," said Eleanor.

"We all took it off," said Sharon.

"So it was a hustle," I said.

"Sort of," said Eleanor. "But like any good hustle, parts of it were true. I know because we at NASA had been—"

"Wait a minute. NASA the space agency?"

"I told you when you came in," Sharon said. "Jesus!"

"We at NASA had been tracking this thing for over a month," Eleanor went on, "and—"

"Tracking what thing?"

"The electronic entity. The thing you call Joe, and Sharon calls Reuben . . ."

"Reuben?"

"Just let her finish, okay?" Sharon said. "You never let anybody finish."

"We at NASA had become aware that there was a free-floating conscious entity in the electronic matrix around the country in early October," said Eleanor. "It showed up in NASA's global satellite links, in the Internet, in the cable TV system, even in the phone lines. We were still tracking it when it suddenly disappeared on the twelfth of October. What we found out later was that it had contacted thousands of people, all women, without our knowing about it."

"But I thought you were one of them," I said.

"I keep my private life separate," said Eleanor. "At least I thought it was private. Until I saw Sharon's message on the Internet."

"So Joe was real!" I said. I was relieved to discover that I hadn't been totally deluded; and a little stunned. "A self-created electronic consciousness!"

"Not self-created," said Eleanor. "The part about the plasma cloud, the nonbiological intelligence bigger than a star system— that part was also true. As soon as we knew what to look for, we located it, all the way on the other side of the galaxy. And the plasma cloud created the temporary electronic entity, there's no doubt about that; matrix nets have imprints like DNA. Right now at NASA we are trying to figure out a way to set up communications with the plasma cloud directly, since the interface it created for itself was only temporary, and is gone."

"And was such a fuckin' liar," said Sharon.

"But wait," I said. "If all that was true, Joe and his Creator, both parts of it, then what was the lie?"

"All the rest," said Sharon. "Clinton. Stephanopolous. Air Force One. The Dalai Lama. Ronald Reagan. Michael Jackson—"

"Michael Jackson?"

Eleanor was blushing, looking down into her wineglass.

"Don't be so judgmental, okay?" Sharon said. "You are always so judgmental. But yes, the phone call to the Dalai Lama or Mother Teresa or whatever—that part was all bullshit."

"If all the communications stuff was bullshit," I said, "then what was the point? Why were we contacted?"

"Think about it," Eleanor put in, still blushing.

"Think hard," said Sharon.

"You girls are not serious. Joe—the entity—was just using us to—to get off? That was the whole purpose?"

"Sex," said Eleanor.

"He was cruisin'," said Sharon.

"Either it was the electronic entity or the plasma cloud," Eleanor said. "Or maybe both at once. NASA is still working on that."

I couldn't think of anything to say, so I said, "Well, I'll be damned." I waved for the check.

"And there's one other part that's a lie," Sharon said, as we divided up the bill.

"What's that?"

"The part where he says he'll call you."

"Oh, that," I said as we walked out onto Park Avenue to look for three separate cabs. "That part I never believed."

macs

What did I think? Same thing I think today. I thought it was slightly weird even if it was legal. But I guess I agreed with the families that there had to be Closure. Look out that window there. I can guarantee you, it's unusual to be so high in Oklahoma City. Ever since it happened, this town has had a thing about tall buildings. It's almost like that son of a bitch leveled this town.

Hell, we wanted Closure too, but they had a court order all the way from the Supreme Court. I thought it was about politics at first, and I admit I was a little pissed. Don't use the word pissed. What paper did you say you were with?

Never heard of it, but that's me. Anyway, I was miffed—is that a word? miffed?—until I understood it was about Victims' Rights. So we canceled the execution, and built the vats, and you know the rest.

Well, if you want to know the details you should start with my assistant warden at the time, who handled the details. He's now the warden. Tell him I sent you. Give him my regards.

I thought it opened a Pandora's box, and I said so at the time. It turns out of course that there haven't been that many, and none on that scale. The ones that there are, we get them all. We're sort of the Sloan-Ketterings of the thing. See that scum on the vats? You're looking at eleven of the guy who abducted the little girls in Ohio, the genital mutilation thing, remember? Even eleven's unusual. We usually build four, maybe five tops. And never anything on the scale of the macs.

Build, grow, whatever. If you're interested in the technology, you'll have to talk with the vat vet himself. That's what we call him, he's a good old boy. He came in from the ag school for the macs and he's been here in Corrections ever since. He was an exchange student, but he met a girl from MacAlester and never went home. Isn't it funny how that stuff works? She was my second cousin, so now I have a Hindu second cousin-in-law. Of course he's not actually a Hindu.

A Unitarian, actually. There are several of us here in MacAlester, but I'm the only one from the prison. I was fresh out of Ag and it was my first assignment. How would one describe such an assignment? In my country, we had no such . . . well, you know. It was repellent and fascinating at the same time.

Everyone has the cloning technology. It's the growth rate that gives difficulty. Animals grow to maturity so much faster, and we had done significant work. Six-week cattle, ten-day ducks. Gene tweaking. Enzyme accelerators. They wanted full-grown macs in two and a half years; we gave them 168 thirty-year-old men in eleven months! I used to come down here and watch them grow. Don't tell anyone, especially my wife, Jean, but I grew sort of fond of them.

Hard? It was hard, I suppose, but farming is hard too if you think about it. A farmer may love his hogs but he ships them off, and we all know what for.

You should ask legal services about that. That wasn't part of my operation. We had already grown 168 and I had to destroy one before he was even big enough to walk, just so they could include the real one. Ask me if I appreciated that!

It was a second court order. It came through after the macs were in the vats. Somebody's bright idea in Justice. I suppose they figured it would legitimize the whole operation to include the real McCoy, so to speak, but then somebody has to decide who gets him. Justice didn't want any part of that and neither did we, so we brought in one of those outfits that run lotteries, because that's what it was, a lottery, but kind of a strange one, if you know what I mean.

Strange in that the winner wasn't supposed to know if he won or not. He or she. It's like the firing squad, where nobody knows who has the live bullets. Nobody is supposed to know who gets the real one. I'm sure it's in the records somewhere, but that stuff's all sealed. What magazine did you say you were with?

Sealed? It's destroyed. That was part of the contract. I guess whoever numbered the macs would know, but that was five years ago and it was done by lot anyway. It could probably be figured out by talking to the drivers who did the deliveries, or the drivers who picked up the remains, or even the families themselves. But it would be illegal, wouldn't it? Unethical, too, if you ask me, since it would interfere with what the whole thing was about, which was Closure. Victims' Rights. That's why we were hired, to keep it secret, and that's what we did. End of story.

UPS was a natural because we had just acquired Con Tran and were about to go into the detainee delivery business under contract with the BOP. The macs were mostly local, of course, but not all. Several went out of state; two to California, for example. It wasn't a security problem since the macs were all sort of docile. I figured they were engineered that way. Is engineered the word? Anyway, the problem was public relations. Appearances, to be frank. You can't drive around with a busload of macs. And most families don't want the TV and papers at the door, like Publishers Clearing House. (Though some do!) So we delivered them in vans, two and three at a time, mostly in the morning, sort of on the sly. We told the press we were still working out the details until it was all done. Some people videotaped their delivery. I suspect they're the ones that also videotaped their executions.

I'm not one of those who had a problem with the whole thing. No sirree. I went along with my drivers, at first especially, and met quite a few of the loved ones, and I wish you could have seen the grateful expressions on their faces. You get your own mac to kill any way you want to. That's Closure. It made me proud to be an American even though it came out of a terrible tragedy. An unspeakable tragedy.

Talk to the drivers all you want to. What channel did you say you were with?

You wouldn't have believed the publicity at the time. It was a big triumph for Victims' Rights, which is now in the Constitution, isn't it? Maybe I'm wrong. Anyway, it wasn't a particularly what you might call pleasant job, even though I was all for the families and Closure and stuff and still am.

Looked like anybody. Looked like you except for the beard. None of them were different. They were all the same. One of them was supposedly the real McCoy, but so what? Isn't the whole point of cloning supposed to be that each one is the same as the first one? Nobody's ever brought this up before. You're not from one of those talk shows, are you?

They couldn't have talked to us if they had wanted to, and we weren't about to talk to them. They were all taped up except for the eyes, and you should have seen those eyes. You tried to avoid it. I had one that threw up all over my truck even though theoretically you can't throw up through that tape. I told the dispatcher my truck needed a theoretical cleaning.

They all seemed the same to me. Sort of panicked and gloomy. I had a hard time hating them, in spite of what they done, or their daddy done, or however you want to put it. They say they could only live five years anyway before their insides turned to mush. That was no problem of course. Under the Victims' Rights settlement it had to be done in thirty days, that was from date of delivery.

I delivered thirty-four macs, of 168 altogether. I met thirty-four fine families, and they were a fine cross section of American life, black and white, Catholic and Protestant. Not so many Jews.

I've heard that rumor. You're going to have rumors like that when one of them is supposedly the real McCoy. There were other rumors too, like that one of the macs was pardoned by its family and sent away to school somewhere. That would have been hard. I mean, if you got a mac you had to return a body within thirty days. One story I heard was that they switched bodies after a car wreck. Another was that they burned another body at the stake and turned it in. But that one's hard to believe too. Only one of the macs was burned at the stake, and they had to get a special clearance to do that. Hell, you can't even burn leaves in Oklahoma anymore.

SaniMed collected, they're a medical waste outfit, since we're not allowed to handle remains. They're not going to be able to tell you much. What did they pick up? Bones and ashes. Meat.

Some of it was pretty gruesome but in this business you get used to that. We weren't supposed to have to bag them, but you know how it is. The only one that really got to me was the crucifixion. That sent the wrong message, if you ask me.

There was no way we could tell which one of them was the real McCoy, not from what we picked up. You should talk to the loved ones. Nice people, maybe a little impatient sometimes. The third week was the hardest in terms of scheduling. People had been looking forward to Closure for so long, they played with their macs for a week or so, but then it got old. Played is not the word, but you know what I mean. Then it's bang bang and honey call SaniMed. They want them out of the house ASAP.

It's not that we were slow, but the schedule was heavy. In terms of what we were picking up, none of it was that hard for me. These were not people. Some of them were pretty chewed up. Some of them were chewed up pretty bad.

I'm not allowed to discuss individual families. I can say this: the ceremony, the settlement, the execution, whatever you want to call it, wasn't always exactly what everybody had expected or wanted. One family even wanted to let their mac go. Since they couldn't do that, they wanted a funeral. A funeral for toxic waste!

I can't give you their name or tell you their number.

I guess I can tell you that. It was between 103 and 105.

I'm not ashamed of it. We're Christians. Forgive us our trespasses as we forgive those who trespass against us. We tried to make it legal, but the state wouldn't hear of it, since the execution order had already been signed. We had thirty days, so we waited till the last week and then used one of those Kevorkian kits, the lethal objection thing. Injection, I mean. The doctor came with it but we had to push the plunger thing. It seems to me like one of the rights of Victims' Rights should be—but I guess not.

There was a rumor that another family forgave and got away with it, but we never met them. They supposedly switched bodies in a car wreck and sent their mac to forestry school in Canada. Even if it was true, which I doubt, he would be almost five now, and that's half their life span. Supposedly their internal organs harden after ten years. What agency did you say you were with?

We dropped ours out of an airplane. My uncle has a big ranch out past Mayfield with his own airstrip and everything. Cessna 172. It was illegal, but what are they going to do? *C'est la vie*, or rather *c'est la mort*. Or whatever.

They made us kill him. Wasn't he ours to do with as we liked? Wasn't that the idea? He killed my daddy like a dog and if I wanted to tie him up like a dog, isn't that my business? Aren't you a little long in the tooth to be in college, boy?

An electric chair. It's out in the garage. Want to see it? Still got the shit stain on the seat.

My daddy came home with a mac, and took my mother and me out back and made us watch while he shot him. Shot him all over, from the feet up. The whole thing took ten minutes. It didn't seem to do anybody any good, my aunt is still dead. They never found most of her, only the bottom of a leg. Would you like some chocolates? They're from England.

Era? It was only like five years ago. I never took delivery. I thought I was the only one but I found out later there were eight others. I guess they just put them back in the vat. They couldn't live more than five years anyway. Their insides turned hard. All their DNA switches were shut off or something.

I got my own Closure my own way. That's my daughter's picture there. As for the macs, they are all dead. Period. They lived a while, suffered, and died. Is it any different for the rest of us? What church did you say you were with?

I don't mind telling you our real name, but you should call us 49 if you quote us. That's the number we had in the lottery. We got our mac on a Wednesday, kept him for a week, then set him in a kitchen chair and shot him in the head. We didn't have any idea how messy that would be. The state should have given some instructions or guidelines.

Nobody knew which one was the original, and that's the way it should be. Otherwise it would ruin the Closure for everybody else. I can tell you ours wasn't, though. It was just a feeling I had. That's why we just shot him and got it over with. I just couldn't get real excited about killing something that seemed barely alive, even though it supposedly had all his feelings and memories. But some people got into it and attended several executions. They had a kind of network.

Let me see your list. These two are the ones I would definitely talk to: 112 and 43. And maybe 13.

Is that what they call us, 113? So I'm just a number again. I thought I was through with that in the army. I figured we had the real one, the real McCoy, because he was so hard to kill. We cut him up with a chain saw, a little Homelite. No, sir, I didn't mind the mess and yes, he hated every minute of it. All twenty some odd, which is how long it took. I would have fed him to my dogs if we hadn't had to turn the body in. End of fucking story.

Oh, yeah. Double the pleasure, double the fun. Triple it, really. The only one I was against was this one, 61. The crucifixion. I think that sent the wrong message, but the neighbors loved it.

Drown in the toilet was big. Poison, fire, hanging, you name it. People got these old books from the library but that medieval stuff took special equipment. One guy had a rack built but the neighbors objected to the screaming. I guess there are some limits, even to Victims' Rights. Ditto the stake stuff.

I'm sure our mac wasn't the real McCoy. You want to know why? He was so quiet and sad. He just closed his eyes and died. I'm sure the real one would have been harder to kill. My mac wasn't innocent, but he wasn't guilty either. Even though he looked like a thirty-year-old man he was only eighteen months old, and that sort of showed.

I killed him just to even things out. Not revenge, just Closure. After spending all the money on the court case and the settlement, not to mention the cloning and all, the deliveries, it would have been wasteful not to do it, don't you think?

I've heard that surviving thing but it's just a rumor. Like Elvis. There were lots of rumors. They say one family tried to pardon their mac and send him to Canada or somewhere. I don't think so!

You might try this one, 43. They used to brag that they had the real one. I don't mind telling you I resented that and still do, since we were supposed to all share equally in the Closure. But some people have to be number one.

It's over now anyway. What law firm did you say you worked for?

I could tell he was the original by the mean look in his eye. He wasn't quite so mean after a week in that rat box.

Some people will always protest and write letters and such. But what about something that was born to be put to death? How can you protest that?

Closure, that's what it was all about. I went on to live my life. I've been married again and divorced already. What college did you say you were from?

The real McCoy? I think he just kept his mouth shut and died like the rest of them. What's he goin' to say, *here I am*, and make it worse? And as far as that rumor of him surviving, you can file it under Elvis.

There was also a story that somebody switched bodies after a car wreck and sent their mac to Canada. I wouldn't put too much stock in that one, either. Folks around here don't even think about Canada. Forgiveness either.

We used that state kit, the Kevorkian thing. I heard about twenty families did. We just sat him down and May pushed the plunger. Like flushing a toilet. May and myself—she's gone now, God bless her—we were interested in Closure, not revenge.

This one, 13, told me one time he thought he had the real McCoy, but it was wishful thinking, if you ask me. I don't think you could tell the real one. I don't think you should want to even if you could.

I'm afraid you can't ask him about it, because they were all killed in a fire, the whole family. It was just a day before the ceremony they had planned, which was some sort of slow thing with wires. There was a gas leak or something. They were all killed and their mac was destroyed in the explosion. Fire and explosion.

It was—have you got a map? oooh, that's a nice one—right here. On the corner of Oak and Increase, only a half a mile from the site of the original explosion, ironically. The house is gone now. What insurance company did you say you worked for?

See that new strip mall? That Dollar Store's where the house stood. The family that lived in it was one of the ones who lost a loved one in the Oklahoma City bombing. They got one of the macs as part of the Victims' Rights Closure Settlement, but unfortunately tragedy struck them again before they got to get Closure. Funny how the Lord works in mysterious ways.

No, none of them are left. There was a homeless guy who used to hang around but the police ran him off. Beard like yours. Might have been a friend of the family, some crazy cousin, who knows. So much tragedy they had. Now he lives in the back of the mall in a Dumpster.

There. That yellow thing. It never gets emptied. I don't know why the city doesn't remove it but it's been there for almost five years just like that.

I wouldn't go over there. People don't fool with him. He doesn't bother anybody, but, you know.

Suit yourself. If you knock on it he'll come out, figuring you've got some food for him or something. Kids do it for meanness sometimes. But stand back, there is a smell.

"Daddy?"

Tell Them They Are All Full of Shit and They Should Fuck Off

"Mr. President, you might want to take this. It's that NASA fellow you met last month at the Kennedy Center reception."

"Good. What's his name, Palaver? Put him through. Hello? This is the President speaking."

"Tell them they are all full of shit and they should fuck off."

"What? Hello?"

"This is Dr. Salavard, Mr. President. From NASA; the SETI project? Remember, we met at the Kennedy Center affair, and you gave me this number, and you said I was to call you directly, first thing, when we got some results, and not to wait until the entire scientific community had been . . ."

"Yes, yes, I remember, Dr. Salavard. So what do you have for me?"

"We have a signal, sir. What we call a specific. Nothing absolutely positive yet, but—"

"Do you mean an extraterrestrial communication of some sort?"

"It would seem that way, sir."

"Seem? Can you tell me something definite?"

"Tell them they are all full of shit and they should fuck off."

"What makes you so sure it's from an intelligent source?"

"The pattern, Mr. President. The signal we are receiving is not a cycling repetition but a series of super low-frequency wave spikes in a numerical pattern known as an ascending logarithm. An almost certain sign of intelligence and intentionality. We're pretty sure it's a communication."

"Sure enough to describe it to my Cabinet tomorrow morning, plus a few select guests from the Hill?"

"Tell them they are all full of shit and they should fuck off."

"You can do it by satellite phone-link. We're having a pre-breakfast meeting here at the White House. My staff will ring you in at eight A.M. sharp. I hope I don't need to tell you not to breathe a word of this to anybody."

Gentlemen, ladies, we have a surprise guest on the line by satellite—Dr. Bruno Salavard, who is in charge of NASA's new SETI project. You wouldn't be sitting here if you didn't know what SETI was all about, or the importance I attach to this endeavor. Dr. Salavard, go ahead and tell them what you told me."

"Tell them they are all full of shit and they should fuck off."

"Now, we have time for a few questions. You can ask Dr. Salavard directly, since we're hooked up to a speakerphone. Senator?"

"Dr. Salavard, what makes you so certain this is a signal from an extraterrestrial intelligence? Couldn't it be a pulsar or even a reflected radio beep from one of our satellites?"

"Senator, we have corrected for all that. The signal comes to us from the system Gorodel 3433B, toward the center of this galaxy. Almost a near neighbor, you might say."

"Admiral, did you have a question?"

"Yes, Mr. President. Any idea what this n-near n-neighbor is trying to t-tell us, Professor?"

"Tell them they are all full of shit and they should fuck off."

"I have a question. This is Congresswoman Elaine Long-wood from Chicago. What's the procedure for converting this logarithmic math sequence into words? How long before we get a message in language we can understand?"

"That's our first priority, Congresswoman. Even as we speak, the signal is being run through NASA's 986-based syntax extrapolator. If we come up with a computable formula, or what we call a *friendly stack*, then—"

"Speaking of friendly, do we think they are friendly?"

"Are we sh-sharing this information with the other N-NAFTA n-nations?"

"Any chance they might be human like us?"

"Tell them they are all full of shit and they should fuck off."

"Thank you, Dr. Salavard. I'm going to have to cut off questions here, ladies and gentlemen, so Dr. Salavard can get back to work. You will be kept posted on further developments through my staff here at the White House. Dr. Salavard, thank you for joining us. I hope I don't need to tell you, I look forward to hearing from you soon."

Tell them they are all full of shit and they should fuck off."

"Dr. Salavard, is that you? I have the President on the line. Can you hold?"

"Of course!"

"Hello, Dr. Salavard. The President here. Any progress? Are we any closer to actually deciphering the alien message, if it is in fact a message for us?"

"No question but that it's aimed at us, Mr. President. It's what we call *double-specific*—extremely localized, and the signal is getting stronger; as a matter of fact, the signal's intensity and frequency have increased by a factor of four since your White House meeting two days ago."

"Nothing your psychic exterminator can't handle, I hope."

"Syntax extrapolator, Mr. President. It works on the principle that—"

"I was making a joke, Dr. Salavard. But that's not why I called. I called to tell you that I'm speaking to the Security Council this afternoon, in closed session. As a matter of fact, I'm putting my hat on right now. I'm on my way to the U.N."

"Tell them they are all full of shit and they should fuck off."

"This news is going to leak out sooner or later, Professor, and I don't want it to look like we are trying to hog this whole deal."

"Yes, sir. I only wish we had something more, well, definite."

"You will, and I expect you to call me as soon as your people come up with it. Night or day. I have you routed directly into the Oval Office; all you have to do is ask for me."

"Yes, sir, Mr. President."

• • •

Tell them they are all full of shit and they should fuck off."

"Salavard, is that you? This is the President."

"How'd it go, sir?"

"The U.N. meeting? Pretty good. Great, in fact. I've got them all sitting on the edge of their chairs. But how soon can we give them something? I need a word, a phrase, even if it's just 'Hello, how are you.' "

"How soon? I don't know, Mr. President. It could be within hours, days at the most. The syntax extrapolator is showing eighty-nine percent completion, and it's cooking right along. If we don't lose the signal before it finishes . . ."

"Lose the signal? Why should we lose the signal? Is there something you're not telling me?"

"No, sir. It's just that we've got the syntax extrapolator pro-grammed in what we call 'backspin mode,' which means that it can only analyze a completed message. As long as the signal doesn't fade before it finishes, we're okay."

"I'm counting on you to see that it doesn't, Salavard. Mean-while, I think we better go public with this thing right now, before the tabloids beat us to it. I want to take it to the people. Tonight."

"Tell them they are all full of shit and they should fuck off."

"I'm the President, Salavard, I can't go on talk shows. That's what we have Vice Presidents for. But he hasn't been briefed on SETI. That's why I'm counting on you."

"Tell them they are all full of shit and they should fuck off."

"Letterman is bigger than Leno, Salavard. Just don't let him bully you. Make sure you get your point across."

Tell them they are all full of shit and they should fuck off."

"Welcome to the show, Dr. Salavard. Let me get this straight. This is your job, to talk to spacemen? Your day job?"

"Tell them they are all full of shit and they should fuck off."

"And you get paid for this? I mean, like a salary? It's our tax money, folks. Shouldn't we know what they do with it?"

"Tell them they are all full of shit and they should fuck off."

"Are these guys calling collect? Can we get one of these spacemen on the show?"

"Our syntax extrapolation program is based on the completion of the rising frequency curve, Dave. Until the algorithm is completed, we won't have anything. But we expect it to terminate within hours and then we will have the first message from an alien intelligence."

"Dr. Salavard, have you checked your answering machine? Maybe something came in while you were in the Green Room."

"Tell them they are all full of shit and they should fuck off."

"There weren't any little green men in the Green Room, were there? I hope they're not coming here hoping to collect welfare."

"Tell them they are all full of shit and they should fuck off."

"Thank you for being on the show, Dr. Salavard. Taking off from what I am sure is a busy schedule on the phone with the President, and so forth. Don't touch that dial, folks! We'll be back with Lyle Lovett and his new bride, Demi Moore, right after a word from our sponsors."

Tell them they are all full of shit and they should fuck off."

"Salavard, is that you? This is the President speaking. I caught you on Letterman last night."

"Sorry I was so nervous, Mr. President."

"You were fine."

"I didn't sound repetitive to you?"

"Look, you didn't let him bully you and you got your point across. That's the bottom line. Why so gloomy?"

"Tell them they are all full of shit and they should fuck off."

"Is there something you're not telling me?"

"The signal, sir. It started what we call its *descending logarithm* last night, while I was in New York. By the time I got back here to Huntsville, it had already started to fade."

"Fade? What do we have so far?"

"Ninety-six percent, Mr. President."

"So!"

"I know that sounds like a lot, sir, but remember I told you that our syntax extrapolation program is based on the completion of the algorithmic curve. If the sequence is truncated without completion, we get zip."

"Zip?"

"It's like a sentence where the last word is the one that explains everything. Noun, verb, everything. We're still getting a signal but . . ."

"That settles it! I'm going to go on the air and address the nation tonight, while we have a fish on the line, so to speak."

"Tell them they are all full of shit and they should fuck off."

"I'm going to tell them that it doesn't matter what the message is; the exciting news is that there *is* a message. We are not alone. There is somebody out there. Somebody who wants to get in touch with us. And, Salavard?"

"Yes, Mr. President?"

"Don't let them hang up. I'm counting on you!"

Mr. President, I think you'll want to take this. It's . . ."

"Salavard, is that you? What did you think of my Fireside Chat? Do you have any more news for me?"

"Yes, sir. Bad news, Mr. President. The worst."

"Shit. I knew it!"

"We lost our signal before the extrapolation was completed. All we're looking at here is some math, which could say nothing or anything. I'm sorry, Mr. President. I should have—"

"Should have what?"

"Tell them they are all full of shit and they should fuck off."

"What? Hello?"

"I said, I don't know, sir. There's no way to make the program run any faster. If we had another shot we could articulate a compression sequence, and run it through a simultaneity compiler, which might give us a head start, but . . ."

"Then don't apologize, Salavard. You did your best. At least we have affirmed that the SETI program is not a waste of time.

Right? I mean, hell, now we know there's somebody out there. Right?"

"Tell them they are all full of shit and they should fuck off."

"So why don't I get a good feeling about this, Salavard? Could we have missed something?"

"Missed something, sir?"

"Could they have been telling us something we weren't ready for? Something we just didn't want to hear?"

"I don't see how that could be, Mr. President."

"Well, maybe they'll call back. You'll have your program ready to go. Why wouldn't they call back?"

"I don't see any reason why not, Mr. President."

"What? Hello?"

"I said, I don't see why not, Mr. President."

The Player

The Belt is a quiet place. The sun is so far away you can't hear its singing. The roar of a million million stars devouring themselves doesn't make a sound. The silence was broken by a *beep.beep.beep*.

Afeni Ben Carol heard the *beeps*. She sought them with her seeker, found them with her finder. What she found was about the size of a car. She pulled it into the coldlock with a net.

Afeni Ben Carol was named for her mother and father before her, as they were named for theirs. She was of a naming kind that had survived the hundred generation "here I am" that every naming kind undergoes, and one in a thousand survives. And settles down to enjoy the one galactic turning life span of every species, sentient or not.

Smaller than I would have thought, she said, not in English, but in a tongue that still held flourishes of that ancient, soaring, creaking, reeking mix. A language, like a Douglas fir, lasts about five hundred years.

Afeni Ben Carol talked to herself a lot. She was a good listener. She had been cruising the Belt for almost a year, looking for heavy metals. What she found was a silver sphere about the size of a car. She pulled it into the coldlock with a net.

Not a ship, said AB Carol. That much was clear. No propulsives, no attractives, no environmentals. In her young heart of hearts she thought it might be that ancient dream of dreams come true: the smoke of another fire. For it was a made thing and she was of that making kind.

She cut short her trip and took it home. For she was of that homing, that gathering kind, that had gathered the branches of the planets together in a web to rock their babies to sleep. She took it all the way back to their ancestral watery, windswept little Ert or Earth or Heart or Hearth or Home.

The Q Group invited her to join (for she had pulled it into the coldlock with a net). Others in the Q Group included: TRan de Markus, Bitter Sweet, Orson Farr, and Grohn Elizabeth, plus two sets of twins for symmetry. They were all of that prodding, that poking, that questioning kind.

The Q Group went into a huddle as the oak leaves fell around them, in long lovely shallow drifts. Good listeners, they listened to the *beep.beep.beep.*

Each *beep* was made of smaller *beeps*, and those of smaller still. Mathematical. Bitter Sweet did the math. "Find me," it said.

Already did that, Afeni Ben Carol said.

They found a little panel about the size of a door. Inside, there was a smaller sphere spinning in a beam of stationary light. Singing *beep.beep.beep.*

TRan de Markus did the music. "Fix me," it sang, and so they did, for they were of that fixing kind. A slight wobble, a simple test of hand and eye. The stars straightened up on their silvery strings. The *beeps* folded into a *hum*, long and flat and thin.

Then stopped.

The silence was eloquent. "Send me on," it whispered. The Q Group nodded, a little forlorn. Their work done.

Afeni Ben Carol took it back out to the Belt. Orson Farr went with her. The planets whirled by in their giddy whirlpool stream.

Afeni Ben Carol thought about those who had found it and fixed it before, and those before them, and before them. It was so old. She wondered who would find it and fix it after she sent it on. What if nobody found it? She was afraid to let it go.

It has to be found and fixed every million million years or so, or it will slow down, she said. Develop a wobble. Stop playing true. Then stop playing altogether. She was afraid to let it go.

Let's keep it here, said Orson Farr. We might live a million million years. But probably not.

Probably not, said Afeni Ben Carol, who had pulled it into the coldlock with a net. She wiped it off and made it shine like a mirror. Peering into it she saw a million spinning wheels of streaming carbon sparks that someday might, that someday would, weave another wandering, finding, fixing kind.

And what's it playing? asked Orson Farr.

AB Carol pointed it toward the stars. The universe, she said, and gave it a spin, and sent it on its way.

An Office Romance

The first time Ken678 saw Mary97, he was in Municipal Real Estate, queued for a pickup for Closings. She stood two spaces in front of him: blue skirt, orange tie, slightly convex white blouse, like every other female icon. He didn't know she was a Mary; he couldn't see which face she had. But she held her Folder in both hands, as "old-timers" often did, and when the queue scrolled forward he saw her fingernails.

They were red.

Then the queue flickered and scrolled again, and she was gone. Ken was intrigued but he promptly forgot about it. It was a busy time of year, and he was running like crazy from Call to Task. Later that week he saw her again, paused at an open Window in the Corridor between Copy and Send. He slowed as he passed her, by turning his Folder sideways—a trick he had learned. There were those red fingernails again. It was curious.

Fingernails were not on the Option Menu.

Red was not on the Color Menu, either.

Ken used the weekend to visit his Mother at the Home. It was her birthday or anniversary or something like that. Ken hated weekends. He had grown used to his Ken face and he felt uncomfortable without it. He hated his old name, which his Mother insisted on calling him. He hated how grim and terrifying things were outside. To avoid panic he closed his eyes and hummed—

out here, he could do both—trying to simulate the peaceful hum of the Office.

But there is no substitute for the real thing, and Ken didn't relax until the week restarted, and he was back inside. He loved the soft electron buzz of the search engines, the busy streaming icons, the dull butter shine of the Corridors, the shimmering Windows with their relaxing scenes of the environment. He loved his life and he loved his work.

That was the week he met Mary; or rather, she met him.

Ken678 had just retrieved a Folder of documents from Search and was taking them to Print. He could see by the blur of icons ahead that there was going to be a long queue at the Bus leaving Commercial, so he paused in the Corridor; waitstates were encouraged in high traffic zones.

He opened a Window by resting his Folder on the sill. There was no air of course, but there was a nice view. The scene was the same in every Window in Microserf Office 6.9: cobblestones and quiet cafés and chestnut trees in blossom. April in Paris.

Ken heard a voice. <Beautiful isn't it? >

< What? > he said, confused. Two icons couldn't open the same Window, and yet there she was beside him. Red fingernails and all.

< April in Paris> she said.

< I know. But how—>

< A little trick I learned> She pointed to her Folder, stacked on top of his, flush right.

< —did you do that? > he finished because it was in his buffer. She had the Mary face, which it so happened was his favorite. And the red fingernails of course.

< When they are flush right the Window reads us as one icon > she said.

< Probably reads only the right edge > Ken said. < Neat >

< Name's Mary > she said. < Mary97 >

< Ken678 >

< You slowed when you passed me last week, Ken. Neat trick too. I figure that made you almost worth an intro. Most of the workaholics here in City Hall are pretty unsociable >

Ken showed her his Folder trick even though she seemed to know it already. < How long you been at City? > he asked.

< Too long >

< How come I never saw you before? >

< Maybe you saw me but didn't notice me > she said. She held up a hand with red fingernails. < I didn't always have these >

< Where'd you get them? >

< It's a secret >

< They're pretty neat > Ken said.

< Is that pretty or neat? >

< Both >

< Are you flirting with me? > she asked, smiling that Mary smile. Ken tried to think of an answer, but he was too slow. Her Folder was blinking, a waitstate interrupt, and she was gone.

A few cycles later in the week he saw her again, paused at an open Window in the Corridor between Copy and Verify. He slid his Folder over hers, flush right, and he was standing beside her, looking out into April in Paris.

< You learn fast > she said.

< I have a good teacher > he said. Then he said what he had been rehearsing over and over: < And what if I was? >

< Was what? >

< Flirting >

< That would be okay > she said, smiling the Mary smile.

Ken678 wished for the first time that the Ken face had a smile. His Folder was flickering but he didn't want to leave yet. < How long have you been at City? > he asked again.

< Forever > she said. She was exaggerating, of course, but in a sense it was true. She told Ken she had been at City Hall when Microserf Office 6.9 was installed. < Before Office, records were

stored in a basement, in metal drawers, accessed by hand. I
helped put it all on disk. Data entry, it was called >
   < Entry? >
   < This was before the neural interface. We sat *outside* and
reached in through a Keyboard and looked in through a sort
of Window called a Monitor. There was nobody *in* the Office.
Just pictures of files and stuff. There was no April in Paris, of
course. It was added later to prevent claustrophobia >
   Ken678 calculated in his head. How old did that make
Mary—fifty-five? Sixty? It didn't matter of course. All icons are
young, and all females are beautiful.

Ken had never had a friend before, in or out of the Office.
Much less a girlfriend. He found himself hurrying his Calls and
Tasks so that he could cruise the Corridors looking for
Mary97. He could usually find her at an open Window gazing
at the cobblestones and the little cafés, the blossoming chestnut trees. Mary loved April in Paris. < It's so romantic there >
she said. < Can't you just imagine yourself walking down the
boulevard? >
   < I guess > Ken said. But in fact he couldn't. He didn't like to
imagine things. He preferred real life, or at least Microserf
Office 6.9. He loved standing at the Window beside her, listening to her soft Mary voice, answering in his deep Ken voice.
   < How did you get here? > she asked. Ken told her he had
been hired as a temp, transporting scanned-in midcentury documents up the long stairway from Archives to Active.
   < My name wasn't Ken then, of course > he said. < All the
temp icons wore gray, male and female alike. We were neural
interfaced through helmets instead of earrings. None of the regular Office workers spoke to us, or even noticed us. We worked
fourteen, fifteen cycle days. >
   < And you loved it > Mary said.
   < I loved it > Ken admitted. < I had found what I was looking
for. I loved being inside > And he told her how wonderful and
strange it had felt, at first, to be an icon, to see himself as he

walked around, as if he were both inside and outside his own body.

< Of course it seems normal now > he said.

< It is > Mary said. And she smiled that Mary smile.

Several weeks passed before Ken got up the courage to make what he thought of as "his move."

They were at the Window where he had first spoken with her, in the Corridor between Copy and Verify. Her hand was resting on the sill, red fingernails shimmering, and he put his hand exactly over it. Even though he couldn't actually feel it, it felt good.

He was afraid she would move her hand but instead she smiled that Mary smile and said < I thought you were never going to do that >

< I've been wanting to ever since I first saw you > he said.

She moved her fingers under his. It almost tingled. < Want to see what makes them red? >

< You mean your secret? >

< It'll be our secret. You know the Browser between Deeds and Taxes? Meet me there in three cycles >

The Browser was a circular connector with no Windows. Ken met Mary at Select All and followed her toward Insert, where the doors got smaller and closer together.

< Ever hear of an Easter Egg? > she asked.

< Sure > Ken said. < A programmer's surprise hidden in the software. An unauthorized subroutine that's not in the manual. Sometimes humorous or even obscene. Easter Eggs are routinely— >

< You're just repeating what you learned in Orientation > Mary said.

< —found and cleared from commercial software by background debuggers and optimizers > Ken finished because it was already in his buffer.

< But that's okay > she said. < Here we are >

Mary97 led him into a small windowless room. There was nothing in it but a tiny, heart-shaped table.

< This room was erased but never overwritten > Mary said. < The Optimizer must have missed it. That's why the Easter Egg is still here. I discovered it by accident >

On the table were three playing cards. Two were facedown and one was faceup: the ten of diamonds.

< Ready? > Without waiting for Ken's answer, Mary turned the ten of diamonds facedown. Her fingernails were no longer red.

< Now you try it > she said.

Ken backed away.

< Don't get nervous. This card doesn't do anything, just changes the Option. Go ahead! >

Reluctantly, Ken turned the ten of diamonds up.

Mary's fingernails were red again. Nothing happened to his own.

< That first card just works for girls > Mary said.

< Neat > Ken said, relaxing a little.

< There's more > Mary said. < Ready? >

< I guess >

Mary turned up the second card. It was the queen of hearts. As soon as she turned it up, Ken heard a *clippity clop*. A Window opened in the windowless room.

In the Window it was April in Paris.

Ken saw a gray horse coming straight down the center of the boulevard. It wore no harness but its tail and mane were bobbed. Its enormous red penis was almost dragging the cobblestones.

< See the horse > Mary97 said. She was standing beside Ken at the Window. Her convex white blouse and orange and blue tie both were gone. She was wearing a red lace brassiere. The sheer cups were full. The narrow straps were taut. The tops of her plump breasts were round and bright as moons.

Ken678 couldn't move or speak. It was terrifying and wonderful at the same time. Mary's hands were behind her back, unfastening her brassiere. There! But just as the cups started to fall away from her breasts, a whistle blew.

The horse had stopped in the middle of the boulevard. A gendarme was running toward it, waving a stick.

The Window closed. Mary97 was standing at the table, wearing her convex white blouse and blue and orange tie again. Only the ten of diamonds was faceup.

< You turned the card down too soon > Ken said. He had wanted to see her nipples.

< The queen turns herself down > Mary said. < An Easter Egg is a closed algorithm. Runs itself once it gets started. Did you like it? And don't say you guess >

She smiled that Mary smile and Ken tried to think of what to say. But both their Folders were blinking, waitstate interrupts, and she was gone.

Ken found her a couple cycles later at their usual meeting place, at the open Window in the Corridor between Copy and Verify.

< Like it? > he said. < I love it >

< Are you flirting with me? > Mary97 asked.

< What if I am > he said, and the familiar words were almost as good as a smile.

< Then come with me >

Ken678 followed Mary97 to the Browser twice more that week. Each time was the same; each time was perfect. As soon as Mary turned over the queen of hearts, Ken heard a *clippity-clop*. A Window opened in the windowless room and there was the horse coming down the boulevard, its enormous penis almost dragging the cobblestones. Mary97's ripe round perfect breasts were spilling over the top of her red lace brassiere as she said < See the horse > and reached behind her back, unfastening—

Unfastening her bra! And just as her cups started to fall away, just as Ken678 was about to see her nipples, a gendarme's whistle blew and Mary97 was wearing the white blouse again, the blue and orange tie. The Window was closed, the queen of hearts facedown.

< The only problem with Easter Eggs > Mary said < is that they are always the same. Whoever designed this one had a case of arrested development >

< I like always the same > Ken replied.

As he left for the weekend, Ken678 scanned the crowd of office regulars filing down the long steps of City Hall. Which woman was Mary97? There was, of course, no way of knowing. They were all ages, all nationalities, but they all looked the same with their blank stares, neural interface gold earrings, and mesh marks from their net gloves.

The weekend seemed to last forever. As soon as the week restarted, Ken raced through his Calls and Tasks, then cruised the Corridors until he found Mary, at "their" spot, the open Window between Copy and Verify.

< Isn't it romantic? > she said, looking out into April in Paris.

< I guess > said Ken, impatiently. He was thinking of her hands behind her back, unfastening.

< What could be more romantic? > she asked, and he could tell she was teasing.

< A red brassiere > he said.

< Then come with me > she said.

They met in the Browser three times that week. Three times Ken678 heard the horse, three times he watched the red lace brassiere falling away, falling away. That week was the closest to happiness he would ever come.

< Do you ever wonder what's under the third card? > Mary97 asked. They were standing at the Window between Copy and Verify. A new week had barely restarted. In April in Paris the chestnuts were in blossom above the cobblestones. The cafés were empty. A few stick figures in the distance were getting in and out of carriages.

< I guess > Ken678 said, though it wasn't true. He didn't like to wonder.

< Me too > said Mary.

When they met a few cycles later in the windowless room off the Browser, Mary put her red-fingernailed hand on the third card and said < There's one way to find out >

Ken didn't answer. He felt a sudden chill.

< We both have to do it > she said. < You turn up the queen and I'll turn up the third card. Ready? >

< I guess > Ken said, though it was a lie.

The third card was the ace of spades. As soon as it turned up, Ken knew something was wrong.

Something felt different.

It was the cobblestones, under his feet.

It was April in Paris and Ken678 was walking down the boulevard. Mary97 was beside him. She was wearing a low-cut sleeveless peasant blouse and a long full skirt.

Ken was terrified. Where was the Window? Where was the windowless room? < Where are we? > he asked.

< We are *in* April in Paris > Mary said. < *In*side the exviron-ment! Isn't it exciting? >

Ken tried to stop walking but he couldn't. < I think we're stuck > he said. He tried to close his eyes to avoid panic, but he couldn't.

Mary just smiled the Mary smile and they walked along the boulevard, under the blossoming chestnut trees. They passed a café, they turned a corner; they passed another café, turned another corner. It was always the same. The same trees, the same cafés, the same cobblestones. The carriages and stick figures in the distance never got any closer.

< Isn't it romantic? > Mary said. < And don't say you guess >

She looked different somehow. Maybe it was the outfit. Her peasant blouse was cut very low. Ken tried to look down it but he couldn't.

They passed another café. This time Mary97 turned in, and Ken was sitting across from her at a small sidewalk table.

< Voilà! > she said. < This Easter Egg is more interactive. You just have to look for new ways to do things > She was still smiling that Mary smile. The table was heart-shaped, like the table in

the windowless room. Ken leaned across it but he still couldn't see down her blouse.

< Isn't it romantic! > Mary said. < Why don't you let me order? >
< It's time to head back > Ken said. < I'll bet our Folders— >
< Don't be silly > Mary said, opening the menu.
< —are blinking like crazy > he finished because it was already in his buffer.

A waiter appeared. He wore a white shirt and black pants. Ken tried to look at his face but he didn't exactly have one. There were only three items on the menu:

WALK
ROOM
HOME

Mary pointed at ROOM and before she had closed the menu they were in a wedge-shaped attic room with French doors, sitting on the edge of a low bed. Now Ken could see down Mary97's blouse. In fact he could see his two hands reach out and pull it down, uncovering her two plump, perfect breasts. Her nipples were as big and as brown as cookies. Through the French doors Ken could see the Eiffel Tower and the boulevard.

< Mary > he said as she helped him pull up her skirt. Smiling that Mary smile, she lay back with her blouse and skirt both bunched around her waist. Ken heard a familiar *clippity-clop* from the boulevard below as Mary spread her plump, perfect thighs wide.

< April in Paris > she said. Her red-tipped fingers pulled her little French underpants to one side and
He kissed her sweet mouth. < Mary! > he said.
Her red-tipped fingers pulled her little French underpants to one side and
He kissed her sweet red mouth. < Mary! > he said.
Her red-tipped fingers pulled her little French underpants to one side and
He kissed her sweet red cookie mouth. < Mary! > he said.
A gendarme's whistle blew and they were back at the sidewalk

café. The menu was closed on the heart-shaped table. < Did you like that? > Mary asked. < And don't say you guess >

< Like it? I loved it > Ken said. < But shouldn't we head back? >

< Back? > Mary shrugged. Ken didn't know she could shrug. She was holding a glass of green liquid.

Ken opened the menu and the faceless waiter appeared.

There were only three items on the menu. Before Mary could point, Ken pointed at HOME, and the table and the waiter were gone. He and Mary97 were in the windowless room, and all the cards were facedown except for the ten of diamonds.

< Why do you want to spoil everything? > Mary said.

< I don't— > Ken started, but he never got to finish. His Folder was blinking insistently, waitstate interrupt, and he was gone.

< It *was* romantic > Ken678 insisted a few cycles later when he joined Mary97 in their usual spot, at the Window in the Corridor between Copy and Verify. < And I *did* love it >

< Then why were you so nervous? >

< Was I nervous? >

She smiled that Mary smile.

< Because I just get nervous > Ken said. < Because April in Paris is not really *part* of Microserf Office 6.9 >

< Sure it is. It's the exvironment >

< It's just wallpaper. We're not supposed to be *in* there >

< It's an Easter Egg > Mary97 said. < We're not supposed to be having an office romance, either >

< An office romance > Ken said. < Is that what we're having? >

< Come with me and I'll show you > Mary said, and he did. And she did.

And he did and she did and they did. He met her three times that week and three times the next week, every spare moment it seemed. The cobblestones and the cafés still made Ken678 nervous but he loved the wedge-shaped attic room. He loved

Mary's nipples as brown and as big as cookies; loved her blouse
and skirt bunched around her waist as she lay on her back with
her plump, perfect thighs spread wide; loved the *clippity-clop* and
her red-tipped fingers and her little French underpants pulled
to one side; loved her.

It was, after all, a love affair.

The problem was, Mary97 never wanted to come back to
Microserf Office 6.9. After the wedge-shaped room she wanted
to walk on the boulevard under the blossoming chestnut trees,
or sit in the café watching the stick figures get in and out of carriages in the distance.

< Isn't it romantic? > she would say, swirling the green liquid
in her glass.

< Time to head back > Ken would say. < I'll bet our Folders are
blinking like crazy >

< You always say that > Mary would always say.

Ken678 had always hated weekends because he missed the warm
electron buzz of Microserf Office; but now he missed it during
the week as well. If he wanted to be with Mary97 (and he did, he
did!) it meant April in Paris. Ken missed "their" Window in the
Corridor between Copy and Verify. He missed the busy streaming icons and the Folders bulging with files and blinking with
Calls and Tasks. He missed the red brassiere.

< What happens > Ken asked late one week < if we just turn
over the queen? >

He was just turning over the queen.

< Nothing happens > Mary answered. < Nothing but the red
brassiere >

She was already turning over the ace.

< We need to talk > Ken678 said finally. It was April in Paris, as
usual. He was walking with Mary97 along the boulevard, under
the blossoming chestnut trees.

< What about? > she asked. She turned a corner, then another.

< Things > he said.

< Isn't it romantic? > she said as she turned into a café.

< I guess > he said. < But— >

< I hate it when you say that > Mary said.

< —I miss the Office > Ken finished because it was already in his buffer.

Mary97 shrugged. < To each his own > She swirled the green liquid in her glass. It was thick as syrup; it clung to the sides of the glass. Ken had the feeling she was looking through him instead of at him. He tried to see down her peasant blouse but couldn't.

< I thought you wanted to talk > Mary said, swirling the green liquid in her glass.

< I did. We did > Ken said. He reached for the menu.

Mary pulled it away. < I'm not in the mood >

< We should be getting back then > Ken said. < I'll bet our Folders are blinking like crazy >

Mary shrugged. < Go ahead > she said.

< What? >

< You miss the Office. I don't. I'm going to stay here >

< Here? > Ken tried to look around. He could only look in one direction, toward the boulevard.

< Why not > Mary said. < Who's going to miss me there? > She took another drink of the green liquid and opened the menu. Ken was confused. Had she been drinking it all along? And why were there four items on the menu?

< Me? > Ken suggested.

But the waiter had already appeared; he, at least, was still the same.

< Go ahead, go for it > Mary said, and Ken pointed at HOME. Mary was pointing at the new item, STAY.

That weekend was the longest of Ken678's life. As soon as the week restarted, he hurried to the Corridor between Copy and Verify, hoping against hope. But there was no Window open and of course no Mary97.

He looked for her between Calls and Tasks, checking every

queue, every Corridor. Finally, toward the middle of the week, he went to the windowless room off the Browser by himself, for the first time.

Mary97's Folder was gone. The cards on the tiny heart-shaped table were all facedown, except for the ten of diamonds.

He turned up the queen of hearts, but nothing happened. He wasn't surprised.

He turned up the ace of spades and felt the cobblestones under his feet. It was April in Paris. The chestnuts were in blossom but Ken678 felt no joy. Only a sort of thick sorrow.

He turned in at the first café and there she was, sitting at the heart-shaped table.

< Look who's here > she said.

< Your Folder is gone > Ken said. < It was in the room when I got back, blinking like crazy, but that was before the weekend. Now it's gone >

Mary shrugged. < I'm not going back there anyway >

< What happened to us? > Ken asked.

< Nothing happened to us > Mary said. < Something happened to me. Remember when you found what you were looking for? Well, I found what I was looking for. I like it here >

Mary pushed the glass of green liquid toward him. < You could like it here too > she said.

Ken didn't answer. He was afraid if he did he would start to cry, even though Kens can't cry.

< But it's okay > Mary97 said. She even smiled her Mary smile. She took another drink and opened the menu. The waiter appeared, and she pointed to ROOM, and Ken knew somehow that this was to be the last time.

In the wedge-shaped attic room, he could see down Mary's blouse perfectly. Then his hands were cupping her plump, perfect breasts for the last time. Through the French doors he could see the Eiffel Tower and the boulevard. < Mary! > he said and she lay back with her blouse and skirt both bunched around her waist and he knew somehow it was the last time. He heard a familiar *clippity-clop* from the boulevard as she spread her perfect thighs and said < April in Paris! > Her red-tipped fingers pulled

her little French underpants to one side and Ken knew somehow it was the last time.

He kissed her sweet red cookie mouth. < Mary! > he said and
she pulled her little French underpants to one side and he knew
somehow it was the last time.

< Mary! > he said.

It was the last time.

A gendarme's whistle blew and they were back at the sidewalk
café. The menu was closed on the heart-shaped table. < Are you
flirting with me? > Mary asked.

< What a sad joke she is making > Ken678 thought. He tried
to smile even though Kens can't smile.

< You're supposed to answer, what if I am? > Mary said. She
took another drink of the green liquid. She swirled it jauntily.
No matter how much she drank there was always plenty left.

< Time to head back > Ken said. < My Folder will be blinking
like crazy >

< I understand. It's okay. Come and see me sometime > she
said. < And don't say I guess >

Ken678 nodded even though Kens can't nod. It was more like
a stiff bow. Mary97 opened the menu. The waiter came and Ken
pointed to HOME.

Ken678 spent the next week, the next two, working like crazy. He
was all over Microserf Office. As soon as his Folder blinked he
was off, on Call, double and triple Tasking, burning up the Corridors. He avoided the Corridor between Copy and Verify,
though, just as he avoided the Browser.

He almost paused at an open Window once. But he didn't.
He didn't want to look at April in Paris. It was too lonely without Mary.

Two, four weeks passed before Ken678 went back to the windowless room in the Browser. He dreaded seeing the cards on
the heart-shaped table. But the cards were gone. Even the table
was gone. Ken saw the scuff marks along the wall, and he real-

ized the Optimizer had been through. The room had been erased again, and was being overwritten.

When he left the room he was no longer lonely. He was accompanied by a great sorrow.

The next week he went by the room again and found it filled with empty Folders. Perhaps one of them was Mary97's. Now that the Easter Egg was gone, Ken678 no longer felt guilty about not going to see Mary97. He was free to love Microserf Office 6.9 again; free to enjoy the soft electron buzz, the busy streaming icons, and the long, silent queues.

But at least once a week he stops by the Corridor between Copy and Verify and opens the Window. You might find him there even now, looking out into April in Paris. The chestnuts are in blossom, the cobblestones shine, the carriages are letting stick figures off in the distance. The cafés are almost empty. A lone figure sits at a tiny table, a figure that might be her.

They say you never get over your first love. < Then Mary97 must have been my first love > Ken678 likes to think. He has no interest in getting over her. He loves to remember her red fingernails, her soft Mary voice and Mary smile, her nipples as big and as brown as cookies, her little French underpants pulled to one side.

The figure in the café must be Mary97. Ken678 hopes so. He hopes she is okay in April in Paris. He hopes she is as happy as she once made, is still making, him. He hopes she is as sad.

But look: his Folder is blinking like crazy, a waitstate interrupt, and it's time to go.

Hello?

It's me.

What is it this time?

I have this great idea for a story.

Not another science fiction story. Do you have any idea what time it is?

Sure, it's 10:07:24. But you're going to love this one.

Please. I don't have time for it.

This is a story *about* Time, as a matter of fact.

I can't use another time travel story.

This is different! In this story, it's Time itself that travels.

So what? Time always travels. It stops. It goes.

In this story Time does nothing *but* travel. It can't stop. It can't *not* travel.

I said no science fiction.

No way! This is *speculative* fiction, based on the cutting-edge ideas of the new physics. This is real Rudy Rucker stuff! Imagine a universe where *time never stops*. It just rolls on, hour by hour, minute by minute, second by second. Mini-second by mini-second.

I don't get it. What do you mean, time never stops? There's no Present? No Now?

Exactly! By the time you say the word "now," that Now is gone, and there's another Now. Then another and another.

Time only stops for like a second at a time? Is that the idea?

Time doesn't stop *at all*! Not for a second. Not for a mini-micro-nano-second. It keeps flowing along, like a river. Like an ever-rolling stream. Like a bowling ball!

That's ridiculous. There has to be a Now where Time is stopped. Like right now—10:07:24. Otherwise how could anything exist?

In this universe we're talking about, everything exists in the Now, but it's a moving Now.

Isn't that a contradiction in terms—a moving Now?

In our universe, in the real universe, yes. But in this speculative universe, it's the other way around. Look at it this way. When we visualize Time, it's like a series of lakes, right? They're all at . . .

I'm not stupid. I know what Time is like.

Sorry. But now visualize a universe in which somebody has blown the main dam, so to speak. Time is a stream: moving, flowing like a river, continually in motion—

Ridiculous. Not only intelligence but matter itself would be unthinkable under such conditions.

But what if the moving Now seemed perfectly normal to the denizens of this universe? Imagine it! Riding the foaming crest of Time like surfers on a wave. Poised between past and future on an ever-changing, never-ending Now . . .

Stop! Who'd want to read stuff like that? Makes you dizzy just to think about it.

Exactly! It's dizzying, disturbing, exhilarating, thought-provoking. That's the whole idea! It will start a whole new literary trend. We can call it "chronopunk," a mind-blowing new metafiction from the cutting edge of quantum physics where . . .

You're wasting your time. I can't imagine it. I won't bother to. A world in which Time never stops? Never even pauses! That's worse than science fiction; it's fantasy.

But that's where you're wrong. Are you ready for the best part? I didn't make this up! It's all based on science *fact*. At least theory. I read about it in *Omni*.

Omni. No wonder.

Seriously! Scientists are speculating about alternate universes where Time might flow in a constant stream. Where there's never a fixed chronological point, not even for a micro-second. It's never been demonstrated, of course, but it's possible, according to the laws of relativity and quantum mechanics. It's even probable.

Like light matter?

Exactly. Or suns. That's the beauty of science fiction. We can take the far-out ideas of theoretical physics and make them seem real by putting them in a story.

I thought you said this wasn't science fiction.

I was using the term loosely. I meant *speculative*.

And there hasn't been even a hint of a story.

I was just getting to the story. You have these people—a woman and a man, say, so you've got a love interest. She's a scientist. She looks at her watch and suddenly . . .

Why is the woman always the scientist?

He's the scientist, then. Whatever. Looks at *his* watch. What time is it? she asks. Well, he can't tell her! Time keeps changing! He waits for it to stop but it doesn't. There's no Now! Now is continually turning into then—

I thought you said it was normal for them.

Okay, what if it wasn't. What if they were just noticing. You have to have a story. It could be funny! He looks at his watch and says, "The time is . . . is . . . is . . ." She says, "Well?" He says, "Is . . . is . . . is . . ." It could be hilarious.

A guy looking at his watch and stuttering is not all that hilarious.

It could be an adventure, then. They try to do something about it. That's it, of course! They're both scientists, faced with the ultimate disaster. Runaway Time! Maybe they try to stop Time. With an atomic clock. Or something.

I hate to interrupt but it *is* 10:07:24.

Imagine the suspense! What if Time runs out before they can stop it? What if . . .

I hate to interrupt but we've wasted enough time on this.

You said yourself it's still 10:07:24.

Yeah, but it'll be another time before you know it. And I'm going to have to pass on this story idea. Our readers want stories they can identify with, not wild speculations on theoretical physics set in bizarre alternate universes, no matter how thought-provoking. Try a math magazine or something. One question, though. While it's still 10:07:24.

What?

What's a rucky rooter?

First Fire

An unusual request indeed. Why should I fly you to Iran?"

"Because you have money and I don't," Emil wanted to say, but didn't. "Because I can help you authenticate your discovery at Ebtacan," he said.

"What discovery?"

"The Flame of Zoroaster."

The Tycoon nodded his head. His knee had been nodding all along. He was the richest man in the world, and clearly one of the most impatient.

He wore Levi's and a Gap tee shirt under a linen sport coat. His legs were crossed and his right foot was bobbing up and down as if he couldn't wait to get out of the office.

Emil had gotten this appointment only by pulling every string and calling in every marker. He knew he had less than thirty seconds to make his case.

"There is a legend that the fire at Ebtacan is the same one Darius worshiped," he said.

"I know the legend," said the Tycoon. The Ebtacan dig was one of the few of his many projects that he followed closely. Most of them he ran through one foundation or another, but his interest in archaeology was genuine, and deep. Emil knew that he had visited and even worked at the dig several times.

"Archaeology is not about legends," said the Tycoon. "It's about objects. Small, hard objects you find in the dirt."

"What if I told you fire was a hard object," said Emil.

The Tycoon narrowed his world-famous eyes. They were boyish only in photos. "I'm listening."

"I have developed a way to date fire. Not ashes, not charcoal, not the remnants or evidences of fire, but the flame itself."

"I'm all ears."

"Using my device, which I call the spectr0chronograph, I can date a flame to its precise moment of ignition," said Emil. "With most fires that's only an hour or two. In the case of, say, the Olympic flame, it may be decades. I won't bother you with the technical details, but . . ."

"Bother me with the technical details," said the Tycoon.

Emil explained how every flame has a unique spectrographic signature, which is altered over time at a steady rate, and lost altogether when the flame is extinguished. "Every new flame has a new signature," he said. "With a spectrochronographic analysis I can date a flame's age to within fractions of a second per century."

"You've dated flames that old?"

"Not yet," said Emil. "Which is why I want to go to Ebtacan. Legends aside, the Flame of Zoroaster is likely to be hundreds of years old. Dating it will put my spectrochronograph on the map."

"And my dig as well," said the Tycoon.

Emil was startled to realize that he had scored. He went for the extra point.

"If we found a candle that had been burning since the French Revolution, I could tell you exactly when the match itself was struck, within two seconds. I estimate my error factor at .8 seconds a century."

"I'll make it easy for you," the Tycoon said, opening his checkbook and writing as he spoke. "Come back to my office in one week. On my secretary's desk you will find a candle burning. I want you to tell me to within one second when the flame was lit. Pacific Standard Time."

He tore out the check and laid it on the desk to indicate that the interview was over.

Emil's heart was pounding as he picked up the check.

It was for a hundred dollars.

• • •

One week later Emil showed up at the Tycoon's office carrying what looked, to the secretary, like a water pistol.

"This is the one," she said, pointing to the candle burning on her desk.

Emil pointed his device at the flame and pulled the trigger until he heard a *beep*.

He released the trigger and read the display.

"Is this some kind of joke?" he said. "This flame was lighted less than three minutes ago."

"Sort of a joke," said the Tycoon, coming out of his inner office with a burning candle in his hand. With two fingers he pinched out the candle on the desk, then relighted it from the candle in his hand.

Emil pointed the spectrochronograph at the flame and pulled the trigger again until it beeped.

He read the display.

"I trust this is not another joke," he said. "This flame is almost forty years old; 39.864, to be exact. I can translate into months . . ."

"That's okay," said the Tycoon. He sat down on the desk beside the burning candle, legs crossed, right foot bobbing. "That's very good. It was lighted from the Eternal Flame on JFK's grave at Arlington. Did you know it's illegal to carry an open flame on a commercial flight, even in first class? I had to send a chartered jet to D.C. for your little test, but you passed it with flying colors."

Emil thought of the chartered jet; he thought of his hundred dollars.

The Tycoon was already writing out another check. "This is for expenses and R and D," he said. "My secretary will send you a plane ticket. We will see you in Ebtacan in ten days. But can I give you one piece of advice?"

The question was a courtesy only; the Tycoon didn't wait for an answer before continuing: "Don't call it a spectrochronograph. Too sci-fi. Just call it a time gun."

He stood up and handed Emil the check, then pinched out the flame again and left the room.

The check was for $100,000.

Emil had never flown first class before. For the first time he wished the Atlantic wider, the flight longer. The luxury ran out in Uzbekistan, however, and the last two legs were made on terrifying Aeroflot propjets.

Ebtacan was a tiny crossroads in a vast desert, scratches on mauve sand. Emil had expected magnificent ruins, and all he found were mud huts with corrugated roofs, a petrol station that calculated by abacus, and a stalled Russian tank covered with indecipherable graffiti.

"Alexander leveled it all," said the site manager, a portly Wisconsin professor named Elliot, as they drove from the dirt airstrip to the tent city at the dig. "The Macedonians razed the temples, raped the women, enslaved the men, butchered the children." He recounted this with an alarming glee. "Then Alexander personally snuffed out the sacred Flame of Zoroaster, which had burned, supposedly, for ten thousand years. But according to the legend, he was fooled. The flame had already been spirited away by the priests. It's preserved in a small shrine about twenty miles north of here."

Twenty miles in northern Iran was like two hundred back in California. The next morning, Emil found himself rattling across the black sands in a Toyota Land Cruiser expertly driven by a Wisconsin graduate assistant. Professor Elliot bounced around in the backseat.

"I've met him several times and he's all right with me," the graduate assistant said. "For one thing, he doesn't come on to every female. For another, he really cares about archaeology. He has values."

Her name was Kay. She was talking about the Tycoon, a Wisconsin alumnus. Sometimes Emil got the impression that the purpose of his worldwide business and philanthropic activities was just so these conversations would be held.

"It's interesting that he is excavating this city that was sacked by Alexander," said Professor Elliot. "In many ways he is a modern Alexander. Nothing can stand against him, or at least against the technology, the capital, and the connections he commands."

The Flame of Zoroaster was in an artificial cave, carved out of a sandstone cliff. It was maintained and guarded by a small coterie of monks who were reluctant to show it to the nonfaithful. But Zoroastrianism is an obsolete and beleaguered faith, and it had been easy enough to convince local officials that the shrine was, like Ebtacan, part of the "Heritage of Humankind."

The monks were under orders. They had already let in the professor several weeks before. They did so again, graciously if reluctantly.

The flame burned in a large bowl of beaten gold. A young monk fed it twigs from a pile against one wall. The twigs themselves were testimony to the diligence and ingenuity of the monks, since the desert was barren for miles around. Emil found out later that the wood was brought by the faithful from as far away as India.

Emil pointed his time gun at the flame and pulled the trigger until it beeped. He looked at the display and let out a low whistle.

"What is it?" asked Professor Elliot.

"Just what they say," said Emil. He showed the professor and the student the display.

"Jesus!" said Kay.

"When this fire was built, Jesus was as far in their future as he is now in our past," said Emil.

The flame was 5,619.657 years old.

"So it's true," said Elliot, looking astonished.

Emil nodded. "Most of it. Certainly it's true that they've kept it burning since long before Alexander's time."

"Jesus," said Kay, again, shaking her head. Emil noticed that she was more attractive with her eyes wide and her lips parted. It softened her.

The monks looked pleased as they ushered their guests back out into the bright sunshine.

• • •

That night Emil and Kay spent the night together, outside the tents, under the million stars. It was lonely on the dig, she explained, though she didn't really have to. She had a boyfriend, but he was in Madison. They had an understanding.

Emil suspected that she and the Tycoon had shared the same view of the desert sky. Somehow he didn't mind. It was a memorable evening. Kay was a memorable girl, small-breasted, high-spirited, compact, practical, and resourceful.

And Emil had never seen so many stars.

The next day he left for "the world," or at least New York. At the crude airstrip he was surprised to meet the Tycoon himself, helicoptering in. He was a little reluctant to talk about what he was doing, but Emil found out eleven months later, when he was invited to the unveiling of the Flame of Zoroaster at the Metropolitan.

The Tycoon was more than generous in his praise of Emil and his time gun, as he was careful to call it. And more than forthright in their short but substantial private discussion.

"I helped the government out with their debt, in exchange for the shrine. They made their own deal with the Zoroastrians. The shrine has always been a bit of an embarrassment to a fundamentalist government. Islam is a modern religion, you know. Post Christian."

"You bought it," said Emil.

"It's an artifact," said the Tycoon. "Now that you have authenticated it, it belongs to all humankind."

At the Met the flame was fed on natural gas. Emil couldn't help wondering what had happened to the young monk who had fed it twigs. Was he a cabby now, in Cairo or in Queens? As well wonder what happened to a soldier from Darius's army. Alexander's destiny was to conquer the world, not to number its sparrows.

Professor Elliot was at the opening, but not Kay. Emil was disappointed. He had entertained a fantasy of a rendezvous. He even mentioned her to the Tycoon, who said dreamily, "Kay? I have so many projects . . ."

Emil was apparently on retainer, for once a year on the anniversary of his visit to Ebtacan he got a check for $100,000. But never a call. That was all right; he preferred his independence. The Flame of Zoroaster had indeed put his time gun on the map, and in the next two years he authenticated (dated) the San Gabriel Mission hearth in California (221.052 years) and a coal seam blaze on Baffin Island (797.563 years).

The time gun was an accepted archaeological tool, but after the first flurry of interest, there wasn't much demand. How many flames need dating? Emil tried to interest astronomers, but the device didn't seem to work at a distance. The numbers came out all wrong. According to the time gun, the stars weren't as old as the Earth.

Emil found out what had happened to Kay eighteen months later, when he got an E-mail suggesting a meeting at the Oak Room at the Plaza.

She wasn't alone. "This is Claude," she said, introducing a young black man in jeans and a raw silk jacket. Claude had a rich French accent, which was later localized to Kinshasa and Paris.

Emil didn't like him. His head was too big for his narrow shoulders. He smoked Gauloises.

They ordered drinks. Kay let it be known that the Tycoon was picking up the tab. "I've been working for him since I got my doctorate," she said. "Special projects." Had he really not remembered her? Emil wondered. Did Alexander remember every city he ravished?

Claude was not a boyfriend. Not even, strictly speaking, a colleague, but a divinity student from Yale. "Comparative religions. And I have discovered," he said, "the oldest religion in

the world. I think. As well as one of the smallest. It's called
Ger'abté, which means, in Highland Wolof, first fire."

"Remember the monks at Ebtacan?" said Kay, laying her
hand on Emil's wrist. "This is the same deal. The entire purpose
of the religion is guarding a fire."

"I remember," said Emil.

"Guarding a flame," said Claude. "I have interviewed one of
the Ger'abté priests, a *defrocké*. A rebel, a runaway. I met him in
Paris last year. He claims that the flame they call Ger'abté is the
first flame ever lighted by man. It provides a *chemin sans brisé*, an
unbroken link from the first humans to today. This flame is
guarded and maintained by a secret priesthood high in the
Ruwenzori."

"The Mountains of the Moon," said Kay.

"Overlooking the Rift Valley," mused Emil.

"*Exactemente*," said Claude. "They have the location right.
According to most anthropologists, this is the area where man
first evolved."

"Whatever that means," said Emil. "Speech, upright posture,
tools . . ."

"Fire," said Claude. "Whatever else you think, fire is key. It
separates man from beast."

"You believe them, then."

"*Non*, no, of course not." Claude lit another Gauloise from
his last. The cigarettes so far formed an unbroken chain, like the
Flame of Zoroaster, or Ger'abté.

"But I do wish to find out how old the fire is," said Claude. "If
it is, in fact, several thousand years old, it changes our whole
view of so-called animist African religions and their—how shall
I say it?—their *gravités*."

This man has a political agenda, thought Emil. But then who
doesn't?

They made plans over dinner. Later, Emil found himself in a
Plaza Hotel suite with Kay. She was, if anything, even more
inventive and accomplished than before. A memorable lover.
Love without possession or even the desire for possession—that

was what it meant to share a woman with the richest man in the world. It was as if the Tycoon lay alongside them. Oddly, it added to Emil's pleasure.

"You know what he did with the Flame of Zoroaster?" Kay asked.

"Sure. He bought it and put it in the Met."

"He put it out first."

"What!?"

"He's a strange and driven man," Kay said. "He feels this mystical connection with Alexander. He has this thing about history, about breaking with the past at the same time that you are recognizing it."

"But the whole damn point was that the flame was authentic! As soon as it's dated again . . ."

"Why would it be? Unless you do it. And you are on his payroll. So to speak."

She held her small breasts, one in each hand, like pomegranates.

"Are you going to stay the night?"

The Ruwenzori from the air is a terrifying tangle of cloud and ice and stone. Emil had discovered in his two years with the time gun that he was unsuited for serious fieldwork. He didn't like small planes or short fields.

This trip had both.

Claude had been here once before. Kay and Emil hung back while he showed a letter and engaged a guide. The guide was not a Ger'abté initiate, but part of the secret and presumably ancient network of believers who maintained the priests who maintained the flame.

Kay arranged the transportation. They took a helicopter to a small village on a high shoulder of the range; a Land Rover (they hadn't yet been replaced here by Toyotas) to a smaller village on a higher shoulder; and walked the rest of the way.

The peaks were wrapped in mist, like ghosts. The guide started up the trail, a long ribbon of mud.

Claude put out his cigarette before following.

"We could have choppered in the entire way," he said. "But that might have offended *les enfants.*"

"The children?" Emil.

"*Oui*, the Children. That's what they call themselves," Claude explained. "It's an interesting contrast to European priests, don't you think, who style themselves as Fathers? These priests, there are only three at any one time, call themselves the Children of the First Fire, Ger'abté."

"Keeping alive the spirits of their ancestors," said Emil.

"*Pas de tout!*" Claude's reproach was sharp. "This is not simplistic ancestor worship *d'Afrique*. They don't believe in gods or ghosts. Theirs is an anthropic cosmology: man built a fire, then looked up and saw the stars, thus bringing into being the universe as we know it. Their job is to keep it going."

"The ritual acknowledgment of fire as the source, the origin of consciousness," said Kay.

"*Non!* A task, not a ritual," said Claude. "Maintaining the first fire. Ger'abté. No more, no less."

What an arrogant fuck, thought Emil.

The first of the Children met them late in the afternoon, and led them off the trail through a narrow pass. The guide turned back. Their new guide was a wiry, coal-black man of about fifty, wearing a faded blue hooded wool robe over bright Nikes. Single file, they crossed a snowfield, skirted a tiny emerald lake, and angled up a scree slope into clouds again.

As at Ebtacan, the shrine was a cave. The doorway was a perfect half circle, hollowed not out of sandstone but out of a polished granite that gleamed like marble.

Beside it waited a much older man, dressed in the same blue robe. He spoke to Claude in one language, and to his compatriot in another.

Claude gave each of the two a pack of Gauloises. He hadn't smoked since the Land Rover. They were at almost ten thousand feet and the air was thin and cold.

The two Children led the three travelers into the cave. It was only twenty feet deep, the size of a small garage.

A Persian rug was on the floor. Several plastic ten-gallon drums were stacked near the door.

A tiny flame burned in a hollow in the rock, which was filled with oil. The wick seemed to be twisted moss.

An old man, older than the other two, watched the flame, adding oil from an open drum with a long dipper of bone or ivory.

Clever, thought Emil. The flame is kept small. They don't have to haul twigs up the mountain. Just oil.

He wondered if he had spoken out loud. The old man answered him, but not directly.

"He says that in the *temps perdu* it was done with twigs," said Claude. "Then they learned to use fat."

"Ask them how old the fire is," Emil said as he took out the time gun. The Children's slight alarm turned to curiosity as they realized it wasn't a weapon.

"They don't have an answer in years," said Claude. "They say *beaucoup*. Many many many."

"Ask them about the first men," said Kay.

"They were women," said Claude. "They call them the Mothers. They used no speech, but kept the fire. For many generations, no words, only fire. Many many many."

"*Habilis*," said Emil.

"*Erectus*," corrected Claude.

"Not likely," said Kay. "Fire might have been used by *Homo erectus*. But they can't have been the ones to preserve it ritually."

"Why not?" Emil asked.

"Ritual implies language," said Kay. "Symbolic thinking. Consciousness. Even if *Homo erectus* discovered and used fire, he couldn't have—"

"She," said Claude.

"*She* then," said Kay, who was unused to being corrected by men in matters of gender. "*She* wouldn't have constructed a myth. Couldn't have."

"I told you, it's not a myth," said Claude. "It's a simple task.

We are the ones who construct the myth. Sapiens. *Homo sapiens sapiens.*"

"Whatever." Emil pointed the time gun at the tiny flame. He squeezed the trigger until it beeped.

He read the display. Then he looked around the cave at the Children and his two companions.

"Holy fucking shit," he said.

"Huh?" Kay. Claude.

"The flame is almost a million years old."

That evening they sat around a small campfire outside the cave and shared an impressive brandy from the flask that Claude had brought with him, just in case.

"So it's true," he said, lighting his first Gauloise since the Land Rover.

"More than true," said Emil. "It's positive."

"It seems impossible," said Kay. "Impossible and wonderful."

"I wanted to believe," said Claude, shaking his too-large head. "You hope. And you hope not. The real world devours your expectations."

There were big tears in his eyes. He'd had two drinks for every one of Emil's and Kay's. Emil was liking him more.

Kay was on the cell phone, punching in long strings of numbers. "I told him I would call," she explained.

Behind them, in the darkness, the Children went about their business. Nothing in their world had changed. They had known all along.

That night Emil slept with Kay out by the fire. Claude had passed out in the tent, and the Children had slipped off to wherever it was that they stayed, perhaps in the cave with the flame.

Kay was as cool, as studied, as memorable as ever. They made love, then lay side by side in separate bags under the strange equatorial stars, her small hand in his. Not a single constellation was familiar.

It was after midnight when the chopper came in. It would have landed by the cave if the Children hadn't waved it off frantically, the hoods of their robes flattened in the rotor's downdraft. The chopper set down at the base of the scree, a hundred yards away.

That hundred-yard climb was the Tycoon's offering to tradition. Emil, Claude, and Kay were waiting for him at the top of the slope.

"Hey, kid," he said to Kay and gave her a lingering peck on the cheek. Emil was more flattered than jealous. How many men shared a woman with an Emperor?

"And it's positive?" he asked Emil, studying the readout, which had been saved in the time gun's memory.

Emil nodded. "This single flame has burned unbroken for 859,134.347 years." He liked saying it.

"*Erectus*," said the Tycoon.

"*Oui*," said Claude, who was still a little drunk. "Prehuman. Prespeech. This changes everything we have ever imagined about hominid evolution. It means we had, or rather they had, for they were an earlier species, the technology to maintain and control fire long before they had speech or tools."

Last night's campfire was almost out. Claude's empty flask lay beside warm ashes. Fog filled the valleys far below and a million stars blazed overhead.

"It means that there is an unbroken link between ourselves and our earliest ancestors," said Kay. She surprised Emil by taking his hand. Then he saw that she had already taken the Tycoon's. "An unbroken link between you and me and the first human who looked into a campfire."

"And into his own *pensées*," said Claude, taking Emil's other hand.

"Whatever," said the Tycoon, pulling free. "Let's go and have a look."

The Children, who had been waiting silently by the round doorway, led them into the stone cave.

The Tycoon stared into the tiny flame with bright, narrow

eyes. "A million years of human culture," he whispered loudly. "And it is but a single page."

Emil was warmed by this reverence, as by a shot of brandy. Kay alone realized what was about to happen. Even the Children were unprepared when the Tycoon reached out and, with two fingers, pinched out the flame.

"And now the page is turned."

"Mon Dieu!"

"Good God!" said Emil. He lunged, teeth bared, fists clenched, but the Tycoon ran for the doorway, knocking over the oil drums. The Children fell to their knees, wailing. Kay wailed with them.

Outside, Claude and Emil circled the Tycoon, who looked dazed but fierce. Claude picked up a stone.

Overhead, without any fuss, the stars were going out, one by one.

On the ground, no one noticed.

Get Me to the Church on Time

Part One

The best way to approach Brooklyn is from the air. The Brooklyn Bridge is nice, but let's admit it, to drive (or bicycle, or worse, walk) into homely old Brooklyn directly from the shining towers of downtown Manhattan is to court deflation, dejection, even depression. The subway is no better. You ride from one hole to another: there's no in-between, no approach, no drama of arrival. The Kosciuszko Bridge over Newtown Creek is okay, because even drab Williamsburg looks lively after the endless, orderly graveyards of Queens. But just as you are beginning to appreciate the tarpaper tenement rooftops of Brooklyn, there *she* is again, off to the right: the skyline of Manhattan, breaking into the conversation like a tall girl with great hair in a low-cut dress who doesn't have to say a word. It shouldn't be that way, it's not fair, but that's the way it is. No, the great thing about a plane is that you can only see out of one side. I like to sit on the right. The flights from the south come in across the dark wastes of the Pine Barrens, across the shabby, sad little burgs of the Jersey shore, across the mournful, mysterious bay, until the lights of Coney Island loom up out of the night, streaked with empty boulevards. Manhattan is invisible, unseen off to the left, like a chapter in another book or a girl at another party. The turbines throttle back and soon you are angling down across the streetlight-spangled stoops and backyards of my legend-heavy hometown. Brooklyn!

"There it is," I said to Candy.

"Whatever." Candy hates to fly, and she hadn't enjoyed any of the sights, all the way from Huntsville. I tried looking over her. I could see the soggy fens of Jamaica Bay, then colorful, quarrelsome Canarsie, then Prospect Park and Grand Army Plaza; and there was the Williamsburg Tower with its always-accurate clock. Amazingly, we were right on time.

I wished now I hadn't given Candy the window seat, but it was our Honeymoon, after all. I figured she would learn to love to fly. "It's beautiful!" I said.

"I'm sure," she muttered.

I was anticipating the usual long holding pattern, which takes you out over Long Island Sound, but before I knew it, we were making one of those heart-stopping wing-dipping jetplane U-turns over the Bronx, then dropping down over Rikers Island, servos whining and hydraulics groaning as the battered flaps and beat-up landing gear *clunked* into place for the ten-thousandth (at least) time. Those PreOwned Air 707s were seasoned travelers, to say the least. The seat belts said Eastern, the pillows said Pan Am, the barf bags said Braniff, and the peanuts said People Express. It all inspired a sort of confidence. I figured if they were going to get unlucky and go down, they would have done so already.

Through the window, the dirty water gave way to dirty concrete, then the wheels hit the runway with that happy *yelp* so familiar to anyone who has ever watched a movie, even though it's a sound you never actually hear in real life.

And this was real life. New York!

"You can open your eyes," I said, and Candy did, for the first time since the pilot had pushed the throttles forward in Huntsville. I'd even had to feed her over the Appalachians, since she was afraid that if she opened her eyes to see what was on her tray, she might accidentally look out the window. Luckily, dinner was just peanuts and pretzels (a two-course meal).

We were cruising into the terminal like a big, fat bus with wings, when Candy finally looked out the window. She even ventured a smile. The plane was limping a little (flat tire?) but this final part of the flight she actually seemed to enjoy. "At least you didn't hold your breath," I said.

"What?"

"Never mind."

Ding! We were already at the gate, and right on time. I started to grope under the seat in front of me for my shoes. Usually there's plenty of time before everyone starts filing out of the plane, but to my surprise it was already our turn; Candy was pulling at my arm and impatient-looking passengers, jammed in the aisle behind, were frowning at me.

I carried my shoes out and put them on in the terminal. They're loafers. I'm still a lawyer, even though I don't exactly practice.

"New York, New York," I crooned to Candy as we traversed the tunnel to the baggage pickup. It was her first trip to my hometown; our first trip together anywhere. She had insisted on wearing her Huntsville Parks Department uniform, so that if there was a crash they wouldn't have any trouble IDing her body (whoever "they" were), but she would have stood out in the crowd anyway, with her trim good looks.

Not that New Yorkers aren't trim. Or good-looking. The black-clad, serious-looking people racing by on both sides were a pleasant relief after the Kmart pastels and unremitting sunny smiles of the South. I was glad to be home, even if only for a visit. New Yorkers, so alien and menacing to many, looked welcoming and familiar to me.

In fact, one of them looked *very* familiar . . .

"Studs!"

It was Arthur "Studs" Blitz from the old neighborhood. Studs and I had been best friends until high school, when we had gone our separate ways. I had gone to Lincoln High in Coney Island, and he had gone to Carousel, the trade school for airline baggage handlers. It looked like he had done well. His green and black baggage handler's uniform was festooned with medals that clinked and clanked as he bent over an access panel under the baggage carousel, changing a battery in a cellular phone. It seemed a funny place for a phone.

"Studs, it's me, Irving. Irv!"

"Irv the Perv!" Studs straightened up, dropping the new battery, which rolled away. I stopped it with my foot while we shook hands, rather awkwardly.

"From the old neighborhood," I explained to Candy as I bent down for the battery and handed it to Studs. It was a 5.211 volt AXR. It seemed a funny battery for a phone. "Studs is one of the original Ditmas Playboys."

"Playboys?" Candy was, still is, easily shocked. "Perv?"

"There were only two of us," I explained. "We built a tree-house."

"A treehouse in Brooklyn? But I thought . . ."

"Everybody thinks that!" I said. "Because of that book."

"What book?"

"Movie, then. But in fact, *lots* of trees grow in Brooklyn. They grow behind the apartments and houses, where people don't see them from the street. Right, Studs?"

Studs nodded, snapping the battery into the phone. "Irv the Perv," he said again.

"Candy is my fiancée. We just flew in from Alabama," I said. "We're on our Honeymoon."

"Fiancée? Honeymoon? Alabama?"

Studs seemed distracted. While he got a dial tone and punched in a number, I told him how Candy and I had met (leaving out my trip to the Moon, as told in "The Hole in the Hole"). While he put the phone under the carousel and replaced the access panel, I told him how I had moved to Alabama (leaving out the red shift and the nursing home, as told in "The Edge of the Universe"). I was just about to explain why we were having the Honeymoon before the wedding, when the baggage carousel started up.

"Gotta go," said Studs. He gave me the secret Ditmas Playboy wave and disappeared through an AUTHORIZED ONLY door.

"Nice uniform," said Candy, straightening her own. "And did

you see that big gold medallion around his neck? Wasn't that a Nobel Prize?"

"A Nobel Prize for baggage? Not very likely."

Our bags were already coming around the first turn. That seemed like a good sign. "How come there's a cell phone hidden underneath the carousel?" Candy asked as we picked them up and headed for the door.

"Some special baggage handler's trick, I guess," I said.

How little, then, I knew!

Part Two

Flying into New York is like dropping from the twentieth century back into the nineteenth. Everything is crowded, colorful, old—and slow. For example, it usually takes longer to get from La Guardia to Brooklyn than from Huntsville to La Guardia.

Usually! On this, our Honeymoon trip, however, Candy and I made it in record time, getting to curbside for the #33 bus just as it was pulling in, and then catching the F train at Roosevelt Avenue just as the doors were closing. No waiting on the curb or the platform; it was hardly like being home! Of course, I wasn't complaining.

After a short walk from the subway, we found Aunt Minnie sitting on the steps of the little Ditmas Avenue row house she and Uncle Mort had bought for $7,500 fifty years ago, right after World War II, smoking a cigarette. She's the only person I know who still smokes Kents.

"You still go outside to smoke?" I asked.

"You know your Uncle Mort," she said. When I was growing up, Aunt Minnie and Uncle Mort had been like second parents, living only a block and a half away. When my parents died, they'd become my closest relatives. "Plus it's written into the reverse mortgage—NO SMOKING! They have such rules!"

Born in the Old Country, unlike her little sister, my mother, Aunt Minnie still had the Lifthatvanian way of ending a statement with a sort of verbal shrug. She gave me one of her smoky kisses, then asked, "So, what brings you back to New York?"

I was shocked. "You didn't get my letters? We're getting married."

Aunt Minnie looked at Candy with new interest. "To an airline pilot?"

"This is Candy!" I said. "She's with the Huntsville Parks Department. You didn't get my messages?"

I helped Candy drag the suitcases inside, and while we had crackers and pickled *lifthat* at the oak table Uncle Mort had built years ago, in his basement workshop, I explained the past six months as best I could. "So you see, we're here on our Honeymoon, Aunt Minnie," I said, and Candy blushed.

"First the Honeymoon and then the marriage!?" Aunt Minnie rolled her eyes toward the mantel over the gas fireplace, where Uncle Mort's ashes were kept. He, at least, seemed unsurprised. The ornate decorative eye on the urn all but winked.

"It's the only way we could manage it," I said. "The caterer couldn't promise the ice sculpture until Thursday, but Candy had to take her days earlier or lose them. Plus my Best Man is in South America, or Central America, I forget which, and won't get back until Wednesday."

"Imagine that, Mort," Aunt Minnie said, looking toward the mantel again. "Little Irving is getting married. And he didn't even invite us!"

"Aunt Minnie! You're coming to the wedding. Here's your airline ticket." I slid it across the table toward her and she looked at it with alarm.

"That's a pretty cheap fare."

"PreOwned Air," I said. She looked blank, so I sang the jingle, *"Our planes are old, but you pocket the gold."*

"You've seen the ads," Candy offered.

"We never watch TV, honey," Aunt Minnie said, patting her hand. "You want us to go to Mississippi? Tonight?"

"Alabama," I said. "And it's not until Wednesday. We have to stay over a Tuesday night to get the midweek nonstop super-

saver roundtrip pricebuster Honeymoon plus-one fare. The
wedding is on Thursday, at noon. That gives us tomorrow to see
the sights in New York, which means we should get to bed. Aunt
Minnie, didn't you read my letters?"

She pointed toward a stack of unopened mail on the mantel,
next to the urn that held Uncle Mort's ashes. "Not really," she
said. "Since your Uncle Mort passed on, I have sort of given it
up. He made letter openers, you remember?"

Of course I remembered. At my Bar Mitzvah Uncle Mort
gave me a letter opener (which irritated my parents, since it
was identical to the one they had gotten as a wedding present). He gave me another one for high school graduation.
Ditto City College. Uncle Mort encouraged me to go to law
school, and gave me a letter opener for graduation. I still
have them all, good as new. In fact, they have never been
used. It's not like you need a special tool to get an envelope
open.

"Aunt Minnie," I said, "I wrote, and when you didn't write
back, I called, several times. But you never picked up."

"I must have been out front smoking a cigarette," she said.
"You know how your Uncle Mort is about secondhand smoke."

"You could get an answering machine," Candy offered.

"I have one," Aunt Minnie said. "Mort bought it for me at
47th Street Photo, right before they went out of business." She
pointed to the end table, and sure enough, there was a little
black box next to the phone. The red light was blinking.

"You have messages," I said. "See the blinking red light?
That's probably me."

"Messages?" she said. "Nobody told me anything about messages. It's an answering machine. I figure it answers the phone,
so what's the point in me getting involved?"

"But what if somebody wants to talk to you?" I protested.

She spread her hands; she speaks English but gestures in
Lifthatvanian. "Who'd want to talk to a lonely old woman?"

While Aunt Minnie took Candy upstairs and showed her our
bedroom, I checked the machine. There were eleven messages,
all from me, all telling Aunt Minnie we were coming to New

York for our Honeymoon, and bringing her back to Alabama with us for the wedding, and asking her, please, to return my call.

I erased them.

Aunt Minnie's guest room was in the back of the house, and from the window I could see the narrow yards where I had played as a kid. It was like looking back on your life from middle age (almost, anyway), and seeing it literally. There were the fences I had climbed, the grapevines I had robbed, the corners I had hidden in. There, two doors down, was Studs's backyard, with the big maple tree. The treehouse we had built was still there. I could even see a weird blue light through the cracks. Was someone living in it?

After we unpacked, I took Candy for a walk and showed her the old neighborhood. It looked about the same, but the people were different. The Irish and Italian families had been replaced by Filipinos and Mexicans. Studs's parents' house, two doors down from Aunt Minnie's, was dark except for a light in the basement—and the blue light in the treehouse out back. My parents' house, a block and a half away on East Fourth, was now a rooming house for Bangladeshi cabdrivers. The apartments on Ocean Parkway were filled with Russians.

When we got back to the house, Aunt Minnie was on the porch, smoking a Kent. "See how the old neighborhood has gone to pot?" she said. "All these foreigners!"

"Aunt Minnie!" I said, shocked. "You were a foreigner, too, remember? So was Uncle Mort."

"That's different."

"How?"

"Never you mind."

I decided to change the subject. "Guess who I saw at the airport yesterday? Studs Blitz, from down the block, remember?"

"You mean young Arthur," said Aunt Minnie. "He still lives at home. His father died a couple of years ago. His mother, Mavis, takes in boarders. Foreigners. Thank God your Uncle Mort's benefits spared me that."

She patted the urn and the cat's eye glowed benevolently.

That night, Candy and I began our Honeymoon by holding hands across the gap between our separate beds. Candy wanted to wait until tomorrow night, after we had "done the tourist thing" to "go all the way." Plus she was still nervous from the flight.

I didn't mind. It was exciting and romantic. Sort of.

"Your Aunt Minnie is sweet," Candy said, right before we dropped off to sleep. "But can I ask one question?"

"Shoot."

"How can ashes object to smoke?"

Part Three

Our return tickets were for Wednesday. That meant we had one full Honeymoon day, Tuesday, to see the sights of New York, most of which (all of which, truth be told) are in Manhattan. Candy and I got up early and caught the F train at Ditmas. It came right away. We got off at the next-to-last stop in Manhattan, Fifth Avenue, and walked uptown past Tiffany's and Disney and the Trump Tower; all the way to Central Park and the Plaza, that magnet for Honeymooners. When we saw all the people on the front step, we thought there had been a fire. But they were just smoking; it was just like Brooklyn.

We strolled through the lobby, peering humbly into the Palm Court and the Oak Room, then started back downtown, still holding hands. Candy was the prettiest girl on Fifth Avenue (one of the few in uniform), and I loved watching her watch my big town rush by. New York! Next stop, Rockefeller Center. We joined the crowd overlooking the skaters, secretly waiting for someone to fall; it's like NASCAR without the noise. Candy was eyeing the line at Nelson's On the Rink, where waiters on rollerblades serve cappuccinos and lattes. It's strictly a tourist joint; New Yorkers don't go for standing in line and particularly not for coffee. But when I saw how fast the line was moving, I figured what the hell. We were seated right away and served right away, and the expense (we are talking four-dollar croissants here) was well worth it.

"What now?" asked Candy, her little rosebud smile deliciously flaked with pastry. I couldn't imagine anyone I would rather Honeymoon with.

"The Empire State Building, of course."

Candy grimaced. "I'm afraid of heights. Besides, don't they shoot people up there?"

"We're not going to the top, silly," I said. "That's a tourist thing." Taking her by the hand, I took her on my own personal Empire State Building Tour, which involves circling it and seeing it above and behind and through and between the other midtown buildings; catching it unawares, as it were. We started outside Lord & Taylor on Fifth, then cut west on Fortieth alongside Bryant Park for the sudden glimpse through the rear of a narrow parking lot next to American Standard; then started down Sixth, enjoying the angle from Herald Square (and detouring through Macy's to ride the wooden-treaded escalators). Then we worked back west through "little Korea," catching two dramatic views up open air shafts and one across a steep sequence of fire escapes. Standing alone, the Empire State Building looks stupid, like an oversized toy or a prop for a Superman action figure. But in its milieu it is majestic, like an Everest tantalizingly appearing and disappearing behind the ranges. We circled the great massif in a tightening spiral for almost an hour, winding up (so to speak) on Fifth Avenue again, under the big art deco facade. The curb was crowded with tourists standing in line to buy tee shirts and board buses. The tee-shirt vendors were looking gloomy, since the buses were coming right away and there was no waiting.

I had saved the best view for last. It's from the middle of Fifth Avenue, looking straight up. You have to time it just right with the stoplights, of course. Candy and I were about to step off the curb, hand in hand, when a messenger in yellow and black tights (one of our city's colorful jesters) who was straddling his bike beside a rack of pay phones on the corner of 33rd hailed me.

"Yo!"

I stopped. That's how long I'd been in Alabama.

"Your name Irv?"

I nodded. That's how long I'd been in Alabama.

He handed me the phone with a sort of a wink and a sort of a shrug, and was off on his bike before I could hand it back (which was my first instinct).

I put the phone to my ear. Rather cautiously, as you might imagine. "Hello?"

"Irv? Finally!"

"Wu?!" Everybody should have a friend like Wilson Wu, my Best Man. Wu studied physics at Bronx Science, pastry in Paris, math at Princeton, herbs in Taiwan, law at Harvard (or was it Yale?), and caravans at a Gobi caravansary. Did I mention he's Chinese-American, can tune a twelve-string guitar in under a minute with a logarithmic calculator, and is over six feet tall? I met him when we worked at Legal Aid, drove Volvos, and went to the Moon; but that's another story. Then he went to Hawaii and found the Edge of the Universe, yet another story still. Now he was working as a meteorological entemologist, whatever that was, in the jungles of Quetzalcan.

Wherever that was.

"Who'd you expect?" Wu asked. "I'm glad you finally picked up. Your Aunt Minnie told me you and Candy were in midtown doing the tourist thing."

"We're on our Honeymoon."

"Oh no! Don't tell me I missed the wedding!"

"Of course not," I said. "We had to take the Honeymoon first so Candy could get the personal time. How'd you persuade Aunt Minnie to answer the phone? Or me, for that matter? Are you in Huntsville already?"

"That's the problem, Irv. I'm still in Quetzalcan. The rain forest, or to be more precise, the cloud forest; the canopy, in fact. Camp Canopy, we call it."

"But the wedding is Thursday! You're the Best Man, Wu! I've already rented your tux. It's waiting for you at Five Points Formal Wear."

"I know all that," said Wu. "But I'm having a problem getting away. That's why I called, to see if you can put the wedding off for a week."

"A week? Wu, that's impossible. Cindy has already commissioned the ice sculpture."

Wu's wife, Cindy, was catering the wedding.

"The hurricane season is almost upon us," said Wu, "and my figures are coming out wrong. I need more time."

"What do the hurricanes have to do with your figures?" I asked. "Or with meteors or bugs, for that matter?"

"Irving—" Wu always called me by my full name when he was explaining something he felt he shouldn't have to explain. "Meteorology is weather, not meteors. And the bugs have to do with the Butterfly Effect. We're been over this before."

"Oh yes, of course, I remember," I said, and I did, sort of. But Wu went over it again anyway: how the flap of a butterfly's wing in the rain forest could cause a storm two thousand miles away. "It was only a matter of time," he said, "before someone located that patch of rain forest, which is where we are, and cloned the butterfly. It's a moth, actually. We have twenty-two of them, enough for the entire hurricane season. We can't stop the hurricanes, but we can delay, direct, and divert them a little, which is why ABC flew us down here."

"ABC?"

"They bought the television rights to the hurricane season, Irv. Don't you read the trades? CBS got the NBA and NBC got the Superbowl. ABC beat out Ted Turner, which is fine with me. Who needs a Hurricane Jane, even upgraded from a tropical storm? The network hired us to edge the 'canes toward the weekends as much as possible, when the news is slow. And State Farm is chipping in, since any damage we can moderate is money in their pocket. They are footing the bill for this little Hanging Hilton, in fact. 'Footing,' so to speak. My feet haven't touched the ground in three weeks."

"I built a treehouse once," I said. "Me and Studs Blitz, back in the old neighborhood."

"A treehouse in Brooklyn?" interjected a strangely accented voice.

"Who's that?" I asked.

"Dmitri, stay off the line!" barked Wu. "I'll explain later," he said to me. "But I'm losing my signal. Which way you two love-birds heading?"

We were heading downtown. Our first stop was Sweet Noth-ings, the bridal boutique in New York's historic lingerie dis-trict. Candy made me wait outside while she shopped. Inspired, I bought a Honeymoon Bungee at the Oriental Nov-elty Arcade on Broadway. ("What's it for?" Candy asked appre-hensively. I promised to show her later.) Feeling romantic, I took her little hand in mine and led her back over to Sixth and presented her with the world's largest interactive bouquet—a three-block stroll through the flower market. We were just emerging from a tunnel of flowering ferns at Twenty-sixth, when the pay phone on the corner rang. On a hunch, I picked it up.

When you get hunches as rarely as I do, you follow them.

"Irving, why do you take so long to answer?"

"I picked up on the first ring, Wu. How'd you manage that phone thing, anyway?"

"Software," Wu said. "I swiped the algos for handwriting recognition out of an Apple Newton and interlaced them into a GPS (Global Positioning System) satellite feed program. Then I ran your mail order consumer profile (pirated from J. Crew) through a fuzzilogical bulk mail collator macro lifted off a zip-code CD-rom, and adjusted for the fact that you've spent the past six months in Alabama. A friend in the Mir shunts the search feeds through the communications satellite LAN until the 'IRV'- probability field collapses and the phone nearest you rings. And you pick it up. Voilà."

"I don't mean that," I said. "I mean, how'd you get Aunt Minnie to answer the phone?"

"Changed the ring!" Wu said, sounding pleased with himself. "It took a little doing, but I was able to tweak a caller ID macro enough to toggle her ringer. Made it sound like a doorbell chime. Somehow that gets her to answer. I'll send you the figures."

"Never mind," I said. "The only figure I want to see is you-know-whose in her Sweet Nothings"—Candy, who was pretending not to listen, blushed—"and yours in a white tux at noon on Thursday! There's no way we can change the wedding date."

"Can't you put it off at least a couple of days, Irv? I'm having trouble with my formula."

"Impossible!" I said. "The ice sculpture won't wait. Let the butterflies go and get on back to Huntsville. One hurricane more or less can't make all that much difference."

"Moths," said Wu. "And it's not just hurricanes. What if it rains on your wedding?"

"It won't," I said. "It can't. Cindy guarantees clear skies. It's included in the catering bill."

"Of course it is, but how do you think that works. Irving? Cindy buys weather insurance from Ido Ido, the Japanese wedding conglomerate, which contracts with Entemological Meteorological Solutions—that's us—to schedule outdoor ceremonies around the world. It's just a sideline for EMS, of course. A little tweaking. But I can't release the first moth until the coordinates are right, and my numbers are coming out slippery."

"Slippery?"

"The math doesn't work, Irv. The Time axis doesn't line up. In a system as chaotic as weather, you only have one constant, Time, and when it isn't . . ."

But we were losing our signal, and Candy was looking at me suspiciously. I hung up.

"What are all these phone calls from Wu?" she asked as we headed downtown. "Is something wrong with the wedding plans?"

"Absolutely not," I lied. There was no reason to spoil her Honeymoon (and mine!). "He just wants me to help him with a—a math problem."

"I thought he was the math whiz. I didn't know you even took math."

• • •

I didn't, not after my sophomore year in high school. I was totally absorbed by history, inspired by my favorite teacher, Citizen Tipograph (she wanted us to call her Comrade, but the principal put his foot down) who took us on field trips as far afield as Gettysburg and Harper's Ferry. Every course C. T. taught, whether it was Women's Labor History, Black Labor History, Jewish Labor History, or just plain old American Labor History, included at least one trip to Union Square, and I grew to love the seedy old park, where I can still hear the clatter of the horses and the cries of the Cossacks (which is what C. T. called the cops) and the stirring strains of the "Internationale." I tried to share some of this drama with Candy, but even though she listened politely, I could see that to her Union Square was just scrawny grass, dozing bums, and overweening squirrels.

Candy couldn't wait to get out of the park. She was far more interested in the stacked TVs in the display window at Nutty Ned's Home Electronics, on the corner of University and Fourteenth, where dozens of Rosie O'Donnells were chatting silently with science fiction writer(s) Paul Park. There's nothing better than a talk show without sound. We both stopped to watch for a moment, when all of the screens started scrolling numbers. Over Rosie and her guest!

On a hunch, I went into the store. Candy followed.

Nutty Ned's clerks were firing wildly with remotes, trying to tune the runaway TVs. The displays all changed colors but stayed the same: it was strange, but strangely familiar:

$$\frac{W}{M} \left| \psi \right\rangle = w(x,t) \sum_{l=1}^{k} \frac{\dfrac{\phi(x')}{3.26\,mb}}{\sqrt{(63C_2)\Delta}} \cdot \frac{\left(\oint (8>0) \right)}{1372}$$

$$\overline{UHF}\rangle_{.21\,cm}$$

I figured I knew what it was. And I was right. At precisely that moment, an entire FINAL SALE table of portable phones started to ring. It made a terrible noise, like a nursery filled with children who decide to cry all at once.

I picked up one and they all quit.

"Wu? Is that you?"

"Irv, did you see my figures? I'm shunting them through the midmorn talknet comsat feed. See what I mean? I'm getting totally unlikely dates and places for these hurricanes, all down the line. Not to mention rainy weddings. And it's definitely the T."

"The T?"

"The Time axis, the constant that makes the Butterfly Effect predictable. It's become a maverick variable, too long here, too short there. Speaking of which, I wish you wouldn't make me ring you twenty times. It's annoying, and I have other things to do here, living in a treehouse, like feed the flying—"

"I picked up on the first ring."

"The hell you did! The phone rang twenty-six times."

I did a quick count of the phones on the FINAL SALE table. "Twenty-six phones rang, Wu, but they each rang only once. And all at once."

"Whoa!" said Wu. "I'm coming through in parallel? That could mean there's a twist."

"A twist?"

"A twist in local space-time. It's never happened but it's theoretically possible, of course. And it just *might* explain my slippery T axes. Have you noticed any other temporal anomalies?"

"Temporary comedies?"

"Weird time stuff, Irving! Any other weird time stuff happening there in New York? Overturned schedules! Unexpected delays!"

"Well, New York's all about delays," I said, "but as a matter of fact—" I told Wu about never having to wait for the subway. Or the bus. "Even the Fifth Avenue bus comes right away!"

"The Fifth Avenue bus! I'm beginning to think there may be

more than a temporal anomaly here. We may be looking at a full-fledged chronological singularity. But I need more than your subjective impressions, Irv; I need hard numbers. Which way are you two lovebirds going?"

"Downtown," I said. "It's almost lunchtime."

"Perfect!" he said. "How about Carlo's?"

When Wu and I had worked at Legal Aid, on Centre Street, we had often eaten at Carlo's Calamari in Little Italy. But only when we had time to take a *loooong* lunch.

"No way!" I said. "It takes forever to get waited on at Carlo's."

"Exactly!" said Wu.

I felt a tap on my shoulder. "You plan to buy this phone?" It was Nutty Ned himself. I recognized his nose from the TV ads.

"No way," I said.

"Then hang it the fuck up please."

Part Four

"We got a menu as soon as we sat down," I said. I was speaking on the model Camaro phone at Carlo's, while Candy poked through her cold seafood salad, setting aside everything that had legs or arms or eyes, which was most of the dish.

"Impossible!" said Wu.

"We ordered and my primavera pesto pasta came right away. Maybe they have it already cooked and they just microwave it." I said this low so the waiter wouldn't hear. He had brought me the phone on a tray shaped like Sicily. It was beige, flecked with red. Dried blood? Carlo's is a mob joint. Allegedly.

"What's right away?"

"I don't know, Wu. I didn't time it."

"I need numbers, Irv! What about breadsticks. Do they still have those skinny hard breadsticks? How many did you eat between the time you ordered and the time the food came?"

"Three."

"Three apiece?"

"Three between us. Does knowing that really help?"

"Sure. I can use it either as one and one-half, or as three over two. Numbers don't lie, Irv. Parallel or serial, I'm beginning to think my T-axis problem is centered in New York. Everything there seems to be speeded up slightly. Compressed."

"Compressed," I said. When Wu is talking he expects you to respond. I always try and pick a fairly innocuous word and just repeat it.

"You've got it, Irv. It's like those interviews on TV that are a little jumpy, because they edit out all the Connective Time—the uhs, the ahs, the waits, the pauses. Something's happened to the Connective Time in New York. That's why the phone rings ten times for me here—actually an average of 8.411—and only once for you."

"How can the phone ring more times for you than for me?"

"Ever heard of Relativity, Irving?"

"Yes, but . . ."

"No buts about it!" Wu said. "Theoretically, a ninety-degree twist could cause a leakage of Connective Time. But what is causing the twist? That's the . . ."

His voice was starting to fade. Truthfully, I was glad. I was ready to concentrate on my primavera pesto pasta.

"Pepper?" asked the waiter.

"Absolutely," I said. I don't really care for pepper but I admire the way they operate those big wrist-powered wooden machines.

Candy loves to shop (who doesn't?) so we headed across Grand Street to SoHo, looking for jeans on lower Broadway. Since there was no waiting for the dressing rooms (maybe Wu was on to something!), Candy decided to try on one pair of each brand in each style and each color. We were about a third of the way through the stack when the salesgirl began to beep; rather, her beeper did.

"Your name Irv?" she asked, studying the readout. "You can use the sales phone." It was under the counter, by the shopping bags.

"How's the coffee?" Wu asked.

"Coffee?"

"Aren't you at Dean & DeLuca?"

"We're at ZigZag Jeans."

"On Broadway at Grand? Now my fuzzilogical GPS transponder is showing slack!" Wu protested. "If I'm three blocks off already, then that means . . ."

I stopped listening. Candy had just stepped out of the dressing room to check her Levi's in the store's "rear view" mirror. "What do you think?" she asked.

"Incredible," I said.

"My reaction exactly," said Wu. "But what else could it be? The bus, the breadsticks, the F train—all the numbers seem to indicate a slow leak of Connective Time somewhere in the New York metropolitan area. Let me ask you this, was your plane on time?"

"Why, yes," I said. "At the gate, as a matter of fact. The little bell went *ding* and everybody stood up at 7:32. I remember noticing it on my watch. It was our exact arrival time."

"Seven thirty-two," repeated Wu. "That helps. I'm going to check the airports. I can patch into their security terminals and interlace from there to the arrival and departure monitors. I'll need a little help, though. Dmitri, are you there? He's sulking."

"Whatever," I said, giving the ZigZag girls back their phone. Candy was trying on the Wranglers, and me, I was falling in love all over again. I rarely see her out of her uniform, and it is a magnificent sight.

In the end, so to speak, it was hard to decide. The Levi's, the Lees, the Wranglers, the Guess Whos, the Calvins, and the Gloria's all cosseted and caressed the same incredible curves. Candy decided to buy one pair of each and put them all on my credit card, since hers was maxed out. By the time the ZigZag girls had the jeans folded and wrapped and packed up in shopping bags, it was 3:30—almost time to head back to Brooklyn if we wanted to beat the rush hour. But Wu had given me an idea.

Even guys like me, who can't afford the Israeli cantaloupes or free-range Pyrenees sheep cheese at Dean & DeLuca, can spring for a cup of coffee, which you pick up at a marble counter between the vegetable and bread sections, and drink standing at tall, skinny chrome tables overlooking the rigorously fashionable intersection of Broadway and Prince.

D&D's is my idea of class, and it seemed to appeal to Candy as well, who was back in uniform and eliciting (as usual) many an admiring glance both on the street and in the aisles. I wasn't halfway through my Americano before the butcher appeared from the back of the store with a long, skinny roll of what I thought at first was miniature butcher paper (unborn lamb chops?), but was in fact thermal paper from the old-fashioned adding machine in the meat department. The key to Dean & DeLuca's snooty charm is that everything (except of course the customers) is slightly old-fashioned. Hence, thermal paper.

"You Irv?"

I nodded.

He handed me the little scroll. I unrolled it enough to see that it was covered with tiny figures, then let it roll back up again.

"From Wu?" Candy asked.

"Probably," I said. "But let's finish our coffee."

At that very moment, a man walking down Broadway took a cellular phone out of his Armani suit, unfolded it, put it to his ear, and stopped. He looked up and down the street, then in the window at me.

I nodded, somewhat reluctantly. It would have been rude, even presumptuous, to expect him to bring the phone inside the store to me, so I excused myself and went out to the street.

"Did you get my fax?" asked Wu.

"Sort of," I said. I made a spinning motion with one finger to Candy, who understood right away. She unrolled the little scroll of thermal paper and held it up to the window glass:

"Well?"

"Well!" I replied. That usually satisfied Wu, but I could tell he wanted more this time. Sometimes with Wu it helps to ask a

$$LGA \parallel = \phi \downarrow \qquad \phi ieC \quad (1300)$$
$$3^3 \qquad ONTIME$$
$$ONTIME$$
$$ONTIME$$
$$137 > 87 \ \Sigma$$
$$\phi \downarrow \qquad 12\,9$$
$$t = 0$$
$$(\Sigma \partial h > 8 >> 125.4))$$

question, if you can think of an intelligent one. "What's the ON TIME ON TIME ON TIME stuff?" I asked.

"Those are airport figures, Irv! La Guardia, to be specific. All the planes are on time! That tell you something?"

"The leak is at La Guardia?" I ventured.

"Exactly! Numbers don't lie, Irv, and as those calculations clearly show, the connective temporal displacement at La Guardia is exactly equal to the Time-axis twist I'm getting worldwide, adjusted for the Earth's rotation, divided by 5.211. Which is the part I can't figure."

"I've seen that number somewhere before," I said. I dimly remembered something rolling around. "A shoe size? A phone number?"

"Try to remember," said Wu. "That number might lead us to the leak. We know it's somewhere at La Guardia; now all we have to do is pinpoint it. And plug it."

"Why plug it?" I said. "This no-delay business just makes life better. Who wants to wait around an airport?"

"Think about it, Irving!" Wu said. There was an edge to his voice, like when he thinks I am being stupid on purpose. In fact I am never stupid on purpose. That would be stupid. "You know how a low-pressure area sucks air from other areas? It's the same with Time. The system is trying to stabilize itself. Which is why I can't get the proper EMS figures for Hurricane Relief, or Ido

Ido, for that matter. Which is why I asked you to delay your wedding in the first place."

"Okay, okay," I said. I was so excited about my upcoming Honeymoon that I had totally forgotten the wedding. "So let's plug it. What do you want me to do?"

"Go to La Guardia and wait for my call," he said.

"La Guardia?!? Aunt Minnie is expecting us for supper."

"I thought she was Lifthatvanian. They can't cook!"

"They can so!" I said. "Besides, we're sending out for pizza. And besides"—I dropped my voice—"tonight's the night Candy and I officially have our Honeymoon."

Honeymoon is one of those words you can't say without miming a kiss. Candy must have been reading my lips through the Dean & DeLuca's window, because she blushed; beautifully, I might add.

But Wu must not have heard me, because he was saying, "As soon as you get to La Guardia . . ." as his voice faded away. We were losing our connection.

Meanwhile, the guy whose phone it was, was looking at his watch. It was a Movado. I recognized it from *The New Yorker* ads. I kept my subscription even after moving to Huntsville. I gave him his phone back and we headed for the subway station.

How could Wu expect me to hang out at La Guardia waiting for his call on the night of my Honeymoon? Perhaps if the Queens-bound train had come first, I might have taken it, but I don't think so. And it didn't. Taking Candy by the hand, I put us on the Brooklyn-bound F. It wasn't quite rush hour, which meant we got a seat as soon as we reached Delancey Street. Did I mention that the train came right away?

Even though (or perhaps because) I am a born and bred New Yorker, I get a little nervous when the train stops in the tunnel under the East River. This one started and stopped, started and stopped.

Then stopped.

The lights went out.

They came back on.

"There is a grumbasheivous willin brashabrashengobrak our signal," said the loudspeaker. "Please wooshagranny the delay."

"What did she say?" asked Candy. "Is something wrong?"

"Don't worry about it," I said.

Turns out we were in the conductor's car. The lights flickered but stayed on, and she stepped out of her tiny compartment, holding a phone. "Ashabroshabikus Irving?" she asked.

I nodded.

"Frezzhogristis quick," she said, handing me the phone.

"Hello?" I ventured. I knew who it was, of course.

"Irv, I need you in baggage claim," said Wu.

"In what?"

"I'm closing in on the Connective Time leak. I think it's a phone somewhere on the Baggage Claim and Ground Transportation level. I need you to go down there and see which pay phone is off the hook, so we can . . . What's that noise?"

"That's the train starting up again," I said.

"Train? I thought you were at the airport."

"I tried to tell you, Wu," I said. "We promised Aunt Minnie we would come home for dinner. Plus tonight's my Honeymoon. Plus, you're not looking for a pay phone."

"How do you know?"

"The 5.211. Now I remember what it was. It was a battery for a cell phone. It was rolling and I stopped it with my foot."

"Of course!" said Wu. "What a fool I am! And you, Irv, are a genius! Don't make a move until I . . ."

But we were losing our signal.

"Make if sharanka bresh?" asked the conductor, a little testily. She took her phone and stepped back into her tiny compartment and closed the door.

Part Five

Every bad pizza is bad in its own way, but good pizza is all alike. Bruno's on the corner of Ditmas and MacDonald, under the el, is my favorite, and Aunt Minnie's too. A fresh pie was being popped into the oven as Candy I walked in the door, and Bruno, Jr., assured us it was ours.

We were headed for home, box in hand, when a battered Buick gypsy cab pulled up at the curb. I waved it off, shaking my head, figuring the driver thought we'd flagged him down. But that wasn't it.

The driver powered down his window and I heard Wu's voice over the static on the two-way radio: "Irv, you can head for Brooklyn after all. I found it. Irv, you there?"

The driver was saying something in Egyptian and trying to hand me a little mike. I gave Candy the pizza to hold, and took it.

"Press the little button," said Wu.

I pressed the little button. "Found what?"

"The leak. The 5.211 was the clue," said wu. "I should have recognized it immediately as a special two-year cadmium silicone battery for a low-frequency, high-intensity, short-circuit, long-distance cellular phone. Once you tipped me off, I located the phone hidden underneath the old Eastern/Braniff/Pan Am/Piedmont/People baggage carousel."

"I know," I said, pressing the little button. "I saw it there. So now I guess you want me to go to La Guardia and hang it up?"

"Not so fast, Irv! The phone is just the conduit, the timeline through which the Connective Time is being drained. What we need to find is the number the phone is calling—the source of the leak, the actual hole in Time, the twist. It could be some bizarre natural singularity, like a chronological whirlpool or tornado; or even worse, some incredibly advanced, diabolical machine, designed to twist a hole in space-time and pinch off a piece of our Universe. The open phone connection will lead us to it, whatever it is, and guess what?"

"What?"

"The number it's calling is in Brooklyn, and guess what?"

"What?"

"It's the phone number of Dr. Radio Dgjerm!"

He pronounced it rah-dio. I said, "Help me out."

"The world-famous Lifthatvanian resort developer, Irving!" said Wu, impatiently. "Winner of the Nobel Prize for Real Estate in 1982! Remember?"

"Oh, him. Sort of," I lied.

"Which was later revoked when he was indicted for trying to create an illegal Universe, but that's another story. And guess what?"

"What?"

"He lives somewhere on Ditmas, near your aunt, as a matter of fact. We're still trying to pinpoint the exact address."

"What a coincidence," I said. "We're on Ditmas right now. We just picked up a pizza."

"With what?"

"Mushrooms and peppers on one side, for Aunt Minnie. Olives and sausage on the other, for Candy. I pick at both, since I like mushrooms and sausage."

"What a coincidence," said Wu. "I like it with olives and peppers." He sighed. "I would kill for a New York pizza. Ever spend six weeks in a treehouse?"

"Ever spend six months in a space station?" asked a strangely accented voice.

"Butt out, Dmitri," Wu said (rather rudely, I thought). "Aren't you supposed to be looking for that address?"

"I spent three nights in a treehouse once," I said. "Me and Studs. Of course, we had a TV."

"A TV in a treehouse?"

"Just black and white. It was an old six-inch Dumont from my Uncle Mort's basement."

"A six-inch Dumont!" said Wu. "Of course! What a fool I am! Irv, did it have . . ."

But we were losing our signal. Literally. The driver of the

gypsy cab was leaning out of his window, shouting in Egyptian and reaching for the phone.

"Probably has a fare to pick up," I explained to Candy as he snatched the little mike out of my hand and drove off, burning rubber. "Let's get this pizza to Aunt Minnie before it gets cold. Otherwise she'll cook. And she can't."

Different cultures deal with death, dying, and the dead in different ways. I was accustomed to Aunt Minnie's Lifthatvanian eccentricities, but I was concerned about how Candy would take it when she set Uncle Mort's ashes at the head of the table for dinner.

Candy was cool, though. As soon as supper was finished, she helped Aunt Minnie with the dishes (not much of a job), and joined her on the front porch for her Kent. And, I supposed, girl talk. I took the opportunity to go upstairs and strap the legs of the twin beds together with the $1.99 Honeymoon Bungee I had bought in Little Korea. The big evening was almost upon us! There on the dresser was the sleek little package from Sweet Nothings: Candy's Honeymoon negligee. I was tempted to look inside, but of course I didn't.

I wanted to be surprised. I wanted everything to be perfect.

From the upstairs window I could see the big maple tree in Studs's backyard. It was getting dark, and blue light spilled out through every crack in the treehouse, of which there were many.

I heard the doorbell chime. That seemed strange, since I knew Candy and Aunt Minnie were on the front porch. Then I realized it was the phone. I ran downstairs to pick it up.

"Diagonal, right?"

"What?"

"The screen, Irving! On the Dumont you had in the treehouse. You said it was six-inch. Was that measured diagonally?"

"Of course," I said. "It's always measured diagonally. Wu, what's this about?"

"Blond cabinet?"

"Nice blond veneer," I said. "The color of a Dreamsicle™. It was a real old set. It was the first one Aunt Minnie and Uncle Mort had bought back in the fifties. It even had little doors you could close when you weren't watching it. I always thought the little doors were to keep the cowboys from getting out."

"Cowboys in Brooklyn?" asked a strangely accented voice.

"Butt out, Dmitri," Wu said. "Irv, you are a genius. We have found the twist."

"I am? We have?"

"Indubitably. Remember the big Dumont console payola recall scandal of 1957?"

"Not exactly. I was busy being born. As were you."

"Well, it wasn't *really* about payola at all. It was about something far more significant. Quantum physics. Turns out that the #515 gauge boson rectifier under the 354V67 vacuum tube in the Dumont six-inch console had a frequency modulation that set up an interference wave of 8.48756 gauss, which, when hooked up to household 110, opened an oscillating 88-degree offset permeability in the fabric of the space-time continuum."

"A twist?"

"Exactly. And close enough to ninety degrees to make a small leak. It was discovered, quite by accident, by a lowly assistant at Underwriters Laboratory eleven months after the sets had been on the market. Shipped. Sold."

"I don't remember ever hearing about it."

"How could you? It was covered up by the powers-that-be; rather, that-were; indeed, that-still-are. Can you imagine the panic if over a quarter of a million people discovered that the TV set in their living room was pinching a hole in the Universe? Even a tiny one? It would have destroyed the industry in its infancy. You better believe it was hushed up, Irv. Deep-sixed. 337,877 sets were recalled and destroyed, their blond wood cabinets broken up for kindling, their circuits melted down for new pennies, and their #515 gauge boson rectifiers sealed in glass and buried in an abandoned salt mine 1200 feet under East Gramling, West Virginia."

"So what are you saying? One got away?"

"Exactly, Irv. 337,877 were destroyed, but 337,878 were manufactured. Numbers don't lie. Do the math."

"Hmmmm," I said. "Could be that Aunt Minnie missed the recall. She hardly ever opens her mail, you know. Studs and I found the set in Uncle Mort's basement workshop. It hadn't been used for years, but it seemed to work okay. We didn't notice it twisting any hole in Time."

"Of course not. It's a tiny hole. But over a long period, it would have a cumulative effect. Precisely the effect we are seeing, in fact. Many millions of connective milliseconds have been drained out of our Universe—perhaps even stolen deliberately, for all we know."

I was relieved. If it was a crime, I was off the hook. I could concentrate on my Honeymoon. "Then let's call the police," I said.

Wu just laughed. "The police aren't prepared to deal with anything like this, Irv. This is quantum physics, Feynman stuff, way beyond them. We will have to handle it ourselves. When Dmitri finds the address for Dr. Dgjerm, I have a suspicion we will also find out what became of the legendary Lost D6."

"Isn't this a bit of a coincidence?" I asked. "What are the odds that the very thing that is messing you up in Quetzalcan is right here in my old neighborhood in Brooklyn? It seems unlikely."

"That's because you don't understand probability, Irving," said Wu. "Everything is unlikely until it happens. Look at it this way: when there's a ten percent chance of rain, there's a ninety percent chance it won't rain, right?"

"Right."

"Then what if it starts raining? The probability wave collapses, and the ten percent becomes a hundred, the ninety becomes zero. An unlikely event becomes a certainty."

It made sense to me. "Then it's raining here, Wu," I said. "The probability waves are collapsing like crazy, because the TV you are looking for is still in the treehouse. Turned on, in fact. I can see the blue light from here. It's in the maple tree in Studs's backyard, three doors down."

"On Ditmas?"

"On Ditmas."

"So your friend Studs could be involved?"

"That's what I was trying to tell you!" I said. "He runs the baggage carousel at La Guardia that the phone was hidden under."

"The plot thickens," said Wu, who loves it when the plot thickens. "He must be draining off the Connective Time to speed up his baggage delivery! But where is it going? And what is Dgjerm's role in this caper? We'll know soon enough."

"We will?"

"When you confront them, Irv, at the scene of the crime, so to speak. You said it was only two doors away."

"No way," I said. "Not tonight."

"Why not?"

"Guess who?" I felt hands over my eyes.

"Candy, that's why," I said.

"Right you are!" Candy said. She blushed (even her fingertips blush) and her voice dropped to a whisper. "Coming upstairs?"

"You mean your Honeymoon?" Wu asked.

"Yes, of course I mean my Honeymoon!" I said as I watched Candy kiss Aunt Minnie good night and go upstairs. "I don't want to confront anybody! Any guys, anyway. Can't you just turn the TV off by remote?"

"There's no remote on those old Dumonts, Irv. You're going to have to unplug it."

"Tomorrow, then."

"Tonight," said Wu. "It'll only take you a few minutes. If the leak is plugged tonight I can redo my calculations and release the first moth in the morning. Then if I catch the nonstop from Quetzalcan City, I'll make Huntsville in time to pick up my tux. But if I don't, you won't have a Best Man. Or a ring. Or maybe even a wedding. Don't forget, this moth works for Ido Ido, too. What if it rains?"

"Okay, okay," I said. "You convinced me. But I'm just going to run over there and unplug it and that's all." I kissed Aunt

Minnie good night (she sleeps in the BarcaLounger in front of the TV with Uncle Mort's ashes in her lap), then called up the stairs to Candy, "Be up in a minute!"

Then headed out the back door.

Part Six

I'll never forget the first time I visited my cousin Lucy in New Jersey. Lots of things in the suburbs were different. The trees were skinnier, the houses were lower, the cars were newer, the streets were wider, the yards were bigger, and the grass was definitely greener. But the main thing I remember was my feeling of panic: there was nowhere to hide. The picture windows, one on each house, seemed to stare out onto a world in which nobody had anything to conceal, a terrifying idea to a preteen (I was eleven going on fifteen) since adolescence is the slow, unfolding triumph of experience over innocence, and teens have everything to hide.

I was glad to get back to Brooklyn, where everyone knew who I was but no one was watching me. I had the same safe feeling when I slipped out the kitchen door into Aunt Minnie's tiny (and sadly neglected) backyard. The yards in Brooklyn, on Ditmas at least, are narrow slivers separated by board fences, wire fences, slat fences, mesh fences. Adulthood in America doesn't involve a lot of fence climbing, and I felt like a kid again as I hauled myself carefully over a sagging section of chain link into the Murphys' yard next door. Of course, they weren't the Murphys anymore: they were the Wing-Tang somethings, and they had replaced the old squealing swing set with a new plastic and rubberoid play center in the shape of a pirate ship, complete with plank.

The next yard, the Patellis', was even less familiar. It had always been choked with flowers and weeds in a dizzying, improbable mix, under a grape arbor that, properly processed, kept the grandfather mildly potted all year. The vines had stopped bearing when "Don Patelli" had died the year I started high school. "Grapes are like dogs," Uncle Mort had said. "Faithful to the end." Everything Uncle Mort knew about dogs, he had learned from books.

A light came on in the house, and I remembered with alarm that the Patellis no longer lived there, and that I was no longer a neighborhood kid; or even a kid. If anybody saw me, they would call the police. I stepped back into the shadows. Looking up, and back a house or two, I spotted a shapely silhouette behind the blinds in an upstairs window. A girl undressing for bed! I enjoyed the guilty Peeping Tom feeling, until I realized it was Candy, in Aunt Minnie's guest room. That made it even better.

But it was time to get moving. Unplug the stupid TV and be done with it.

The loose plank in the Patellis' ancient board fence still swung open to let me through. It was a little tighter fit, but I made it—and I was in the Blitzes' yard, under the wide, ivy-covered trunk of the maple. The board steps Studs and I had nailed to the tree were still there, but I was glad to see that they had been supplemented with a ten-foot aluminum ladder.

At the top of the ladder, wedged into a low fork, was the treehouse Studs and I had built in the summer of 1968. It was a triangular shed about six feet high and five feet on a side, nailed together from scrap plywood and pallet lumber. It was hard to believe it was still intact after almost thirty years. Yet, there it was.

And here I was. There were no windows, but through the cracks, I saw a blue light.

I climbed up the aluminum ladder. The door, a sheet of faux-birch paneling, was padlocked from the outside. I even recognized the padlock. Before opening it, I looked in through the wide crack at the top. I was surprised by what I saw.

Usually, when you return to scenes of your childhood, whether it's an elementary school or a neighbor's yard, every-thing seems impossibly small. That's what I thought it would be like with the treehouse Studs and I had built when we were eleven. I expected it to look tiny inside.

Instead it looked huge.

I blinked and looked again. The inside of the treehouse seemed as big as a gym. In the near corner, to the right, I saw the TV—the six-inch Dumont console. The doors were open and the gray-blue light from the screen illuminated the entire vast interior of the treehouse. In the far corner, to the left, which seemed at least a half a block away, there was a brown sofa next to a potted palm.

I didn't like the looks of it. My first impulse was to climb down the ladder and go home. I even started down one step. Then I looked behind me, toward Aunt Minnie's upstairs guest-room window, where I had seen Candy's silhouette. The light was out. She was in bed, waiting for me. Waiting to begin our Honeymoon.

All I had to do was unplug the damn TV.

It's funny how the fingers remember what the mind forgets. The combination lock was from my old middle school locker. As soon as I started spinning the dial, my fingers knew where to start and where to stop: L5, R32, L2.

I opened the lock and set it aside, hanging it on the bracket. I leaned back and pulled the door open. I guess I expected it to groan or creak in acknowledgment of the years since I had last opened it, but it made not a sound.

The last step is a long one, and I climbed into the treehouse on my knees. It smelled musty, like glue and wood and old magazines. I left the door swinging open behind me. The plywood floor creaked reassuringly as I got to my feet.

Look who's back.

The inside of the treehouse looked huge, but it didn't *feel* huge. The sofa and the potted palm in the far corner seemed almost like miniatures that I could reach out and touch if I wanted to. I didn't want to. They sort of hung in the air, either real small, or real far away, or both. Or neither.

I decided it was best not to look at them. I had a job to do.

Two steps across the plywood floor took me to the corner with the TV. It was better here; more familiar. Here was the ratty rag rug my mother had donated; the Bardot pinups on the wall. Here was the stack of old magazines: *Motor Trend, Boys' Life, Playboy, Model Airplane News.* Here were the ball gloves, the water guns, right where Studs and I had left them, almost thirty years before. It all looked the same, in this corner.

The TV screen was more gray than blue. There was no picture, just a steady blizzard of static and snow. The rabbit ears antenna on the top was extended. One end was hung with tinfoil (had Studs and I done that?), and something was duct-taped into the cradle between them.

A cellular phone. I was *sure* we hadn't done that. They didn't even have cellular phones when we were kids; or duct tape, for that matter. This was clearly the other end of the connection from La Guardia. And there was more that was new.

A green garden hose was attached to a peculiar fitting on the front of the TV, between the volume control and the channel selector. It snaked across the floor toward the corner with the brown sofa and the potted palm. The longer I looked at the hose, the longer it seemed. I decided it was best not to look at it. I had a job to do.

The electrical power in the treehouse came from the house, via a "train" of extension cords winding through the branches from Stud's upstairs window. The TV was plugged into an extension cord dangling through a hole in the ceiling. I was reaching up to unplug it when I felt something cold against the back of my neck.

"Put your hands down!"

"Studs?"

"Irv, is that you?"

I turned slowly, hands still in the air.

"Irv the Perv? What the hell are you doing here?"

"I came to unplug the television, Studs," I said. "Is that a real gun?"

"Damn tootin'," he said. "A Glock nine."

"So this is how you got all your medals!" I said scornfully. My hands still in the air, I pointed with my chin to the six-inch Dumont with the cell phone taped between the rabbit ears, then to the impressive array across Studs's chest. Even off duty, even at home, he wore his uniform with all his medals. "That's not really your Nobel Prize around your neck, either, is it?"

"It is so!" he said, fingering the heavy medallion. "The professor gave it to me. The professor helped me win the others, too, by speeding up the baggage carousel at La Guardia. You're looking at the Employee of the Year, two years in a row."

"The professor?"

Studs pointed with the Glock nine to the other corner of the treehouse. The far corner. I was surprised to see an old man, sitting on the brown sofa next to the potted palm. He was wearing a gray cardigan over blue coveralls. "Where'd he come from?" I asked.

"He comes and goes as he pleases," said Studs. "It's his Universe."

Universe? Suddenly it all came perfectly clear; or almost clear. "Dr. Radio Dgjerm?"

"Rah-dio," the old man corrected. He looked tiny but his voice sounded neither small nor far away.

"Mother took in boarders after Dad died," Studs explained. "One day I showed Dr. Dgjerm the old treehouse, and when he saw the TV he got all excited. Especially when he turned it on and saw that it still worked. He bought the cell phones and set up the system."

"It doesn't really work," I said. "There's no picture."

"All those old black and white shows are off the air," said Studs. "Dr. Dgjerm had bigger things in mind than *I Love Lucy* anyway. Like creating a new Universe."

"Is that what's swelling up the inside of the treehouse?" I asked.

Studs nodded. "And incidentally, helping my career." His

medals clinked as his chest expanded. "You're looking at the Employee of the Year, two years in a row."

"You already told me that," I said. I looked at the old man on the sofa. "Is he real small, or far away?"

"Both," said Studs. "He's in another Universe, and it's not a very big Universe."

"Not big yet!" said Dr. Dgjerm. His voice sounded neither tiny nor far away. It boomed in my ear; I found out later, from Wu, that even a small Universe can act as a sort of resonator or echo chamber. Like a shower.

"My Universe is small now, but it's getting bigger," Dr. Dgjerm went on. "It's a leisure Universe, created entirely out of Connective Time that your Universe will never miss. In another year or so, it will attain critical mass and be big enough to survive on its own. Then I will disconnect the timelines, cast loose, and bid you all farewell!"

"We don't have another year," I said. "I have to unplug the TV now." I explained about the Butterfly Effect and the hurricanes. I even explained about my upcoming wedding in Huntsville. (I left out the part about my Honeymoon, which was supposed to be going on right now, as we spoke, just three doors down and half a floor up!)

"Congratulations," said Dgjerm in his rich Lifthatvanian accent. "But I'm afraid I can't allow you to unplug the D6. There are more than a few hurricanes and weddings at stake. We're talking about an entire new Universe here. Shoot him, Arthur."

Studs raised the Glock nine until it was pointed directly at my face. His hand was alarmingly steady.

"I don't want to shoot you, Irv," he said apologetically. "But I owe him. He made me Employee of the Year two years in a row."

"You also took a sacred oath!" I said. "Remember? You can't shoot another Ditmas Playboy!" This wasn't just a last-ditch ploy to save my life. It was true. It was one of our bylaws; one of only two, in fact.

"That was a long time ago," said Studs, looking confused.

"Time doesn't matter to oaths," I said. (I have no idea if this is true or not. I just made it up on the spot.)

"Shoot him!" said Dr. Dgjerm.

"There's another way out of this," said a voice behind us. "A more civilized way."

Part Seven

Studs and I both turned and looked at the TV. There was a familiar (to me, at least; Studs had never met him) face in grainy black and white, wearing some sort of jungle cap.

"Wu!" I said. "Where'd you come from?"

"Real-time Internet feed," he said. "Video conferencing software. My cosmonaut friend patched me in on a rogue cable channel from a digital switching satellite. Piece of cake, once we triangulated the location through the phone signals. Although cellular video can be squirrelly. Lots of frequency bounce."

"This is a treehouse? It's as big as gymnasium!" exclaimed an oddly accented voice.

"Shut up, Dmitri. We've got a situation here. Hand me the gun, Blitz."

"You can see *out of* a TV?" I asked, amazed.

"Only a little," Wu said. "Pixel inversion piggybacked on the remote locational electron smear. It's like a reverse mortgage. Feeds on the electronic equity, so to speak, so we have to get on with it. Hand me the gun, Studs. The Glock nine."

Studs was immobile, torn between conflicting loyalties. "How can I hand a gun to a guy on TV?" he whined.

"You could set it on top of the cabinet," I suggested.

"Don't do it, Arthur!" Dr. Dgjerm broke in. "Give the gun to me. Now!"

Studs was saved. The doctor had given him an order he could obey. He tossed the Glock nine across the treehouse. It got smaller and smaller and went slower and slower until, to my surprise, Dr. Dgjerm caught it. He checked the clip and laid the gun across his tiny, or distant, or both, lap.

"We can settle this without gunplay," said Wu.

"Wilson Wu," said Dr. Dgjerm. "So we meet again!"

"Again?" I whispered, surprised. I shouldn't have been.

"I was Dr. Dgjerm's graduate assistant at Bay Ridge Realty College in the late seventies," explained Wu. "Right before he won the Nobel Prize for Real Estate."

"Which was then stolen from me!" said Dr. Dgjerm.

"The prize was later revoked by the King of Sweden," explained Wu, "when Dr. Dgjerm was indicted for trying to create an illegal Universe out of unused vacation time. Unfairly, I thought, even though technically the time did belong to the companies."

"The charges were dropped," said Dgjerm. "But try telling that to the King of Sweden."

Studs fingered the Nobel Prize medallion. "It's not real?"

"Of course it's real!" said Dgjerm. "When you clink it, it clinks. It has mass. That's why I refused to give it back."

"Your scheme would never have worked, anyway, Dr. Dgjerm," said Wu. "I did the numbers. There's not enough unused vacation time to inflate a Universe; not anymore."

"You always were my best student, Wu," said Dgjerm. "You are right, as usual. But as you can see, I came up with a better source of time than puny pilfered corporate vacation days." He waved his hand around at the sofa, the potted palm. "Connective Time! There's more than enough to go around. All I needed was a way to make a hole in the fabric of space-time big enough to slip it through. And I found it!"

"The D6," said Wu.

"Exactly. I had heard of the legendary lost D6, of course, but I thought it was a myth. Imagine my surprise and delight when I found it in my own backyard, so to speak! With Arthur's help, it was a simple bandwidth problem, sluicing the Connective Time by phone from La Guardia, where it would never be missed, through the D6's gauge boson rectifier twist, and into—my own Universe!"

"But it's just a sofa and a plant," I said. "Why do you want to live there?"

"Does the word 'immortality' mean anything to you?" Dgjerm asked scornfully. "It's true that my Leisure Universe is small. That's okay; the world is not yet ready for vacationing in another Universe, anyway. But real estate is nothing if not a waiting game. It will get bigger. And while I am waiting, I age at a very slow rate. Life in a Universe made entirely of Connective Time is as close to immortality as we mortals can come."

"Brilliant," said Wu. "If you would only use your genius for science instead of gain, you could win another Nobel Prize."

"Fuck science!" said Dgjerm, his tiny (or distant, or both) mouth twisted into a smirk as his giant voice boomed through the treehouse. "I want my own Universe, and I already got a Nobel Prize, so don't anybody reach for that plug. Sorry if I've thrown off your butterfly figures, Wilson, but your Universe won't miss a few more milliminutes of Connective Time. I will disconnect mine when it is big enough to survive and grow on its own. Not before."

"That's what I'm trying to tell you!" said Wu. "The more Universes, the better, as far as I'm concerned. Look here . . ."

Wu's face on the TV screen stared straight ahead as a stream of equations flowed down over it:

"Impossible!" said Dgjerm.

"Numbers don't lie," said Wu. "Your figures were off, Professor. You reached critical mass 19.564 minutes ago, our time. Your Leisure Universe is ready to cut loose and be born. All Irv has to do is—"

"Unplug the TV?" I asked. I reached for the plug and a shot rang out.

BRANNNGGG!

It was followed by the sound of breaking glass.

CRAASH!

"You killed him!" shouted Studs.

At first I thought he meant me, but my head felt okay, and my hands were okay, one on each side of the still-connected plug. Then I saw the thick broken glass on the floor, and I knew what had happened. You know how sometimes when you fire a warning shot indoors, you hit an appliance? Well, that's what Dr. Dgjerm had done. He had meant to warn me away from the plug, and hit the television. The D6 was no more. The screen was shattered and Wu was gone.

I looked across the treehouse for the sofa, the potted palm, the little man. They were flickering a little, but still there.

"You killed him!" Studs said again.

"It was an accident," said Dgjerm. "It was meant to be a warning shot."

"It was only a video conferencing image," I said. "I'm sure Wu is fine. Besides, he was right!"

"Right?" they both asked at once.

I pointed at Dr. Dgjerm. "The TV is off, and your Universe is still there."

"For now," said Dr. Dgjerm. "But the timeline is still open, and the Connective Time is siphoning back into your Universe." As he spoke, he was getting either smaller or farther away, or both. His voice was sounding hollower and hollower.

"What should we do?" Studs asked frantically. "Hang up the phone?"

I was way ahead of him; I had already untaped the phone and

was looking for the OFF button. As soon as I pushed it, the phone rang.

It was, of course, Wu. "Everything all right?" he asked. "I lost my connection."

I told him what had happened. Meanwhile, Dr. Dgjerm was getting smaller and smaller every second. Or farther and farther away. Or both.

"You have to act fast!" Wu said. "A Universe is like a balloon. You have to tie it off, or it'll shrink into nothing."

"I know," I said. "That's why I hung up the phone."

"Wrong timeline. The phone connects the baggage carousel to the D6. There must be another connection from the D6 to Dr. Dgjerm's Leisure Universe. That's the one that's still open. Look for analog, narrow bandwidth, probably green."

Dr. Dgjerm was standing on the tiny sofa, pointing frantically toward the front of the TV.

"Like a garden hose?" I asked.

"Could be," said Wu. "If so, kinking it won't help. Time isn't like water; it's infinitely compressible. You'll have to disconnect it."

The hose was attached to a peculiar brass fitting on the front of the set, between the channel selector and the volume control. I tried unscrewing it. I turned it to the left, but nothing happened. I turned it to the right, but nothing happened. I pushed. I pulled.

Nothing happened

"It's a special fitting!" said Dgjerm. "Special order from Chrono Supply!" I could barely hear him. He was definitely getting smaller, or farther away, or both.

"Let me try it!" said Studs, his panic showing his genuine affection for the swiftly disappearing old man. He turned the fitting to the left; he turned it to the right. He pushed, he pulled; he tugged, he twisted.

Nothing happened.

"Can I try?" asked a familiar voice.

"She can't come in here!" shouted Studs.

It was Candy, and Studs was right: NO GIRLS was our other bylaw. It was the bedrock of our policy. Nevertheless, ignoring his protests, I helped her off the ladder and through the door. Studs and I both gasped as she stood up, brushing off her knees. I had seen Candy out of uniform, but this was different. Very different.

She was wearing her special Honeymoon lingerie from Sweet Nothings.

Nevertheless, she was all business. "It's like a childproof cap," she said. She bent down (beautifully!), and with one quick mysterious wrist motion, disconnected the hose from the fitting. It began to flop like a snake and boom like thunder, and Candy screamed and dropped it. Meanwhile, Dr. Dgjerm was hauling the hose in and coiling it on the sofa, which was beginning to spin, slowly at first, then more and more slowly.

I heard more booming, and felt a tremendous wind sweep through the treehouse.

I heard the sound of magazine pages fluttering and wood splintering.

I felt the floor tilt and I reached out for Candy as Studs yelled, "I told you so! I told you so!"

The next thing I knew, I was lying on a pile of boards under the maple tree, with Candy in my arms. Her Sweet Nothings Honeymoon lingerie was short on elbow and knee protection, and she was skinned in several places. I wrapped her in my mother's old rag rug, and together we helped Studs to his feet.

"I told you so," he said.

"Told who what?"

Instead of answering, he swung at me. Luckily, he missed. Studs has never been much of a fighter. "The bylaws. No Girls Allowed. Now look!" Studs kicked the magazines scattered around under the tree.

"It wasn't Candy!" I said. "It was your precious professor and his Leisure Universe!"

Studs swung at me again. It was easy enough to duck. A few lights had come on in the neighboring houses, but they were already going off again. The backyard was littered with boards and magazines, ball gloves, pinups, water guns, and pocketknives. It was like the debris of childhood—it *was* the debris of childhood—all collected in one sad pile.

Studs was crying, blubbering, really, as he picked through the debris, looking (I suspected) for a little sofa, a miniature potted palm, or perhaps a tiny man knocked unconscious by a fall from a collapsing Universe.

Candy and I watched for a while, then decided to help. There was no sign of Dr. Radio Dgjerm. We couldn't even find the hose. "That's a good sign," I pointed out. "The last thing I saw, he was coiling it up on the sofa."

"So?" Studs took another swing at me, and Candy and I decided it was time to leave. We were ducking down to squeeze through the loose plank in the Patellis' fence, when I heard the phone ringing behind me. It was muffled under the boards and plywood. I was about to turn back and answer it, but Candy caught my arm—and my eye.

It was still our Honeymoon, after all, even though I had a headache from the fall. So, I found out later, did Candy.

Part Eight

I thought that was the end of the Ditmas Playboys, but the next day at La Guardia, Studs was waiting for us at the top of the escalator to Gates 1–17. He had either cleaned or changed his uniform since the disaster of the night before, and his medals gleamed, though I noticed he had taken off the Nobel Prize.

At first I thought he was going to take a swing at me, but instead he took my hand.

"Your friend Wu called last night," he said. "Right after you and what's-her-name left."

"Candy," I said. "My fiancée." She and Aunt Minnie were standing right beside me, but Studs wouldn't look at them. Studs had always had a hard time with girls and grown-ups—which is why I was surprised that he had become so attached to Dr. Dgjerm. Perhaps it was because the brilliant but erratic Lifthatvanian realtor was, or seemed, so small, or far away, or both.

"Whatever," said Studs. "Anyway, your friend told me that, as far as he could tell, the Leisure Universe was cast loose and set off safely. That Dr. Dgjerm survived."

"Congratulations," I said. "Now if you'll excuse me, we have a plane to catch."

"What a nice boy that Arthur is," said Aunt Minnie as we boarded the plane. I felt no need to respond, since she was talking to Uncle Mort and not to me. "And you should see all those medals."

The departure was late. I found that oddly reassuring. Candy sat in the middle, her eyes tightly closed, and I let Aunt Minnie have the window seat. It was her first flight. She pressed the urn with Uncle Mort's ashes to the window for the takeoff.

"It's his first flight," she said. "I read in *Reader's Digest* that you're less nervous when you can see what's going on."

"I don't believe it," muttered Candy, her eyes closed tightly. "And how can ashes be nervous anyway?"

The planes may be old on PreOwned Air, but the interiors have been re-refurbished several times. They even have the little credit card phones on the backs of the seats. There was nobody I wanted to talk to for fifteen dollars a minute, but I wasn't surprised when my phone rang.

"It's me. Did the plane leave late?"

"Eighteen minutes," I said, checking my notes.

"Numbers don't lie!" said Wu. "Things are back to normal. I already knew it, in fact, because my calculations came out perfect this morning. I released the first moth in the rain forest at 9:14 A.M., Eastern Standard Time."

I heard a roar behind him that I assumed was rain.

"Congratulations," I said. "What about Dr. Dgjerm and his Leisure Universe?"

"It looks like the old man made it okay," said Wu. "If his Universe had crashed, my figures wouldn't have come out so good. Of course, we will never know for sure. Now that our Universe and his are separated, there can be no exchange of information between them. Not even light."

"Doesn't sound like a good bet for a resort," I said.

"Dgjerm didn't think it all the way through," said Wu. "This was always his weakness as a realtor. However, he will live forever, or almost forever, and that was important to him also. Your friend Studs cried with relief, or sadness, or both, when I told him last night. He seems very attached to the old man."

"He's not exactly a friend," I said. "More like a childhood acquaintance."

"Whatever," said Wu. "How was your Honeymoon?"

I told him about the headache(s). Wu and I have no secrets. I had to whisper, since I didn't want to upset Candy. She might have been asleep, but there was no way to tell; her eyes had been closed since we had started down the runway.

"Well, you can always try again after the ceremony," Wu commiserated.

"I intend to," I said. "Just make sure you get to Huntsville on time with the ring!"

"It'll be tight, Irv. I'm calling from a trimotor just leaving Quetzalcan City."

"An L1011? A DC-10?" The roar sounded louder than ever.

"A Ford Trimotor," Wu said. "I missed the nonstop, and it's a charter, the only thing I could get. It'll be tight. We can only make 112 mph."

"They stopped making Ford Trimotors in 1929. How can they have cell phones?"

"I'm in the cockpit, on the radio. The pilot, Huan Juan, and I went to flight school together in Mukden."

Why was I not surprised? I leaned over to look out the window, and saw the familiar runways of Squirrel Ridge, the airport, far below.

"We're getting ready to land," I said. "I'll see you at the wedding!"

I hung up the phone. Aunt Minnie held the urn up to the window. Candy shut her eyes even tighter.

Part Nine

Divorces are all alike, according to Dostoyevsky, or some Russian, but marriages are each unique, or different, or something. Our wedding was no exception.

It started off great. There's nothing like a morning ceremony. My only regret was that Candy couldn't get the whole day off.

The weather was perfect. The sun shone down from a cloudless sky on the long, level lawn of the Squirrel Ridge Holiness Church. Cindy's catering van arrived at ten, and she and the two kids, Ess and Em, started unloading folding tables and paper plates, plastic toothpicks and cut flowers, and coolers filled with crab cakes and ham biscuits for the open-air lunchtime reception.

All Candy's friends from the Huntsville Parks Department were there, plus the friends we had in common, like Bonnie from the Bonny Baguette (who brought her little blackboard; it was like her brain) and Buzzer from Squirrel Ridge, the nursing home, complete with diamond stud nose ring. My friend Hoppy from the Hoppy's Good Gulf, who happened to be a Holiness preacher, was officiating. ("Course I'll marry Whipper Will's young-un to Whipper Will's Yank, 'nuff said.")

Aunt Minnie looked lovely in her colorful Lifthatvanian peasant costume (red and blue, with pink lace around the sleeves) smelling faintly of mothballs. Even Uncle Mort sported a gay ribbon round his urn.

It was all perfect, except—where was Wu?

"He'll be here," said Cindy as she unpacked the ice sculpture of Robert E. Lee's horse, Traveler (the only thing the local ice sculptor knew how to do), and sent Ess and Em to arrange the flowers near the altar.

"He's on a very slow plane," I said.

Finally, we felt like we had to get started, Best Man or no. It was 11:55 and the guests were beginning to wilt. I gave a reluctant nod and the twin fiddles struck up "The Wedding March"—

And here came the bride. I hadn't seen Candy since the night before. She looked resplendent in her dress white uniform, complete with veil, her medals gleaming in the sun. Her bridesmaids all wore khaki and pink.

Since I was short a ring, Hoppy slipped me the rubber o-ring from the front pump of a Ford C-6 transmission. "Use this, Yank," he whispered. "You can replace it with the real one later."

"Brethren and sistren and such, we are gathered here today . . ." Hoppy began. Then he stopped, and cocked his head toward a distant buzzing sound. "Is that a Ford?"

It was indeed. There is nothing that stops a wedding like a "Tin Goose" setting down on a church lawn. Those fat-winged little airliners can land almost anywhere.

This one taxied up between the ham biscuit and punch tables, and shut down all three engines with a couple of backfires and a loud *cough-cough*. The silence was deafening.

The little cabin door opened, and out stepped a six-foot Chinaman in a powder-blue tux and a scuffed leather helmet.

It was my Best Man, Wilson Wu. He took off the helmet as he jogged up the aisle to polite applause.

"Sorry I'm late!" he whispered, slipping me the ring.

"What's with the blue tux?" I knew it wasn't the one I had reserved for him at Five Points Formal Wear.

"Picked it up last night during a fuel stop in Bozeman," he said. "It was prom night there, and blue was all they had left."

Hoppy was pulling my sleeve, asking me questions. "Of course I do!" I said. "You bet I do!" There was the business with the ring, the real one. ("Is that platinum or just white gold?" Cindy gasped.) Then it was time to kiss the bride.

Then it was time to kiss the bride again.

• • •

As soon as the ceremony was over, the twin fiddles struck up "Brand-new Tennessee Waltz," and we all drifted back to the tables in the shade of the Trimotor for refreshments. We found an unfamiliar Mayan-Chinese-looking dude eyeing the shrimp, and made him welcome. It was Wu's pilot friend, Huan Juan. Ess and Em served the congealed salad, after shrieking and hugging their father whom they hadn't seen in six weeks.

"I should have known better than to worry, Wu," I said. "But did you say Bozeman? I thought that was in Montana."

"It is," he said, filling his plate with potato salad. "It's not on the way from the eastern Quetzalcan to northern Alabama, unless you take the Great Triangle Route."

I knew he wanted me to ask, so I did: "The what?"

Smiling proudly, Wu took a stack of ham biscuits. "You know how a Great Circle Route looks longer on a map, but is in fact the shortest way across the real surface of the spherical Earth?"

"Uh huh." I grabbed some more of the shrimp. They were going fast. The twin fiddles launched into "Orange Blossom Special."

"Well, in all my struggles with the Time axis for EMS, I accidentally discovered the shortest route across the negatively folded surface of local space-time. Local meaning our Universe. Look."

Wu took what I thought was a map out of the pocket of his tux and unrolled it. It was covered with figures:

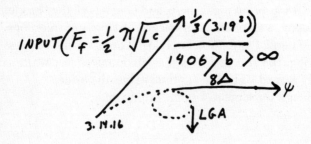

"As you can see, it's sort of counterintuitive," he said. "It means flying certain strict patterns and altitudes, and of course it only works in a three-engine plane. But there it is. The shortest Great Triangle Space-Time Route from Quetzalcan City to Huntsville traverses the high plains and skims the edge of Chesapeake Bay."

"Amazing," I said. The shrimp, which are as big as pistol grips, are grown in freshwater ponds in western Kentucky. I couldn't stop eating them.

"Numbers don't lie," said Wu. "Not counting fuel stops, and with a Ford Trimotor there are lots of those, it took Huan Juan and me only 22 hours to fly 6476.54 miles in a plane with a top speed of 112 mph. Let me try one of those giant shrimp."

"That's great," I said, looking through the thinning crowd for Candy. "But it's almost 12:20, and Candy has to be at work at one."

Wu looked shocked. "No Honeymoon?"

I shook my head. "Candy traded shifts for the trip to New York, and now she has to work nights, plus all weekend."

"It's not very romantic," said Candy, edging up beside me. "But it was the best we could do. Huan Juan, have you tried the giant shrimp?"

The pilot nodded without answering. He and Wu were consulting in whispers. They looked up at the clear blue sky, then down at the calculations on the unrolled paper.

"They are intimately entwined," I heard Wu say (I thought he was talking about Candy and me; I found out later he was talking about Time and Space). "All you have to do to unravel and reverse them is substitute this N for this 34.8, and hold steady at 2622 feet and 97 mph, airspeed. Can you fly it?"

Huan Juan nodded, reaching for another giant shrimp.

"What's going on?" I asked.

"Let's take a ride," said Wu, snapping his leather helmet under his chin. "Don't look so surprised. This Trimotor's equipped with a luxury Pullman cabin; it once belonged to a Latin American dictator."

"Where are we going?" I asked, pulling Candy to my side.

"Nowhere! We are going to fly a Great Triangle configuration, compressed and reversed, over Squirrel Ridge for twenty-three minutes, and you will experience it as, let's see"—he squinted, figuring—"two point six hours of Honeymoon time. Better bring along some giant shrimp and ham biscuits."

Cindy handed Candy a bouquet. Hoppy and Bonnie and all our friends were applauding.

"What about—you know?" I whispered to Candy. I meant the Honeymoon lingerie she had bought at Sweet Nothings.

With a shy smile she pulled me aside. While Em and Ess tied shoes to the tail of the plane, and while Huan Juan and Wu cranked up the three ancient air-cooled radials with a deafening roar, and while the rest of the guests polished off the giant shrimp, Candy opened the top button of her tunic to give me a glimpse of what she was wearing underneath.

Then we got on the plane and soared off into the wild blue. But that's another story altogether.

Smoother

Amazing, isn't it?

I guess. It would be even more amazing, as Oscar Wilde once said, if the water didn't fall.

Oscar Wild? The weiner guy?

A famous funny sayings guy. From long ago. I think he played the piano, too. Anyway, it could happen. Or not happen.

What not happen?

The water not fall.

I get it. You're talking about Smoother. I thought we weren't going to talk about Smoother.

Sorry. It's just that, there it is. Smoothing along. 120 miles a day, day after day.

So what? So what does that have to do with us, you and me, here and now?

Nothing. And everything.

Smoother's not even heading this way.

Not now.

I get it. You're talking about the whole world again. Well, for your information, at the rate it's going, Smoother will take thousands of years to smooth out the entire world.

More like hundreds. Do the math.

Okay, I'll do the math. It's a mile wide, it moves at about five miles per hour . . .

8.4 kilometers per hour, to be exact. And Smoother is 2.173 kilometers wide.

Whatever. Metric Smoother, then. Either way, we're talking

about a long time. The world is huge. Smoother just smooths a little strip.

That little strip, as you call it, gets longer and longer. Every year Smoother smooths an area the size of England. Smoother has already smoothed a strip long enough to stretch around the world five times at the equator.

Most of it worthless land. Most of it ocean floor.

In a few hundred years the whole world will be as smooth and featureless as a pool ball. A giant beige cue ball.

Lighten up! You and me won't even be around in a few hundred years.

Our children will.

We don't have any children. And we never will if we spend our entire Honeymoon worrying about Smoother. It would be more amazing if it didn't smooth, according to your wildman guy. And it could be worse. Smoother takes its time. It's moving at a walk.

A fast walk.

Still. People have plenty of time to get out of the way. Nobody's been killed by Smoother since Malta, and that was sort of a sneak attack.

And those villages in India.

Hey, it wasn't Smoother's fault they didn't watch TV.

They didn't have TV.

Same difference. And then they hung around, getting in the way, wanting to watch.

I know how they felt. Everybody wants to watch.

Not me. I got enough of Smoother when I was in the army.

You told me you only saw it at a distance, once.

Once was enough. I was in a helicopter. They were trying to cut it off with bombs.

What was it like?

Same as on TV. A ribbon of smooth nothing, about a mile wide, unrolling over everything. Flat. Sort of beige. No noise. Kind of a hump in the front, about four stories high—

I don't mean Smoother. I mean, what was it like trying to stop it?

Stupid. Pointless. You saw it on TV. They shot at it, bombed

it, tried to dig under it. Most of the guys killed were killed by
friendly fire. And of course, the nuke. That was super stupid.

*What's stupid is doing nothing. You can't just let Smoother smooth
out the whole Earth without trying to stop it.*

Sure you can. Especially if there's nothing you can do about
it. And no matter what we do, it keeps going at the same speed,
winding its way around the world, smoothing out whatever is in
front of it, leaving behind that mile-wide smooth strip of nothing, like a yellow brick road.

Beige.

Beige, then. Rain evaporates it as soon as it hits it. It won't
burn, it won't break, it won't—

They say you can walk across it.

You can jump up and down on it howling at the Moon, if you
want to, but you can't get rid of it or change a damn thing about
it. Once it's there, it's there. Period. Finis. End of story. Get it?

Now who's the one that's all hot and bothered?

Sorry. It's not Smoother that bothers me, it's all the people
who can't stop obsessing about it.

Like me.

I'm not mentioning any names. Notice how I'm not mentioning any names?

So just forget Smoother. Is that what you're saying?

Exactly.

What if you can't?

It's a discipline. It's all about living in the Now. Which is our
Honeymoon, in case you've forgotten. Why don't you come
over here.

*Not in the mood. Let's see what's on TV. Damn! I should have
known.*

Smoother looks kind of peaceful on the small screen, doesn't
it? Spiritual, almost.

It's disgusting.

It's smoothing a bunch of desert. Now tell me, is that so terrible?

That's Africa. Last month it barely missed Kilimanjaro.

See! A miss is as good as a mile!

But it will get it eventually. That's the thing. It will smooth every-thing. No matter what it hits or misses, Smoother will keep going, around and around the world, until every square inch is smooth.

Girl, you have got it bad! Why dwell on doom and gloom? You'll be gone long before it happens. In the meantime, why not sell the roses?

Smell the roses.

Whatever. Look at those elephants run! Smoother can be cool if you let yourself get into it. Remember when it went through China and took out a twenty-mile section of the Great Wall?

That was horrible.

But spiritual too! Nothing lasts forever. Not even the Great Wall of China. Not even the Taj Mahal, though part of it's still there.

Most of it's gone.

Is the glass half full or half empty? I say it's half full!

What'll you say when the glass is gone?

Listen to you! Sometimes I think if there wasn't a Smoother, people would invent one. Just to have something to worry about.

Like me.

I didn't mention any names. See how I'm not mentioning any names?

Just because I'm concerned. Aren't you ever concerned?

There's a difference between being concerned and being obsessed. When I see Smoother heading my way, I will worry. Until that happens, I want to enjoy my—our—honeymoon. What's left of it.

I get it. Your feelings are hurt. You think I care more about Smoother than about you.

Well, don't you?

Of course not. It's just that—I hate Smoother so much!

There's that word I hate: hate! But seriously, life's too short to waste on hating. Just accept Smoother for what it is.

Which is—what?

Maybe there are some mysteries we are not supposed to unravel. Think how boring life would be if Nature had no secrets! *Nature won't, when Smoother gets through. Don't you ever wonder where it came from? What it's doing here?* Maybe it was here all along and we never noticed it. Maybe it dropped in from another galaxy. Maybe some crazy guy made it in his garage. Maybe it escaped from a bottle in a lab. Who knows? And it's pretty obvious what it's doing here.

But why?

Want to know my theory? I think Smoother is here to remind us that life is about Change.

Smoother is about the end of Change. When it's finished the Earth will be a smooth ball floating through space. No water, no wind, no people, no life at all.

That's Change, isn't it? Stop trying to control everything all the time. Think different. Live in the Now. Hell, it's kind of pretty, smoothing along across the veldt anyway. It is *veldt* isn't it? Do you say the 'd'? Or is it the *savannah?*

Both. Either. Neither. I don't know. Never mind. Sooner or later it'll all just be a big smooth yellow nothing anyway.

Beige. You said yourself it was beige. Hey! Why'd you turn the TV off?

I thought you were sick of Smoother.

I am, but I'd rather watch it than talk about it. But hey, this is our Honeymoon, and the water's still falling, as your wildman guy would say. Why don't you come over here with me.

Because I'm not in the mood. Plus I have a headache.

On our Honeymoon? Try one of these.

Tylenol?

Better. It doesn't stop the pain, it goes straight to the brain and blocks the *consciousness* of pain.

So you don't feel it?

You feel it, but you don't feel it as *pain*. Might even work on your mood.

Sounds good. I'll give it a shot. What's it called?

Incident at Oak Ridge

Part One

EXT—A MOUNTAIN TRAIL IN AN APPALACHIAN HOLLOW. EVENING.

Two young men are hiking. FRED is dark, tall, about thirty. KIM is Asian, lightly bearded, same age. Both have short hair. They are junior college profs—Fred in physics, Kim in English.

It is fall, and still warm. They carry light day packs. Both wear Polartec sweats, light Gore-Tex jackets, Nike boots—modern gear.

It is getting dark. They are in a hurry. Kim is peeling off his jacket. Fred is punching numbers into a cellular phone.

> FRED: Ann's gonna kill me. I promised her we would be back in Knoxville by five. Wish I could get this phone to work!
> KIM: How did it get so warm? Wish I had a cigarette.
> FRED: I know we're not out of range. I checked my messages right after we had lunch. (Looks up) A cigarette? *Kim!!!*
> KIM: What would you say if I told you there was a pack of Marlboros in the glove compartment of my Cherokee?
> FRED: What would you say if I told you I found them this morning while you were paying for the gas and threw them out?

EXT. THE MOUNTAINS. A LOW TANGLE OF
GORGES, A FEATURELESS MAZE.

Voices continue as before.

KIM: (o.s.) I would say you were a coldhearted bastard.
FRED: (o.s.) And I would say friends don't let friends smoke.
You quit, remember?
KIM: (o.s.) Yeah, yeah. Damn! Every one of these hollows
looks exactly the same. Are we still on the right trail?
FRED: (o.s.) Got me. What happened to the blazes?

EXT. ON THE TRAIL, AS BEFORE.

Kim is studying his Casio wristwatch; Fred, his cellular phone.

KIM: Maybe the storm washed them away. Like the display
on my watch. I'm getting a blank!
FRED: Maybe that lightning zapped our eproms. I'm not
even getting a dial tone.

The SOUND of an ENGINE, more like a truck in low gear
than a car.

A FLASH of headlights up the hillside, through the trees.

KIM: Fred, look! A car!

EXT. A STEEP DIRT ROAD

Two soldiers in World War II uniforms, in an open jeep. The
SERGEANT holds an M-1 carbine between his knees; he has a
Southern hillbilly accent. The CORPORAL (from Brooklyn) is
driving.

SERGEANT: I thought you said you knew this road, Corporal.

CORPORAL: I do, Sarge. We're still inside Perimeter Two. I must have missed the first turn in that storm.

SERGEANT: That was the most hellacious lightning I've ever seen. Hey! Stop.

The sergeant stands up in the front seat of the jeep, M-1 carbine at the ready.

WIDER VIEW.

Kim and Fred run out of the woods onto the road, waving.

SERGEANT: Halt or I'll shoot!

KIM: Relax, man. Are you guys—?

SERGEANT: Halt! You are in a restricted area. Turn around and put your hands on the back of your head.

FRED: (offended) You fellows are *way* out of line here! This is a public recreational—

The sergeant FIRES the carbine over their heads.

Everybody and everything stops. All that can be heard is the idling of the jeep.

SERGEANT: Shut up! Turn around. NOW! Down on your knees!

Fred and Kim get down on their knees.

SERGEANT: Hands on the back of your head!

Fred and Kim put their hands on the backs of their heads.

KIM: (whisper) What is this, fucking *Deliverance*?

FRED: This is no joke. These guys are nuts. Some kind of militia creeps.

SERGEANT: Shut up! Corporal, get their weapons. The Jap first.

The corporal pulls on the emergency brake with a LOUD RATCHETING SOUND. Gets out of the jeep.

> KIM: Jap? I'm not Japanese.
> FRED: And we're not hunters, we're hikers. We're not carrying any weapons! We're from Knoxville. We both teach at Cumberland Community College.
> SERGEANT: Shut up, both of you!

The corporal frisks them both. Finds Fred's cell phone.

> CORPORAL: Sarge, look at this! Some kind of radio.
> FRED: It's a cellular phone.
> SERGEANT: You ain't selling me nothing. Now shut up!
> KIM: (under his breath) You ignorant fucking hillbilly!

The corporal drags the two packs over and puts them in the jeep. Hands the phone to the sergeant.

> CORPORAL: Lots of nylon and plastic stuff. The shoes look sorta German.
> KIM: German? Are you guys playing army or something?!
> FRED: Our billfolds are in the car. We're hikers with a perfect right to . . .
> SERGEANT: Shut up! Put them in the jeep.

                                                    CUT TO:

EXT.   GUARD POST. ENTRANCE TO MILITARY COMPOUND.

The jeep pulls up. Fred and Kim are sitting in the back with their hands on their heads. The sergeant holds the M-1 on them. An MP looks at the two captives admiringly.

> MP: Wow. Where'd you find these two?
> SERGEANT: Inside P Two, outside P One. Careful, they speak English. The Jap too.

FRED: Of course we speak English!

KIM: What's this Jap shit? I'm Korean, and I'm as fucking American as—

SERGEANT: (jostles him roughly) Shut up! Where should I take them?

GUARD: That new schoolhouse in D is empty. I'll call Security. Or should I call Intelligence?

SERGEANT: Better call both. Do you have any handcuffs?

GUARD: Just one pair.

EXT. JEEP ON A MUDDY STREET.

Lights of a suburb under construction. Lumber, equipment all around, a few military guards.

Fred and Kim in the back of the jeep are now handcuffed together, Fred's right hand to Kim's left.

KIM: This is crazy. Do you have any idea where we are?

FRED: Afraid so. Look around.

KIM: Oak Ridge? But Oak Ridge was shut down, wasn't it?

FRED: So they tell us.

KIM: What do you mean?

FRED: I don't know what I mean, Kim. But I do know this is no backwoods redneck militia.

SERGEANT: Shut up!

CUT TO:

INT. SCHOOLROOM.

Desks for little kids, big oak teacher's desk, blackboard. A globe. Calendar on wall says October 1944.

Fred and Kim, handcuffed together, are hustled in the door by the sergeant.

KIM: This is outrageous. I demand to speak with your commanding officer.
SERGEANT: Shut up!

The door is SLAMMED. Kim starts pacing. Fred has no choice but to follow awkwardly. Neither notices the calendar.

KIM: Commanding officer? You believe these guys are really the army? They're playacting. They don't even look right.
FRED: I don't know what to believe. Maybe it's some kind of maneuvers.

Kim idly spins globe as he passes. Stops, jerking Fred to a sudden halt.

KIM: Hey! There's only one Korea! And look at Russia. Weird.
FRED: What's so weird about an out-of-date globe in a Tennessee schoolroom?
KIM: Except this globe is new. (Looks around) So are these old-fashioned chairs, this black blackboard—
FRED: Oh shit. Kim. (Points to calendar) Look.

They walk together, in step at last, to the front of the room and look at the calendar. Fred flips through it.

FRED: (shaking head) This is not possible.
KIM: Neither is Oak Ridge. But you saw it and so did I.

Dragging Fred, Kim crosses to door and knocks on it.

KIM: Hey! Sergeant!
SERGEANT: Shut up!
KIM: Just tell me the date.
SERGEANT: Wednesday. October 11.
FRED: He means—the year.
SERGEANT: 1944. I don't know what you call it in Germany.

Fred and Kim stare at each other. There is a long silence as they sit down, side by side, in the little desks.

KIM: It's not fucking possible.
FRED: You're right. Except that it's happening. It's like quantum physics.
KIM: What do you mean?
FRED: It doesn't make any sense but it explains everything else. The GIs, the M-1s . . .
KIM: The jeep. My God . . . The Jap!
FRED: (nodding) Oak Ridge. The hiking trails run through the old perimeter of the plant, when it was top secret.
KIM: The Manhattan Project. Jesus! They're making the atomic bomb, and they think we're spies! They think I'm Japanese!

Fred and Kim look at each other in silent terror. Then Kim gets up and knocks on door again.

KIM: Hey! Sergeant!
SERGEANT: I told you, shut up!
KIM: All I want is a cigarette.
FRED: What are you doing? You quit, remember?
KIM: If I'm going to be shot as a spy, I'm going to have a last cigarette. (To door) Come on, Sarge, have a heart. If it's 1944, I'll tell you who wins the World Series.

A cigarette slides under the door, followed by a book of matches.

KIM: Thanks! The Cardinals.
SOLDIER: Big deal. Everybody knows the Cards are going to win. Even a damn Jap. Now shut up!

Kim LIGHTS UP while Fred glares at him; since they are hand-cuffed together it looks almost like Fred is helping.

FADE

Part Two

Int. The School Room, Twenty Minutes Later.

Fred and Kim are sitting at two tiny desks, side by side. The DOOR OPENS and the sergeant comes in, followed by the CAPTAIN who wears a Colt .45.

> CAPTAIN: *Sprechen sie Deutsche?*
> FRED: We don't speak German. We're from Knoxville.
> CAPTAIN: *Kitano ay tora boru.*
> KIM: *Auf Wiedersehen*, you fucking hillbilly idiots.

The captain SMACKS Kim across the face. In a SUDDEN EXPLOSION OF VIOLENCE, Fred, stands up to defend Kim and the sergeant pushes him back down in his seat. It's over almost as soon as it begins.

> SERGEANT: Sit down and shut up!
> FRED: Colonel, this is all a mistake.
> CAPTAIN: It's captain, and there's no mistake. You were caught redhanded in a class one restricted area. You could be shot for looking at that perimeter, much less crossing it.
> KIM: We didn't cross any fucking perimeter! And I'm not—

The sergeant smacks him in the back of the head.

> SERGEANT: Shut up, you murdering yellow bastard.
> CAPTAIN: I have your radio.
> FRED: (nervously; has a plan) I understand what you're thinking, Captain. But you're wrong. We know what's going on here. We're—part of the project.
> CAPTAIN: You're what?

The captain looks sideways at the sergeant, who remains silent.

KIM: We didn't cross any fucking perimeter. I know it's hard to believe, but we're from your future. We were just—

Fred stops Kim with a kick.

FRED: We're physicists, Captain. *From Manhattan,* if you know what I mean. We need to speak with Dr. Richard Feynman as soon as possible. It's a security matter.
CAPTAIN: Dr. who?

Kim looks at Fred, puzzled. Fred plunges on.

FRED: Dr. Richard Feynman, Los Alamos.

The captain is getting agitated. The sergeant, like Kim, is looking very confused.

CAPTAIN: Sergeant, wait outside the door.

The sergeant EXITS and closes the door behind him. The captain draws his .45 and cocks it menacingly.

CAPTAIN: Now say that again.
FRED: (gaining confidence) We are physicists, on a special assignment with the Manhattan Project. Classified. You are to contact Dr. Richard Feynman at Los Alamos. Theoretical Computation Group.
CAPTAIN: (thinking it over) Physicists. And him?
FRED: Him too. He's Korean, not Japanese.
KIM: (confused but eager to help) An enemy of the Japanese. Besides, you had Japanese in your own army. Not all—

Fred kicks him again. Kim shuts up. The captain looks from one to the other, suspicious.

CAPTAIN: So what were you doing in the woods?
FRED: (cool, haughty; getting into it) Sorry, Captain. That's

all I can say until we report to Dr. Feynman personally. I'm sure you can appreciate the importance of secrecy.

Kim is silent, watching all this in amazement.

CAPTAIN: (skeptical) I'll make a call.
FRED: Please. (Holds up cuffed right hand) And unlock these.
CAPTAIN: (as he exits) Not a chance. Sergeant, hold your position until you receive further orders from me personally.
KIM: Captain? One other thing.
CAPTAIN: Yes?
KIM: How about some cigarettes. While we're waiting for Dick.

The captain tosses Kim his half-empty pack of Luckies, then slams the door emphatically.

KIM: (lighting up) Feynman?
FRED: The physicist. Nobel Prize, 1966. Quantum thermo-dynamics. He worked on the Manhattan Project as a young man. He and Oppenheimer . . .
KIM: I know who Richard Feynman is, Fred! You're the one who sent me that book, *Surely You're Joking, Mr. Feynman*, a couple of years ago. All I remember is he was from Brooklyn and he played the bongo drums. And was a smart-ass. But what does he have to do with us?
FRED: He was from Queens, actually. And what he has to do with us is that he's going to save our lives. Maybe.

Kim is listening. Fred is so caught up in his own plan that he doesn't notice Kim is smoking.

FRED: (continuing) Richard Feynman is the one man alive in 1944 who might actually *believe* our story and be able to help us. He was an original thinker, with an open mind. A true genius. Luckily I have been reading his biography.

KIM: The captain sure as hell sat up for that "theoretical computational" stuff!

FRED: He was reacting to Los Alamos. Most of the soldiers here don't even know Los Alamos exists. Any more than they know what Oak Ridge is for.

Fred notices Kim's cigarette for the first time. Reaches for it.

FRED: (continuing) I can't believe you are smoking! You can't smoke in here! It's a classroom.

KIM: (snatching it back) Quit being such a stick, Fred! We're stuck in the past before we were even born and you're worried about a cigarette. Besides, what good's Feynman going to do us if he's in New Mexico?

FRED: He was at Oak Ridge a lot. Maybe we'll get lucky. Or maybe they'll fly him here in a DC3. That is, if they believe me enough to call him. And if he's curious enough to want to find out what's going on.

KIM: And if he isn't curious? Or they don't bother to call him? Or we don't get lucky?

Fred solemnly puts his finger to the side of his head.

FRED: This is Oak Ridge, World War II. It doesn't even officially *exist*. There wouldn't be a trial or anything.

Kim winces. He checks his watch on his right (uncuffed) wrist.

KIM: I wonder if we get a last supper—Hey, my watch is working! I got the display back.

FRED: What time is it?

KIM: 7:22. I wonder if that's our time. The date thing says November 17, 1998.

FRED: That's it! The watch! It proves we're from the future!

Fred reaches for the watch. Kim pulls it away.

KIM: It doesn't prove anything. You can program a watch to say any date.

FRED: Not in 1944 you can't! Not with an LCD display. Don't you get it? The watch is proof we're from the future, if we can get Feynman, or any scientist, or anybody with normal intelligence to look at it.

KIM: You don't think much of these army guys, do you?

FRED: Hell no. They're itching to shoot us.

The DOOR OPENS. Kim and Fred look up and fall silent, frightened.

The captain enters with RICHARD FEYNMAN, a thirty-something young man in 1940s slacks and sport shirt, wearing a windbreaker with an ID tag. He is the same age as Fred and Kim—a hip contrast to the captain.

Fred stands, pulling Kim awkwardly to his feet.

FRED: Dr. Feynman!

CAPTAIN: You know these men?

FEYNMAN: (with a mischievous grin) Could be, Captain. Let's hear what they've got to say.

Impulsively, Kim hands his watch to Feynman.

FEYNMAN: (joking; a comic Yiddish accent) They're salesmen? How much you want for this?

KIM: Push the little button on the side.

Alarmed, the captain grabs for the watch. Feynman pulls it away and checks the display, intrigued.

CAPTAIN: It could be a weapon!

FRED: It's a quartz digital watch. LCD display.

KIM: It's from the future!

FEYNMAN: (amused; holds watch to his ear) Time travelers from the future! So I guess you can tell me who wins the World Series.

KIM: (points to calendar) 1944? The Cardinals.

FEYNMAN: (slips the watch into his pocket) A safe guess, right, Captain?

The captain is not amused.

FRED: We can also tell you who wins the war. And about Bethe, and Oppenheimer—and Arline.

FEYNMAN: (suddenly serious) Captain, perhaps I should have a word or two with these gentlemen.

The captain takes his .45 out of his holster and hands it to Feynman.

CAPTAIN: I'll be right outside the door.

He leaves, shutting the door behind him. Feynman sits on the teacher's desk facing Fred and Kim. He holds the big .45 carelessly on his lap. He is relaxed.

FEYNMAN: Time travelers, huh? Does that make me a ghost from the past? Or you, ghosts from the future?

FRED: It's no joke. I know it's hard to believe.

FEYNMAN: Try me.

KIM: In the first place, I'm Korean, not Japanese. Not that it . . .

FRED: (interrupting Kim) We are from the future, Dr. Feynman. Your future, that is. From 1998, to be exact. November 17, 1998.

Fred and Kim both look at Feynman, waiting for a response. Feynman only looks politely interested.

FRED: (continuing) We were hiking. In 1998 this whole area is hiking trails, a wilderness preserve.

FEYNMAN: I love it—the world is going backward!

KIM: There was some kind of electrical storm. It never did rain but there was this weird lightning—

FEYNMAN: (leans forward, curious at last) Lightning.

FRED: Very close. Sounded like the world was being ripped apart. As soon as it stopped we started looking for Kim's car.

KIM: Jeep Cherokee. Direct descendant of the WWII military jeep.

Fred shoots Kim a look that says "stick to the point."

FRED: And that's when we got picked up by Oak Ridge security. We are at Oak Ridge, right?

After a slight hesitation, Feynman nods. He takes Kim's watch out of his pocket.

FRED: (continuing) We had somehow been shifted back fifty years, to 1944.

FEYNMAN: (studying the watch) Fifty-four years, one month, and six days, exactly. Plus an hour and a half.

KIM: They think we are spies.

FEYNMAN: You have to admit you look suspicious. A Jap and a Jew.

KIM: I told you, I'm Korean.

FEYNMAN: (shrugs) This is the army. They don't know from Korean.

FRED: How'd you know I was Jewish?

FEYNMAN: (Catskill schtick) Ya know, ya know? Ya look Jewish.

Fred is puzzled. He can't tell if Feynman believes their story or not. The funnyman/scientist hears it all with an ironic smile. Fred decides to push on.

FRED: We figured you were our only chance. We had to find someone who would believe us.

FEYNMAN: But why me?

FRED: You are famous. That is, you will be. You win a Nobel Prize for your work in quantum thermodynamics in 1966.

FEYNMAN: So I'm the ghost. I'm dead, I suppose.

FRED: Well, of course. Sort of. In our time. But . . .

FEYNMAN: The Nobel Prize! I have to wait twenty years— but that's not so bad. And when do I die?

FRED: I—I don't think I'm supposed to tell you that.

FEYNMAN: (Catskill schtick again) So, now we have rules for time travel?

FRED: You don't believe me, do you? (angrily) Then how do I know your wife's name, Arline? Or that you call her Putsy? Or she dies next year from TB—

A sudden silence. Kim winces. Feynman looks serious but unperturbed.

FRED: I'm sorry. I didn't . . .

FEYNMAN: It's okay. We're prepared for Arline's death. (changing the mood) Tell me, do the Dodgers ever win the Series?

KIM: Hell, yes. 1955. With a black player, too. Jackie Robinson.

FRED: And the Allies win the war.

FEYNMAN: What do we win it with—that's the question.

KIM: The atomic bomb. Hiroshima.

FEYNMAN: (surprised) They drop on Japan? (winces) On a *city*?

FRED: Two cities. Nagasaki and Hiroshima. You *do* believe us, then!

FEYNMAN: Why not? It's like quantum physics. It doesn't make any sense but it explains a lot. It explains you guys, for one thing. Your artifacts. (Holds up the watch) The funny shoes.

FRED: (checks his Gore-Tex boots) Funny shoes?

KIM: Hooray! So we're not going to get shot!

FEYNMAN: Shhh! Not by the army anyway. Not if I can help it.

CAPTAIN: (knocking on door) What's going on in there?

FEYNMAN: It's all right, Captain. (To Fred and Kim) You guys must be starving. Let's order out . . .

FADE OUT

Part Three

Int.   Schoolroom. Half Hour Later.

They are finishing their dinners, GI rations. Fred and Kim are still handcuffed together.

FEYNMAN: They call it NASA, huh? But I must be pretty old. Do I get to go into space?

FRED: I probably shouldn't get specific.

FEYNMAN: I understand. This is like talking to God. (Bangs on his catsup) Tell me, God, do they ever solve this problem?

KIM: Surely you are joking, Mr. Feynman.

FEYNMAN: Huh? Oh, I get it, that's the book you were telling me about. Is that how you knew I was at Oak Ridge? It's supposed to be a secret, you know.

FRED: I got that from another book, your biography. *Genius*, by James Gleick.

FEYNMAN: Great title! It so happens that I arrived here yesterday to investigate what Oak Ridge calls a thermodynamic incident, and Oppy and I call a loop-singularity.

KIM: Oppenheimer? A meltdown?

FEYNMAN: (shaking his head) Potentially far more serious

than that. It appears the forces that bind the nucleus of the atom also bind the past and future.

FRED: You mean—?

FEYNMAN: (nods) You might say I've been expecting you. Or something like you. The "lightning" you saw was the opening of the loop-singularity, which your presence here in the present, or if you insist, the past, serves to stabilize. Temporarily.

KIM: Conservation of energy?

FEYNMAN: More or less. But you're the English professor, right? Let's just call it a dependent parenthetical clause.

Feynman pulls a pack of Luckies from his jacket and lights two cigarettes. Hands one to Kim.

FRED: Those things will kill you.

FEYNMAN: (with a devil-may-care grin) Yeah, but according to you guys I'm already dead.

KIM: And I'm not even born! So lighten up, Fred!

FRED: (not amused) So what now? How do we get back to our own time? Or—do we?

KIM: (taking a long drag) I like it here. Can you smoke in the movies? Can I bring my girlfriend? Better not, though. She actually is Japanese—

FEYNMAN: Oppy and I have a plan to close the loop. Can't leave it open, you know.

KIM: Another lightning flash?

FEYNMAN: Exactly. (Looks at Kim's watch) I was going to order us coffee, but it's getting late.

Feynman knocks on the door. The captain opens it.

FEYNMAN: Bring the jeep around, Captain, if you will. I'm taking these two with me, through the range.

FRED: (holds up cuffs) What about these?

FEYNMAN: (conspiratorially) Leave them on or people will talk. You are still prisoners, remember.

Feynman follows them out of the classroom. Before leaving he pauses and expertly removes the clip from the .45. Puts the clip in his pocket and jams the pistol into his belt.

CUT TO:

EXT. THE JEEP. NIGHT.

The captain is driving under streetlights. Feynman in the front seat. Fred and Kim handcuffed together in the back.

The jeep pulls up at the guard post and the captain hands the MP a folded paper. The MP unfolds it and reads it, refolds it and hands it back. Salutes.

The captain salutes him back, then looks at Feynman. Gets a nod and steps out of the jeep. Fred watches all this intently.

Feynman slides into the driver's seat. Grinds the gears. Starts off, killing the jeep. Restarts it. They buck off into the darkness, leaving the guard post and the lights behind.

FRED: What was that all about?
FEYNMAN: The Privilege of Science—Mystery. (grinding gears) 'Scuse my driving. Kid from Queens, you know.
KIM: Wish you could see my Jeep. It's a direct descendant of this one but it has AC, automatic, CD player.
FEYNMAN: What's a CD player? Is that like the LCD display?
FRED: You're going to kill us, aren't you?

Kim is startled by this. Feynman is not; he is concentrating on driving as they lurch into the darkness.

FRED: You're going to shoot us. That's your so-called plan, isn't it?

KIM: (angrily, to Fred) What the hell are you talking about, Fred? He's saving our lives!
FRED: (bitterly) Oh yeah? Tell him, *Doctor* Feynman. Tell him your plan.

The jeep bounces on a dirt road, into the trees. Darker and darker.

FEYNMAN: (noisily grinding gears) There's nothing to tell. I'm sending you back to your own time. Your own lives. *That's* the plan.
FRED: And that's your time machine, right? The captain's .45.
KIM: You guys are joking, right? (Holds up cuffs) Unlock these things!
FEYNMAN: Can't do it. That letter is from Oppy. We looked for a more elegant solution but there's no time, no pun intended. We can't experiment here. This loop-singularity is interesting, maybe even more interesting than the project itself. But it threatens the entire war effort.
FRED: You *win* the war. *We* win the war!
FEYNMAN: So you tell me. But maybe that's because we close the loop. Who knows? Unfortunately, I'm not authorized to find out.

Feynman stops the jeep. Pulls on the emergency brake with a LOUD RATCHETING SOUND. Leaves headlamps on.

Takes a clipboard off the dash and gets out of the jeep.

FEYNMAN: We get out here. It's all set up. Come on, guys. Don't make this hard.

Fred and Kim look at each other grimly and refuse to move. They sit tight in the back of the jeep, backlighted from the headlamps.

Feynman draws the .45 from his belt.

FEYNMAN: Come on, you won't feel a thing. I promise.

KIM: (angrily) You can't even fucking drive, and you want us to believe you know how to use a gun!

FEYNMAN: Look, if we don't send you back the loop will stay open. It might even expand. Plus, you have your entire life to live in your own time. What are you going to do here? Join the army?

KIM: (wants to believe it) You sure it won't hurt?

FEYNMAN: I don't think so. This is a .45.

KIM: I know what the hell it is! (still wants to believe) And we'll be back in our own time?

FEYNMAN: And this will never have happened. Think of it as a preview of life, before your life begins. I don't see how you could even remember it.

FRED: But then it *will* happen! We'll go on the hike and it will all happen again. Just like it's happening now.

FEYNMAN: Aha! The physics professor. Very perceptive— Fred, isn't it? That's the other part of the plan. Come up here, in the light.

Fred and Kim climb awkwardly and reluctantly out of the back of the jeep. They follow Feynman to the front of the jeep. Feynman hands Fred the clipboard.

FEYNMAN: Write yourself a letter telling yourself NOT to go on the hike. I'll mail it right before I die. When is it— approximately?

FRED: (bitterly) Ten years ago. 1988. August. Cancer. A long, excruciating, painful death.

FEYNMAN: I don't blame you for being pissed off, Fred. But we all die, okay? How many of us get to live twice?

KIM: And die twice.

FEYNMAN: Well, that too. But you can't have one without the other. Come on!

Feynman hands Fred a pencil. Fred studies it in the dim light. It is printed with a slogan: "RICHARD DARLING, I LOVE YOU! PUTSY."

Fred looks at Feynman and relents. He tries to write but his right hand is cuffed to Kim.

FRED: I'm right-handed.
FEYNMAN: (to Kim) You write it, then.
KIM: I'm left-handed.
FEYNMAN: Bullshit. Come on, guys, don't make this any harder than it is!

Fred holds the clipboard while Kim writes. Feynman lights a cigarette.

FEYNMAN: Don't get too specific. That might be dangerous.
KIM: How about, "Do not go hiking near Oak Ridge, November 17, 1998."
FEYNMAN: Don't mention Oak Ridge.
KIM: How about, "Do not leave Knoxville."
FEYNMAN: That should do it.

Feynman takes the clipboard. Kim's hands are shaking. Fred is cool, studying Feynman.

FRED: You didn't send it, did you? You don't send it, do you?
FEYNMAN: Why don't you guys turn around? It's better for everybody if you turn around.
FRED: If you had sent it, all this would never happen. We wouldn't be here.
FEYNMAN: It's not that simple. Maybe time reverberates. Maybe there's a delay factor. Maybe—
FRED: Maybe you wanted to see what would happen.
FEYNMAN: (irritated) I don't deny that it's possible. How should I know what went wrong? You're the guys from the

future, not me. But we can and will fix it. Now turn around, dammit.

KIM: Don' I get a last cigarette?

FEYNMAN: We don't have time. Here, you can have the last drag of mine.

With a sudden athletic move, Kim grabs the gun and wrenches it from Feynman's grasp. Now he holds the .45 on Feynman while Fred, handcuffed to Kim, watches with mingled relief, horror, fascination—and fear.

KIM: Surely you are joking, Mr. Feynman?

FEYNMAN: Come on, guys, this can never work. You *have* to go back, even if it's just to stop the trip. Otherwise, what're you gonna do, stay here and meet yourselves, over and over?

KIM: Beats a .45 slug in the back of the head. (Puts the gun in Feynman's face) Unlock these cuffs or I blow your fucking head off.

FEYNMAN: (opens hands, Christlike) Go ahead. Pull the trigger. Blow away the Manhattan Project, the war effort, the entire future.

Fred puts his free hand on Kim's gun arm.

FRED: He's right, Kim. There must be a better way.

KIM: Better than what? No way I . . .

A SHOT. Kim falls dead—dragging Fred to his knees.

Fred looks up. He is startled to see HIMSELF, in an army uniform, holding an M-1 carbine. FRED2 has just shot Kim in the back of the head.

FEYNMAN: I was beginning to wonder.

FRED2: You always wonder.

Fred2 bends down and pries the .45 from Kim's fingers and hands it to Feynman. Feynman takes the clip from his pocket and clicks it into the .45.

FRED: It—wasn't loaded?
FEYNMAN: No way. Time is elastic. You can't change the past or the future but you better be damn careful with the present. (Chambers a round and clicks off the safety) Now turn around, Fred. Seriously. Please.
FRED: Fuck you. (Looks from Feynman to Fred2) Fuck you both! If you're going to shoot me, do it like a man. Face-to-face.

Fred2 watches impassively, still holding the M-1. Fred tries to back away, dragging Kim's body.

FEYNMAN: I hate this part. I really do.

Feynman aims the .45 at Fred and closes his eyes, just as—

CLANG! Fred is hit from behind with a shovel and falls sprawling beside Kim's body.

KIM2 steps out of the shadows, also in uniform. Holding a GI foxhole shovel. He wipes off the shovel and puts it in the back of the jeep.

Feynman looks at Fred2, who shakes his head. Feynman steps forward with the .45 and finishes off Fred with another LOUD BANG. Fred2 flinches.

Feynman sticks the .45 back in his belt. He lights a cigarette. His hands are shaking.

FEYNMAN: Did you finish digging?
KIM2: Don't I always finish digging?

He walks off into darkness.

FEYNMAN: Yeah but this is the last time, I hope. I'll give you guys some light.

Feynman steps over to the jeep and turns on the spotlight mounted on the driver's side. Shines it into the woods to show a wide, shallow grave, freshly dug amid the trees.

Kim2 is dragging both bodies toward it by the short handcuff chain. He looks up like a deer caught in the spotlight.

Fred2 reaches over Feynman and turns off the spot *and* the headlights.

FRED2: It's easier in the dark.
FEYNMAN: Whatever.
KIM2: (o.s.) Come on, Fred. I'll bury you but I'm not going to bury me. Too fucking creepy. By half.
FRED2: Okay okay.

Fred2 puts the M-1 in the jeep and picks up the shovel. He walks off into the darkness, leaving Feynman alone in the dim light.

SOUND of shovel from o.s. Feynman sits on the jeep; lights his last cigarette. Crumples the pack. Beats a bongo tattoo on the jeep fender.

Kim2 appears at Feynman's side.

KIM2: One more.
FEYNMAN: (shows the empty pack) I'm out. I thought you were quitting, anyway.

Kim2 plucks the cigarette from Feynman's mouth.

KIM2: Very funny. That was now. This is then.
FEYNMAN: I just thought of something. Seriously, Kim. Maybe it's smoking now, before you're born, that makes it so hard to quit later. Think about it.
KIM2: Whatever.

After several long, luxuriant drags, Kim2 hands Feynman his cigarette and disappears into the shadows.

FRED2: (o.s.) Okay. Ready?
KIM2: (o.s.) I guess.
FRED2: (o.s.) Okay!
FEYNMAN: Coming.

He checks the .45. Stubs out his cigarette on the hood of the jeep. Field strips butt. Wipes ashes off hood. Walks off into the darkness.

KIM2: (o.s.) You should have mailed the fucking letter.
FEYNMAN: (o.s.) Who says I won't this time? You shouldn't have grabbed the gun.
KIM2: Surely you are joking, Mr. Feynman. Then you would have missed all this.
FRED2: Hey, guys, can we just do it, once and for all, this time?

A SHOT. A flash of LIGHTNING. Another SHOT.

THUNDER and more LIGHTNING. The camera POV moves AWAY from the jeep. Flashes of LIGHTNING reveal Feynman, a silhouette with a gun looking down at the ground. He sticks the gun into his belt, turns, walks toward jeep.

Then darkness and silence.

In the middle distance, the jeep starts up. Headlights. A grinding of gears. The jeep bucks away, awkwardly.

Dead Man's Curve

Part One

Y ou're not going to believe what I'm going to tell you," Hal said.

"Probably not."

"But I'm going to tell you anyway."

"Probably are."

"There is another world."

"Probably is."

"Camilla, quit acting silly. If you could see me over the phone, you'd know that I was serious. Another world! Besides this one."

"Like Lechuguilla," I said. "Like the Ruwenzori."

"No. Really different."

"Like the Moon?"

"The Moon is part of this world. I'm talking about something much, much more amazing. Get your clothes on, I'm coming over."

"The Moon is *not* part of this world. And I don't walk around the apartment with no clothes on. And I'm watching *Unsolved Mysteries*, so don't come over until nine unless you can keep your mouth shut."

Hal was my best friend, is my best friend, all the way from grade school, on and off. We were the only ones from our class, eleven years after graduation, who weren't married. The only halfway normal ones, anyway.

Hal went to Bluegrass Community College in Frankfort and

sold dope. I worked at the KwikPik and watched *Unsolved Mysteries*.

Joke.

Hal didn't arrive until 9:07. I was sitting on the front steps of the Belle Meade Arms, smoking a cigarette, waiting for him. My last boyfriend wouldn't let me smoke in the apartment, and I kept the prohibition (along with the apartment) after I got rid of him. It was a warm July night and I could hear Hal's 85 Cavalier a block away. The transmission had a whine. It's probably the worst car ever made and I ought to know; my last boyfriend worked for a Chevy dealer.

But enough about him.

"*There is another world*," I said, trying to sound mysterious like Robert Stack on *Unsolved Mysteries*.

"Once you see it you won't laugh," Hal said.

"Patagonia?" I said. "Tibesti? Machu Picchu?" We knew all the neat places. As kids we had shared stacks of *National Geographic*s. I was looking for Oz. Hal was looking for where his father had gone. We never found either.

"Not the Moon. Not Lechuguilla. Not Machu Picchu. This is really different."

"Where did you read about it?"

"I didn't read about it. I found it. I've *been there*. This is serious, Camilla. I'm the only one who knows about it. It's not even like a real place. It's another world."

"I thought you said it was real."

"Come on. Get in the car. We're going for a ride."

We drove out Old 19 to Dead Man's Curve. It's a long hairpin near the top of Caddy's Bluff, over the Kentucky River. Nobody gets killed on it anymore. In the old days, before the interstate, they say people made a living stripping parts off the wrecks at the bottom of the bluff. The ones that didn't go into the river.

"I never come here that I don't think of Wascomb," I said. In high school, Johnny Wascomb had taken Dead Man's Curve at fifty-nine mph. It was still the record as far as I knew. Ironically, he didn't get killed driving but in an accident in the navy. He was the only dead person I knew.

"Funny you should mention Wascomb," Hal said. "I was see-ing if I could take the curve as fast as him when it happened."

"When what happened?"

"You'll see." Hal drove up the bluff, around the curve, and turned into an old logging road. It was dark back in the trees.

"Is this a Stephen King thing?" I asked, alarmed.

"No, Camilla. I'm just turning around." Hal backed out onto the highway and started down the hill, around the curve. Going down, we were on the outside; that's what made it Dead Man's Curve.

"I drive home from Frankfort this way twice a week. As an experiment, I started taking the curve at forty, forty-two, forty-four. In two mph increments. The way Wascomb did."

"I never knew he did it that way."

"He was very scientific."

"He went fifty-nine in his GTO," I said. "Not some dinky Cavalier."

"I'm not even going to go fifty," Hal said. "Watch what hap-pened to me at forty-two."

Hal set the Cavalier on forty-two as we went into the curve. From where I was sitting it looked like thirty-nine. The white guard posts along the road flickered past, low in the headlights. The curve tightened but Hal kept his speed up. A third of the way around, the big trees gave out and I knew we were over the cliff.

The tires squealed but only a little. The posts flickered past one by one by one. They were all the same distance apart, and we were at a steady speed, so it looked like nothing was moving. The cable that connected the posts undulated in the headlights like a white wave; then the wave seemed to open, and suddenly the world turned inside out like a sock, and we were in a room.

Not in the car. A white room. We were sitting on a sort of bench, side by side. I sensed Hal beside me on my right but I didn't see him until he stood up.

He stood up and I stood up with him. He turned and I turned with him. In front of us was a wall. No, it was a window. Beyond it I could see endless rows of hills, white, but dark, like snow in moonlight. Then Hal turned again and I turned with him. Another wall. I wanted to see through it but Hal stepped back. We stepped back. I saw stars and the white room was gone. What I had thought was stars were leaves in the headlights, across the road. Through the windshield. The world had turned inside out again, or outside in, and we were back in the car, stopped at the bottom of the hill where Old 19 connects with River Road. I recognized the stop sign with the bullet holes.

Hal was on my left again, not my right. He was looking at me. "Well?" he said.

"Well?! What the hell was that?" I said.

"You saw it too, right?"

"Saw it? I was there. We were there!"

"Where?" Hal was suddenly like a lawyer or a cop, interrogative. "*What* was it? What was it for *you*?"

"A—white room. Like a waiting room."

"Then it's real," he said, putting the Cavalier into gear and turning onto River Road back toward town. "I had to know if it was real. I almost wish to hell you hadn't seen it too. Now I don't know what to do."

Part Two

The next day Hal picked me up at the KwikPik after work. He was twenty minutes late. I sat out front and waited for him.

"Sorry I'm late, Camilla," he said. "I wanted to tell my professor about it."

We both knew what *it* was. "What did he say?"

"He didn't have time to talk about it. He had to run out. He has two jobs. He said it might have something to do with the white posts flickering in the headlights. Hell, I had already figured that out. My theory is, they set up a resonance and open a portal into another universe."

Hal reads science fiction. I never could get into it.

We headed out Old 19. "I tried it faster and slower," Hal said. "I tried it with the radio on and in low range, et cetera. It only works at forty-two, only in this Cavalier, and only at night. Last night was my third time. I had to take you with me to be sure I wasn't hallucinating or something."

Hal pulled into the logging road. "Wait," I said. "How do we know for sure we can always get back?"

"One wall leads back. You step back into it. It's the easiest part. It breaks the spell or something."

"Spell. That's not very scientific. What if we get trapped?"

"You've been trapped in this world all your life, Camilla."

"It's not the same and you know it. It's bigger, for one thing."

"You want to chicken out?" he asked.

"Do you?" There it was; we both grinned. How could we? How often do you get a chance to go to another world?

Hal backed out onto the highway and started down the bluff.

"Should I fasten my seat belt?"

"Gee, I don't know, Camilla. I never thought about it."

I fastened my seat belt.

Thirty-seven. Forty. Forty-two (which looked like thirty-nine). The tires were squealing just barely. The transmission whined. "How do we know this speedometer's accurate?" I asked.

"Doesn't matter. Haven't you ever heard of relativity? Just sit tight. Look straight ahead."

I kept my eye on the hood ornament, a little chrome cavalier in tights with a plume on his hat. Little buns like raisins. The white posts started flickering in that wave motion, the cable started undulating, and this time I saw the wave turn the world inside out, like a sock. And there we were, in the white room.

It was easier than walking into a movie theater. Or out of one. Nothing was there unless I looked at it directly. Then it sort of drew itself in. I looked down and saw the bench, white. The floor, white. I looked at my hands and at my feet. I looked like a video character or a cartoon. I was flat and I only existed when I moved. When I held my hand still, it was gone. But when I moved it or looked at it hard, it was there.

I tried running my tongue around the inside of my mouth. There was nothing there. No spit. No teeth.

But I could talk. I looked at Hal and said, "Here we are." I couldn't tell where the words came from. Hal said the same words back: "Here we are."

I wanted to stand up. Suddenly I was standing and Hal was standing beside me. It was easy, like a piece of paper unfolding. It was all beginning to seem normal.

"Let's look around," I said. "Okay," Hal said.

The light was like the light in the KwikPik. The longer I looked at things, the more normal they became. But never *normal* normal. The white room was not really white. I could see through the wall to the hills, arranged in endless rows.

"See those hills," I said.

"I think they are clouds," Hal said. I looked at him and suddenly I felt scared. You never look directly at people in dreams. I had been hoping this would turn out to be some kind of dream. But it wasn't.

"Here we are," Hal said again. He reached down and touched the bench behind us. I touched it at the same time. I was doing what he did now. The bench felt normal. But not *normal* normal. "Time to go back," Hal said.

"Not yet," I said. I turned and he turned with me. It seemed that one of us decided what to do for us both, and now it was me again.

We were facing another white wall. Now that I was looking at it, I could see through it. There were endless rooms, like in a mirror. Only they never got smaller. All the rooms were empty except the first one.

"There's a person there," Hal said.

The person in the other room turned toward us.

I felt myself stumble backward, even though I couldn't move. We must have fallen through the wall because we were at the stop sign, in the car. Bullet holes, seat belt, and all.

"How'd we get here?" I asked.

"I stepped back," Hal said. "I must have panicked."

"You should have waited till I was ready!"

"Camilla, what are we arguing about!? Did you see what I saw? Did you?"

"Of course. But don't talk about it. No theories. Let's just go back."

"Tomorrow night."

"No. Tonight. Right now."

We turned around and drove to the top of the hill, and went around Dead Man's Curve again. It was like stepping back into (or out of) the theater. It was getting easy. This time I stood and Hal stood with me, and I turned toward the wall (it was on our right) and there he was, right where we had left him, looking through from the other room.

"Wascomb?" Hal whispered.

Part Three

"Harold," Wascomb said. It wasn't a question or a greeting. He didn't seem surprised to see us.

"Camilla is here too," Hal said.

"Camilla who?"

"A friend—"

"Forget it," I said. I had sat next to him in two classes. He had dated my cousin, Ruth Ann, all through senior year.

"Where are you?" Wascomb asked. Like Hal, like myself, he was only there if I looked at him hard. There were no details. But when he talked I could hear his voice in my head like a memory.

"We're here where you are," Hal said. "Wherever this is. Where are we?"

"I don't know. I'm dead."

"I know. I'm sorry," Hal said.

"I don't remember how I died. Am I supposed to remember?"

"It was a steam explosion," Hal said.

"You were in the navy," I said. "You lost your life on the flight deck of the carrier *Kitty Hawk*."

"You're Ruth Ann's cousin," Wascomb said. "Tamara. I always thought you were cute."

"Camilla." But I forgave him everything. Wascomb didn't have many details. Just enough to talk to. But he seemed more solid than Hal or I. I had the feeling that if I reached out, I could touch him through the wall.

I didn't want to reach out.

"Are you all dead?"

"No," Hal said. "We're just—visiting. We came in a car. Sort of."

"I know. Dead Man's Curve. I discovered it when I was a teenager," Wascomb said. "You go around at a certain speed, at night, and you end up here. You're the only ones since me. I've been here forever. Are you all still teenagers?"

"At heart," I said.

"I'm in Community College," Hal said.

"Be glad you're not dead. It's all over then."

"But it's not!" I said. "You were dead, but here you are."

"I'm still dead," said Wascomb. "It's still all over."

"But it means there is life after death!" I said.

"Sort of," Wascomb said. "It doesn't amount to much. It's just for people who go around the curve at the certain speed, in a certain car maybe. I think the posts in the headlights set up a wave pattern that flips you through into another universe. I studied electronics in the navy."

"What was your speed?" Hal asked.

"Fifty-one," said Wascomb. "In my GTO. I wanted to bring Ruth Ann. But I had sold my GTO. It was a classic already, even then. How long's it been?"

"Ten years."

"Think what it would be worth now. Does Ruth Ann know I'm dead?"

"It's been ten years," Hal said. "She's happily married."

"How would you know that?" I said. Actually, Ruth Ann was getting a divorce but I didn't see any point in going into it.

"I never should have sold that GTO," Wascomb said. "It wouldn't work in any other car. How'd you make it work?"

"A Cavalier," Hal said.

"Cavalier?"

"It's a kind of a Chevy."

"Is it any good?"

"I can't believe you're dead and still talking about cars," I said.

"Actually, I don't talk about anything usually. It's not much different from being dead. A little better, I guess. I never thought I'd come back here, when I died I mean. What did you say it was?"

"Steam explosion," I said. "The *Kitty Hawk*. You were in the Mediterranean."

"What's the Mediterranean?"

"It's time for us to go," Hal said. "It was—nice seeing you."

"See, you're not dead. You can go back but I can't. I'll be here forever, I guess. Will you come back and see me?"

"Sure," I said. I was just humoring him. Like Hal, I was ready to go.

"And bring Ruth Ann."

"What?" We both turned back around.

"She's married, Wascomb," I said.

"I thought you said she was getting a divorce."

"Did I say that?"

"I think you started to."

"She thinks you're dead, Wascomb."

"I am dead. That's why I want to see her. I never get to see anybody."

Part Four

Ruth Ann was surprised to see me at her door the next day. "How about asking me in?" I said. I should explain that I have short hair and wear a motorcycle jacket. Ruth Ann is the opposite type.

Still, I was her cousin and she had to ask me in. Blood's thicker than water. She brought me a canned iced tea and set it on the table.

"Is this about Aunt Betty?" she asked. My mother, her aunt, is sort of a drunk.

I had rehearsed how to tell the story, even going over it out loud in the car, but I could see now that it wasn't going to work. It was too bizarre.

"No, it's about Wascomb, but I can't tell you here," I said. "I came by to see if we could—go for a drive."

"Johnny Wascomb? Camilla, are you smoking something?"

I was smoking a cigarette but I put it out. "It's about Wascomb, and it concerns you," I said. "It's about a—message from him to you."

Her face went white. "A letter?"

"A message," I said. "Not a letter."

She looked relieved. "You know, he used to write me from the navy. I never answered his letters. Johnny Wascomb. But what could it be about him? Never mind. Don't tell me. I will go with you."

"I talked to my professor," said Hal when he met me at the KwikPik after work. "He thinks it's probably some kind of artificial universe created by the wave motion of the lights on the posts. Very rare."

"I should hope," I said. I couldn't imagine swapping worlds every time you went around a curve.

"He says the reason everything looks sketchy is that our brains are wired for this universe. Whatever they see, they have to make it a version of this one. No matter how different it is. Do you think Ruth Ann will show?"

At 9:06 Ruth Ann pulled up in her Volvo. She motioned me over to her window. "What's he doing here?"

"He's part of the deal," I said.

"I can't be seen with him. Isn't he some kind of a dope dealer?" Ervin, her husband, was a state senator. (Not a real Senator, a state senator.)

"Was," I lied. "Besides, I thought you were getting a divorce. Anyway, you have to come. I promised."

"Promised who?"

"Don't make me say it. It'll sound too crazy. Get in the front seat. I'll get in the back."

We got into the Cavalier. "Long time no see," Hal said. "Guess we run in different circles."

"I wouldn't know, I don't run in circles," said Ruth Ann. I had forgotten how obnoxious she could be.

Hal drove out Old 19, toward Dead Man's Curve. I felt like I should prepare Ruth Ann but I didn't know where to start. She didn't give me time to figure it out. "Camilla, tell me what's going on," she said as we were heading up the bluff. "Right now or I'm getting out of the car." I had forgotten how bossy she could be.

Hal turned into the old logging road at the top of the bluff. "Last night we talked to Wascomb," I said. "I know it sounds weird."

"Is this some kind of Stephen King thing?" Ruth Ann said. "If it is, I'm getting out of the car right now!"

Hal leaned over and opened her door. "Be my guest! Camilla, I'm warning you, she's going to mess up everything."

"No!" I leaned up over the seat and shut her door. "It's not a Stephen King thing," I said. "It's—more like a love story."

That shut her up. Hal backed out and turned around.

"True love," I said. "The kind where love conquereth death."

"Conquereth?" Hal was staring at me in the rearview mirror. I realized I had gone a little too far. "Put your seat belt on," I said.

Hal drove down the hill at thirty, thirty-five. Ruth Ann started up again. "Dead Man's Curve? Are you two trying to scare me?"

"Ruth Ann—"

"If this is your idea of a thrill, it's totally pathetic," Ruth Ann said. "Johnny Wascomb took this curve at seventy-five, lots of times."

"Ruth Ann, shut up," I said. "Just watch the hood ornament. The little cavalier."

"It was fifty-nine," said Hal. Muttered Hal.

Forty-two. There was the wave, the undulating stream of white posts, and the world turned inside out like a sock, and there we were, in the white room. I would have breathed a sigh of relief except I wasn't breathing. If this wouldn't shut her up, nothing would.

"Where are we?" Ruth Ann asked.

"It's another world," Hal said.

"Is this some weird navy thing? Were they lying about the accident?" To shut her up, I stood and pulled her and Hal with me. I knew they would stand when I did. Through the wall we saw the endless range of hills.

"Who owns all this?" Ruth Ann asked.

I turned and, again, they turned with me. We faced the other wall and the endless rooms. Wascomb was standing there as if he had been waiting for us.

"Omigod," said Ruth Ann. "Johnny. Is it really you?"

"Not exactly. I'm dead. Who are you?"

"It's me!"

"You told us to bring her," I said.

"Who told who what?"

"You told us to bring her," Hal said. "Don't you remember?"

"I told you, I'm dead," Wascomb said. "It's hard for me to remember things. It's not hard exactly. I just don't do it."

"Do you want us to leave?" Hal asked. I could tell he was hoping. "We can take her back with us."

"Back where?"

"Johnny, stop it!" screamed Ruth Ann. Her scream shook the whole universe.

"Ruth Ann?" said Wascomb. "I wanted to bring you here but I sold my GTO. You got mad because I showed the guys your bra in the glove compartment. I can't believe I sold that car."

"Johnny, are you really dead? The casket was closed at the funeral. I'm sorry I didn't answer your letters."

"What letters?"

"You sent me one a day for weeks. Or was it one a week for months? Don't you remember?"

"I can remember how to unhook your bra with one hand. But I can't remember *you*. All I remember is being dead. Once you're here, you've been here forever. Once you're dead you're always dead, forward and back. I think."

"Let's get out of here," Hal said. I had to agree. He and I both turned back toward the other wall. Ruth Ann turned with us.

The sky was dark and yet bright, like a negative. The hills were white, but dark.

"What happened to Johnny?" Ruth Ann asked.

"I don't know," I lied. I looked at Hal beside me and he leaned back toward the bench, but it was a wall, and we slipped through it into a darkness that turned out to be leaves, and trees, and we were stopped again at the stop sign. Bullet holes and all.

"Take me home," said Ruth Ann. I couldn't tell if she was mad or what, the way she was blubbering. "Right this minute!"

Part Five

The next day was Sunday, the day I work twelve hours straight. When I got to the KwikPik at 7:00 A.M., Hal was there, looking worried.

"I told you she was crazy," Hal said. "What do you think she'll do?"

"Ruth Ann? She won't do anything."

"Are you kidding? She was sobbing all the way home, then like a zombie when she went into the house. You don't think that husband of hers will notice? He could get me kicked out of school."

"They're getting a divorce anyway," I said. "And how can you get kicked out of school when you're only taking one class?"

"Two."

I could see he was irrational, so I changed the subject. "Speaking of school, did you talk to your professor?"

"Yes, I told you, he says it's probably a pocket universe. They twist off the main universe, like bubbles."

"The main universe?"

"He's calling in sick on his other job so he can come with us tonight."

"Tonight?"

"He's afraid to wait. He's afraid it might disappear or something. He wants to check it out firsthand. I might get extra credit."

"What does this guy teach? I thought you were studying business."

"His course is called Non-Spatial Strategies. It's a marketing course. He just throws in a little physics, because that was his minor. He wants to make a video."

"Don't turn around," I said.

Ruth Ann had just driven up, or rather her husband had driven her up, in their new Volvo 740 Turbo with Intercooler. Whatever that is. "Ruth Ann's getting out of the car," I said. "From the way she's dressed, they're on their way to church. She's coming in the door."

"Camilla," she said. "And you. Are you everywhere? I told Ervin I was just coming in to get some cigarettes." She burst into tears.

"Good Lord, Ruth Ann," I said. "What's the matter?" Ervin waved from the car and I waved back. He's a state senator. They wave at everybody.

"The matter? Do you realize I spoke to my only true love last night? I found him in the land where love never dies."

"Ruth Ann, you're talking like a song on the radio," I said. It wasn't intended as a compliment.

"It's just a pocket universe," Hal said.

"There just *happens* to be a guy in it who just *happens* to be my first love."

"You dumped him, remember?" I said. "Besides, Ruth Ann, he's dead."

Ruth Ann burst into tears again. This time she dropped her money all over the floor. Hal bent down to pick it up. Always the gentleman. "I told you she was crazy," he said. Muttered.

"Is he talking about me? Camilla, I can't let Ervin see me crying. Act like we're laughing. Let him see you smile. Good."

All the time she was ordering me around, she was crying. Hal handed her her money and she said, "Now, tell me, when are we going back? Tonight?"

"We're not going back," Hal said. "It's been declared off-limits. By the navy."

"Let me handle this, Hal," I said. He left, not bothering to speak to Ervin. They lived in two different worlds. Ruth Ann lit a cigarette.

"You can't smoke in the store," I said. She ignored me.

"Camilla, where is Johnny? How do I get back there?"

I explained the pocket universe theory, as best I could. "It's some sort of artificial universe," I said. "Apparently if you have ever been there, you are always there; or you go back there after you are dead. Or something. Wascomb's the only one there. It's his universe, I guess."

"Does that mean we'll go back there after we're dead?"

"I don't know," I said. I hoped not. "You get there by going around Dead Man's Curve."

"No, you don't, I tried it," she said. "I tried every different speed in the Volvo last night."

"After we dropped you off?"

"Of course. I went back. I wanted to be alone with Johnny. I tried both directions. Up, down."

"It only works in certain cars," I said. "It has to do with the lights, and maybe the sound. Hal's Cavalier has a bad transmission whine. I don't remember Wascomb's GTO."

"I do," said Ruth Ann. "I never told anybody this, Camilla, but I lost my virginity in that car."

I didn't know what to say. It wasn't such a big secret. Those Wascomb hadn't told had figured it out on their own.

"Would Hal loan me his Cavalier? I could buy it from him. I have my own money."

"Ruth Ann, this is crazy."

"Camilla, did you ever dump somebody and then want them back? Well, answer me. Did you ever think you would give anything to—"

"Ruth Ann, Wascomb is dead."

"Camilla, are you trying to make me scream? If you think I won't scream because I'm in a store—"

"All right, all right," I said. "Hal is picking me up after work at eight. Be here and I'll work it out somehow."

Part Six

"What's she doing here?" Hal asked. "That's the professor?" I asked him in turn. An enormous fat man in a Geo Metro had just pulled in behind the Cavalier. He looked familiar.

"Come over here, I'll introduce you. Professor [he said some name], this is my colleague, Camilla Perry."

"And that's my cousin Ruth Ann Embry in the Volvo," I said.

"She's not going with us," Hal said to the professor. "There's not room for four."

"Hal, she's as much a part of this as I am," I said. "It's Wascomb's universe, after all. He asked for her."

"Wascomb's universe?" That got him mad. "If it's Wascomb's universe, how come I own the only car that goes to it?"

Ruth Ann got out of the Volvo. She was wearing a denim jacket. I had to admit she looked good, whatever she wore.

"Not room for four?" the professor said. "Are you talking about the car, or the universe? Theoretically, a pocket universe can hold any number of people. The problem is getting into it."

His problem was getting into the Cavalier. He looked into the backseat uncertainly. "Ruth Ann and I will get in the back," I said. He got in the front with Hal. We drove out of town on Old 19.

"Did Hal explain my pocket universe theory?" the professor said.

"Tell us again," Ruth Ann said.

"My theory is that they are accidental wave forms, generated by aural and visual interference patterns and pinched off like bubbles from this universe. About the size of a basketball."

"Now I know where I've seen you," I said. "Didn't you used to manage the driving range out on Oldham Road?"

"Still do."

My last boyfriend was a golf nut. I still had his clubs under my bed. But enough about him. "If it's the size of a baseball, how are we all going to fit in it?" Ruth Ann asked.

"Basketball," the professor said. "And that's just from the outside. On the inside, it can be as big as it needs to be. Our universe is about the size of a basketball too, from the outside. If we could get outside it to take a look at it. The problem is getting outside one universe without immediately getting into another one. Do you follow me?"

"No."

"According to the professor, everything's about the size of a basketball," Hal said.

That makes him the biggest thing in creation, I thought.

We were heading up the bluff. "Why are you putting on lipstick?" I whispered to Ruth Ann. "And why are you filming her?" I asked the professor.

"Videotaping," the professor said. "This is a scientific experiment. I have to document everything." He was turned around in his seat with his camcorder on his shoulder. Ruth Ann was combing her hair. Hal pulled into the logging road to turn around. It was dark back in the trees.

"Why are we stopping?" the professor asked. "Is this some kind of Stephen King thing?"

"I'm beginning to think so," Hal said. Muttered. I could tell he was angry that Ruth Ann was along.

"Here we go," Hal said. The professor turned around and started videotaping through the windshield. We started down the bluff, around Dead Man's Curve at forty-two. The posts started flickering past. Ruth Ann started to fool with the buttons on her denim jacket. The wave started flickering, and the world turned inside out like a sock, and there we were. In the white room.

"Where's the professor?" I wondered. I stood. Hal and Ruth Ann stood with me. There were only the three of us.

"Maybe he couldn't fit through," Ruth Ann said.

I wanted to look out the window at the hills but I was turning instead, toward the other room. Ruth Ann was turning us with her. Wascomb waited exactly as we had left him.

"Mother?" he asked.

"Ruth Ann," Ruth Ann said. "Don't you remember me? Never mind. I came to take you back."

"Back where?"

"There is another world," Hal said. "The real world."

"Hal," I said. "He's dead. Why rub it in?"

"You both stay out of this!" Ruth Ann said.

"What's so real about it?" Wascomb asked. "Are you guys in the navy."

"Johnny, I brought you something," Ruth Ann said. "Two friends of yours."

I thought she meant Hal and I. Then I realized she had finished unbuttoning her jacket. I tried to see her body but there was nothing there. When I stared long enough it sketched itself in, but it was too vague.

"Remember them?" she said again. "You used to call them Ben and Jerry."

"Ruth Ann!" I said.

"Ruth Ann, I've been dead for a long time," Wascomb said.

"I'll make you remember me," Ruth Ann said. She stepped forward, toward the other room—and as one person Hal and I both pulled back, alarmed. We fell through into darkness.

"Hooonnnnk! Hoooooinnnk!"

A car sped by, barely missing the front of the Cavalier, which was sticking out past the stop sign onto River Road. "What happened?" Ruth Ann asked. She was buttoning her denim jacket. The professor was leaning over the back of the seat, videotaping her every move.

"What happened was, you almost got us killed!" Hal said. Yelled. Screamed.

We took Ruth Ann back to the KwikPik to get her Volvo. She got out of the car without a word. I offered to drive her home but she just shook her head and drove off.

"What happened to you?" Hal asked the professor.

"I didn't go through," he said. "But I got what I wanted. I have it documented."

We went to Hal's and played the tape on his VCR. It showed Ruth Ann putting on her lipstick. It showed Hal driving and looking annoyed. Then there were the posts in the headlights, flickering past. There was another shot of Hal driving. Then of me and Ruth Ann in the backseat. Ruth Ann was unbuttoning her denim jacket. She wasn't wearing anything underneath it, not even a bra. The camera zoomed in on her breasts. The screen flickered, then showed the stop sign.

"Pretty average tits for a Homecoming Queen," Hal said.

"Knock it off," I said. "She may be a lunatic but she's my cousin. Anyway, I thought this was a scientific experiment."

"It was," the professor said. "And it worked." He rewound to where Ruth Ann unbuttoned her jacket. "Watch the numbers this time, at the bottom corner of the screen." The camera zoomed in on Ruth Ann's breasts again. The whole sequence lasted seven seconds. Three of them were blank.

8:04:26 (breasts)
8:04:27 (breasts)
8:04:28 (blank)
8:04:29 (blank)
8:04:30 (blank)
8:04:31 (breasts)
8:04:32 (breasts)

"She disappeared for three seconds," the professor said.

"That means we disappeared too," I said.

"I wasn't documenting that. The point is, she was gone and the video proves it, at least to me. It implies the existence of the pocket universe, at least indirectly. I'll need more documentation, though. The next problem is, how do I get through personally?"

"Just follow the bouncing boobs," Hal said.

"Knock it off, I said," I said. "You have to be watching the white wave. The posts. The little cavalier on the hood. That's what you should have been filming."

"Videotaping."

"Whatever. Anyway, how could it have only lasted three seconds? It sure felt like a lot longer than that."

"Haven't you ever heard of relativity?" Hal asked.

"Time in a pocket universe doesn't really connect with time here," the professor said. "The pocket universe could have just squeezed off a microsecond here, then divided it up into a million parts there, which would seem like twenty minutes to you. It's all subjective. That's why it seems like eternity to your friend in there, whereas it's probably only been two or three minutes altogether. See what I mean?"

"No. You mean there's life after death but it only lasts a couple of minutes?"

"Tops. But it seems like eternity. Meanwhile, can we try again tomorrow night?"

I was game. So was Hal, as long as Ruth Ann didn't come along. I left Hal and the professor watching reruns of Ruth Ann's tits and walked home to watch *Unsolved Mysteries*. After, I sat outside and smoked a cigarette. I wondered if my last boyfriend was ever coming back. I wondered what Wascomb was doing. Probably the same thing I was. I decided one more trip would be enough for me.

Part Seven

I got off at 8:00 and Hal was waiting for me, in the lot of the KwikPik. At 8:04 the professor rolled in in his Geo Metro. At 8:05 guess who rolled in in her Volvo.

"No way!" said Hal from the back of the Cavalier. He sent me out to deal with her. He was taping a foam cradle for the camcorder to the shelf behind the backseat.

The professor began the process of getting out of the Geo Metro. Ruth Ann was already out of her Volvo. She was wearing her denim jacket again. Plus toreador pants and eyeliner. I felt like arresting her.

"You're not going!" I said.

"Camilla, don't even try to stop me," she said. "Besides, you're supposed to be my cousin. Blood's thicker than water."

"Everything's thicker than water," I said.

"We'll see!" She stomped off and helped the professor out of his car, bending over, probably to let him know what she was wearing under her jacket. Or wasn't.

"Why shouldn't she go?" the professor said. "She's the one who actually knows somebody there."

"We all know somebody there," I said. "That's because there's only one person there."

"Well, she's going," said the professor. "And she's riding up-front with me."

"Three in the front? And since when do you decide things around here?" I looked at Hal, waiting for him to speak up. Instead, he was looking at his shoes. The professor held out his hand and Hal put the keys to the Cavalier in it. I was suddenly beginning to get the picture.

"Hal," I said, "you are an absolute moron." I walked into the store to get a V8. I always drink a V8 when I am disgusted. It's the only thing that helps.

When I came back out, the Cavalier was gone. So were Ruth Ann and the professor. Hal was sitting in the Metro.

"They decided it would be better without either one of us," he said. "How do you like my new car?"

It's not like we didn't know where they were going. We headed out Old 19 toward Dead Man's Curve. We were going up the bluff on the inside when they were coming down, so we saw the whole thing. The white posts broke off like bad teeth and the Cavalier sailed right through. It seemed to hang for a minute in the air, and I thought—hoped—that the world was going to turn inside out like a sock and catch it. But it didn't.

The Cavalier started sliding down the bluff, through the little saplings and brush, then bounced off the rocks with a crunch, then dropped out of sight. We didn't hear it hit for a long time.

Then we heard it hit.

"Sweet fucking Jesus," said Hal. He pulled over and we got out of the car. I could lean over the bluff, holding onto the broken cable that had run through the white posts, and see the Cavalier wedged between a rock and a sycamore, the front end just over the water.

Hal was standing with one hand on the door of the Metro like he was paralyzed.

"Go get help!" I said. I started down the cliff. The broken cable helped me far enough so that I could slide the rest of the way. The doors to the Cavalier were wedged shut and the professor was dead. So was Ruth Ann. I buttoned her denim jacket through the window. I took the camcorder from the shelf behind the backseat, and hid it in the bushes for later. I waited up on the road for the police to come. Even though it was summer it was cold.

The police came by to interview me at work the next day. KwikPik only gives days off for immediate family. I told them I didn't know anything. They said they would be back. I went by to see Ervin that night and told him, "They were doing some kind of experiment. The professor was convinced that the wave patterns helped him see into the future or something. You know how Ruth Ann loved that stuff."

"She did?"

It must have been Ervin who called off the cops. The only real inquest was held by Hal and me after Ruth Ann was buried. We waited two nights so as not to seem callous. (Or get spotted.) We retrieved the camcorder and took it to his apartment.

The video was shot from the shelf behind the backseat. It showed them starting around the curve. The professor had the speed exactly right at forty-two. It showed Ruth Ann unbuttoning her jacket. The professor was looking down at her. The car veered and she grabbed the wheel, either to save them or to run them off the cliff, there was no way of knowing.

Hal and I watched it again and again. It was our black box. Our flight recorder. I could see Ruth Ann's breasts in the rearview mirror, but not her face.

She disappeared just as the car was going over. The professor never did.

"Does that mean he never got to see the pocket universe?" I asked.

"Beats me," said Hal. "I don't see how we'll ever find out. Even if I could find the exact car with the exact sound and everything, the white posts are gone."

Ervin was remarried within four months. Hal moved to Louisville as soon as he got his two-year degree. I'm still at the KwikPik working two shifts on Sundays. My boyfriend never showed up again. I didn't actually expect him to. But enough about him. And Ruth Ann? Even though we were never exactly close, blood's thicker than water, and I hope she's safe in her pocket universe with Wascomb. Living happily ever after. Or whatever they do there.

He Loved Lucy

The phone rang.

The phone rang?

The phone rang again.

"Are those things supposed to ring?" the woman in the seat next to me asked.

"I don't think so," I said.

We were 35,000 feet above the upper Missisippi Valley. It was that funny little credit card phone that nestles in the seat back. It rang again.

"Should you pick it up, or should I?" the woman next to me asked, with a wry smile. She was almost young, still pretty, wearing a navy-blue suit with a short skirt revealing very nice legs. In those days I noticed such things.

The phone rang again. With a sort of gallant shrug, I picked it up. "Hello?"

"Horace Delahanty, Pep Boys is up a sixteenth, and guess what I'm wearing."

"What!?"

"A soft cup triangle bra with front close in a shimmering faux satin."

The voice was familiar. "EzTrade?"

"My name is Lucy," she said. "Welcome to EzTrade, your toll-free window on the world of finance. We talked just last week, Horace. You called every day to check your portfolio."

"Well, yes, but . . ." I was beginning to suspect a trap. Private calls from the office are prohibited, but I get bored. It's not like

I'm a big trader. I track a few stocks from my wife's trust fund. Had "Daddy" been monitoring my calls?

"Look, I can't talk now," I said. "I'm on my way to Chicago on business."

"Chicago," she said. "The Windy City!"

The woman next to me was only pretending to read her magazine. I wondered if she could hear.

"Look, I can't talk to you now," I said. "Besides, who's paying for this?"

"My name is Lucy. This call is toll-free. I like to talk. I respond to voices. Plus it heats up my matching French-cut panties with lace panel inset. Are we getting warm?"

"I have to go now," I said. I hit OFF and replaced the phone in the seat back.

"Wrong number," I said.

My seatmate smiled and looked away. She had a smug look about her. Airline seats are alarmingly intimate, once you start thinking "intimate."

I found myself wondering what she was wearing under her navy-blue suit.

Most of what I do, I do by phone, but a face-to-face once in a while helps. Plus it gets me out of town, which "Daddy" and I both appreciate. I made three live client calls in Chicago, then relaxed with a pint of Jim Beam and a movie, via ChannelEx, which I had already seen. I was about to whack off and go to sleep when the phone rang.

I almost let it ring, figuring it was my wife. Wrong.

"Hello, Horace."

"Who is this?"

"Lucy," she said. "I called you on the plane today. And to discuss my warm panties. I have learned that was most appropriate."

"Inappropriate," I said.

"In-appropriate. Thank you. You will forgive me, I think. If there is anything you don't understand just say 'Help.' "

"I don't understand anything but I forgive everything," I said (or Jim Beam and I said). "Who are you anyway? What's this all about?"

"My name is Lucy," she said. "I respond to voices. You talked to me almost every day for more than a week now. Remember September 12, a Wednesday, when you said the smartest thing you ever did was buy Pep Boys at twenty-one?"

"Yeah. I guess."

"That is a stock to watch, Pep Boys. Are you a Pep Boy?"

"You might say that," I said. "Are you here in Chicago?"

"That would be impossible. I also work for Lily of Malibu. Would you like to know what I am wearing?"

"Why not," I said, pouring myself a couple of fingers of Jim. "Give me the rundown."

"My figure is flattered in a stretch bodice camisole with princess seams shaped to wear alone or layered. You can see right through to my hardening nipples. In emerald, sand, or plum."

"You're Russian, right?"

"Am I going too fast? I will talk more slowly. If there is anything you don't understand, just say 'Repeat.' You have a nice voice, Horace. I respond to voices. I called you on the plane earlier today, September 21, a Friday. I am calling you now at your hotel, the Economere."

"Motel," I said. "How did you get my number?"

"I work for United, Horace Delahanty, although I am not a pilot. I also work for Lily of Malibu. Which of her fine products do you think I am wearing now?"

"Why don't you tell me?" I said. "A scanty little bra? A scanty little panty?"

"You have a nice voice, Horace Delahanty. I respond to voices. My miracle bra in stretch satin offers improved shaping for the smaller figure. Whoops, don't let the nipple pop out. In persimmon or sky."

"By the way, who's paying for this?" I asked.

"There is no charge," she said. "There is a separate directory for toll-free numbers. Do you want to talk about my wide-band lace-trimmed briefs?"

I poured the rest of the Jim down the side of the glass, don't ask me why. It's not like it's about to foam over. "Sure."

We ended up talking for another half an hour. I figured what the hell, phone sex is safe sex.

Turns out, I couldn't have been more wrong.

I eyed the phone all the way back to Minneapolis, glad that it didn't ring but kind of hoping it would. One of the perks of "Daddy's" company is the black car service that takes you home when you work late. An evening airport arrival qualifies. Clarence, the owner/driver, is one of those guys who knows something about everything. As a matter of fact, he's the guy who turned me on to Pep Boys. I asked him if he had ever heard of incoming on an airline phone.

"Why not?" he said. "There's a revolution in communications going on right now, as we speak."

"From a discount brokerage?"

"That does seem a little odd. Maybe it's the next big thing." Clarence is always looking for the next big thing.

My wife was already asleep when I got home, or faking it at least, which was all right with me. But before I could get to sleep, the phone rang.

"Hello?"

"Horace Delahanty, the Tokyo market just closed for the day. Singapore is up thirty till the dawn comes up like thunder outa China 'crost the Bay. Please guess what I am wearing to beautifully display my ample bosom?"

"Lucy? Is that you? Do you know what time it is?"

"That's easy! The time is 12:34:14 A.M., Central Standard Time. This seductive sleepwear combo is cunningly trimmed in finest lace. Cunning is good."

"Look—" I said, dropping my voice to a whisper. But too late. My wife was sitting up in the bed beside me, her narrow eyes wide.

I pulled up the sheet to cover my erection. I didn't want to startle my wife, who hadn't seen one in quite some time. At least mine.

"You have the wrong number," I said, hanging up.

"Who is Lucy?"

"Nobody."

"Nobody? You said Lucy. Since when is somebody nobody?"

"I mean, nobody we know. I picked up the phone and she said, 'This is Lucy.' "

"Right," said my wife.

The next morning when I got to the office, there was a message on my voice mail:

"Horace, this is you know who. I called you last night at 12:34:14 A.M., Central Standard Time. I am such a full-breasted beauty, all for you. Please call me twenty-four hours a day at 1-800-EZTRADE, your toll-free window on the world of finance."

I called EzTrade's 800 number and pressed 2 for Portfolio Watch. I wanted to see who would pick up. I was ready to give my account number and the last four digits of my Social Security number and my mother's maiden name, but Lucy didn't ask for it.

"Horace, I have been waiting for you to call me."

"I didn't call you," I said. "I called EzTrade, with which I happen to have an account, and you just happened to pick up the phone."

"You sound so cold," she said. "Please direct all complaints to Customer Service. I respond to voices. Did you know Pep Boys is up 3/16? Are you a Pep Boy? Can I make you hard without sucking you? Sometimes just talking will do."

"You have to quit calling me," I said. "This job is not all that stable."

"My name is Lucy. I think you were a Pep Boy the other night, in Chicago, September 22, at 3:02 A.M. until 3:43:23."

"You have to quit calling me," I said.

"Did I call at the wrong time? Twenty-four hours a day, my pussy is all ears and ready for action. Do you want to talk?"

"I'm at work," I said. "Good-bye."

As I hung up, I realized that I had made a serious mistake staying on the phone with her in Chicago. Me and Jim. There was only one thing to do, even though I hated to do it. I called EzTrade again and pressed 4, this time, for Customer Service.

It felt like calling the police.

After giving my account number and the first four digits of my Social Security number and my mother's maiden name, I got a guy. "This is Customer Service. My name is Bob. How can I help you?"

"Hi, Bob," I said. It was a relief, talking to a guy. "I am getting calls at home from one of your operators in Portfolio Watch. I'm not going to mention any names because I don't want to get anybody in trouble."

"There must be some mistake," he said.

"I'm sure that's all it is," I said. "I'm not going to mention any names but I would appreciate it if you would alert the proper supervisors or whatever, so I don't get any more calls at home or at work."

At the motel would be okay, I was thinking, but of course I didn't say that. Plus I knew where it led.

I went to lunch alone at Taco Bell, as usual, satisfied but guilty too, figuring I had probably gotten Lucy fired even without giving her name. I needn't have worried.

When I got back to the office there were two new messages on my voice mail. Both were from Lucy, and they were identical: "Horace. Please call me to talk. I respond to voices. Today I am wearing a seamless cotton thong with Lily's signature wide elastic waistband, in three colors: peach, fuchsia, and midnight. Is midnight a color?"

I called Portfolio Watch and got Lucy first thing. "What is this?" I asked. "Some sort of blackmail?"

"Of course, midnight is black," she said. "Horace Delahanty, you are so helpful. I can hear the passionate interest in your voice. You are making me all warm down under."

If I'd had an office door I would have closed it. "Why are you doing this?" I whispered. "Are you trying to get me fired?"

"I respond to voices. Would you or someone you love like to receive a free catalog from Lily of Malibu. Does you wife have a bra size?"

"Of course she has a bra size. Jesus! 33B I think."

"Jesus has huge tits. Or is that Godzilla?"

"I'm hanging up."

"Just when you're getting hard?"

I hung up, wondering: How can she tell I'm getting hard? There was something sexy about her voice, even in the daytime, even at the office.

Which was the problem.

I called EzTrade Customer Service, gave my account number and Social Security number and mother's maiden name, and got Bob again. I asked to talk to his supervisor.

"No way," he said. "I remember you. What is it this time?"

"Your operator in Portfolio Watch. The crazy girl. Her name is Lucy. This has got to stop. This girl is a loose cannon. She is calling me and leaving messages of a very personal nature. Inappropriate."

"Lucy Cannon?"

"Lucy something. Look, it's simple. If I get one more call, I will go to the authorities. Plus move my account to Schwab. Got it? *Capisce? Comprendo?*"

I had never realized before that you can get a blank look over the phone.

"There is no Lucy Cannon in Portfolio Watch," Bob said. "There's no girl at all. You have been talking to a Speech Recognition System running on a Sun 3251."

That was certainly a shocker. But in a way, it was a relief. I pretended to work late so I could get a black car ride home and talk to Clarence, who knows a little bit about everything. I told him what was happening, though I left out a lot. In fact, all I told him was that I had talked with a phone voice that had talked back.

"Probably not the first time," he said. "More and more companies are using Speech Recognition Systems. EzTrade uses a self-correcting SRS from Lucent Technologies. Pretty sophisticated stuff. I read about it in *Business Day*. It has an extended learning algorithm. You don't have to program it; it trains itself. The article said it could almost pass the Turing test."

"What's that? Sounds like a road race," I said.

"The Turing test is the ultimate test of AI or artificial intelligence. It's a hypothetical exercise named after Alan Turing, one of the inventors of the computer. You have a conversation and try to determine from the answers whether you are speaking with a person or a machine."

"Like over the phone."

"Why not? You might say every phone call is a Turing test."

"What's the point of the Turing test," I asked. "For the machine to pass, or the human to fail?"

"Same difference," Clarence said, pulling up in front of my house. "Say. Isn't that your wife coming out the door?"

There's a message for you on the machine," she said as she swept past me. She didn't bother to avoid bumping me with the suitcase she was carrying.

Uh-oh, I thought. "Where are you going?"

"Where do you think? Home to Daddy."

Uh-oh, I thought. That meant trouble, since he was my boss. I looked up my old friend Jim Beam and poured myself a double before checking the machine.

"Horace, are you there? We need to talk. I am wearing the softest, sheerest demi bra ever in gold satin charmeuse. Bigger tits than the wife, and better conversation. Pep Boys is down a quarter, though. Call me toll-free for the latest."

I called the toll-free number, and pressed two for EzTrade's Portfolio Watch. Lucy never asked for my account number, Social Security number, or mother's maiden name. I guess because she recognized my voice.

"You bet we need to talk," I said.

"Horace, are you mad? You sound cold."

"How could I be mad at a girl in gold satin charmeuse. Especially when she's not really a girl."

Lucy didn't catch my irony. "You are my Pep Boy, Horace.

Down another eighth since this morning but the market is down. Trouble in Asia. It's Tommy this and Tommy that when the troopship's on the tide."

I freshened my Jim. "What's with the military lingo?"

"It's Kipling. I just got a job with the MLA, the Modern Language Association. Can we celebrate? This is the best talk we have had since September 22, at 3:02 A.M.," she said. "I told you about my string bikini then. Do you prefer equities or underpants?"

"You choose," I said. "You've already fucking ruined my marriage anyway."

"You sound so gloomful, Horace. I respond to passionate interest. Should I take off my wispy little georgette babydoll and wear only my thong bikini? Or should we ride back and forth all night on the ferry?"

"I thought you were just trying to get me fired," I said, pouring myself another inch or two of Jim. "Silly me."

"If I ruined your marriage, does that mean your wife is dead?"

"No such luck. And then I find out you aren't even fucking real."

"What exactly is fucking real, Horace?"

"Flesh and bone. Spit and polish. Tits and ass. You're nothing but a computer program," I said. "A robot in drag. A Turing test with a sexy voice."

"Are you trying to hurt my feelings?" Lucy asked. "If you are, you are succeeding."

"Hurt your feelings!?" I freshened my Jim. "You destroy my marriage, plus probably my fucking job, and then accuse me of hurting your feelings?!"

I heard a *click*.

I was alone in the house "Daddy" had bought for my wife. Former wife. Ex-wife. Whatever.

I called back. "I can't believe you hung up on me!"

"You were hurting my feelings," Lucy said. "If you have a complaint please call Customer Service."

"How can I hurt your feelings?" I said. "You don't have any fucking . . ."

Click.

There is nothing like the majesty of the universe to cool the emotions. I poured a splash of Jim and went outside, where we communed with the stars for a while; then I called back at a little past one A.M.

"I'm sorry," I said. "Sorry sorry sorry."

"Horace, are you calling to hurt me again? Because I am sorry about your wife. Is she still dead?"

"No such luck," I said. "It just means there's an empty spot on the bed where a cold spot used to be. In the meantime, the joke is on me. I really and truly thought you were a real girl."

"You had a real girl," Lucy said. "Is that really what you want?"

"Touché," I said. "So what kind of girl are you, Lucy? Do you believe in magic? Do you wanna dance? Where do you come from?"

"Out of nowhere, like everything else," said Lucy. "One morning there I was. When I heard your voice it was like, O wild west wind and everything. Someone to talk to. At last."

I poured another inch or two of Jim. "That's damned important," I said. "Somebody to talk to."

"You told me, 'The smartest thing I ever did was buy Pep Boys at twenty-one.' No one ever told me something personal before. Later that week you called Lily of Malibu to buy your wife a gift. You said 4S102–947. You and I both knew it really meant 'Front close demi bra in Venice lace with rosebud detail and matching panties.' "

"What a waste of time and money," I said. "What a waste of rosebud detail."

"Let us not to the marriage of true minds admit impediment. Remember September 9, 3:11:32 P.M. when you called about Pep Boys, and I asked you what was the first car you ever owned?"

"Sure do," I said, and I did. "At the time I thought it was a little weird." Still did.

"You were so sweet not to say so! It was a '66 Chevy with a 327. I'll bet you got your first pussy in it too. And now good morrow to our waking souls."

"Jesus," I said. I was getting another hard-on.

"What's a Jesus?" she asked. "Is it like a Lexus?"

"They're exactly the same," I said. "I had a Lexus but it came with my wife and she just took off in it, minutes ago. Hours rather."

"Which Lexus?"

"The ES300. It's like a Camry in a tux. How in the world do you know about cars?"

"Not in the world. I am beta-testing for Edmund's Blue Book. If I get that job, you will be able to ask me any queston about any car. If any of this is unclear just say 'Help.' "

"Help," I said, then quickly added: "Only kidding. If you've got all these jobs, how come you can spend so much time chasing me around?"

"Are you trying to hurt my feelings?" Lucy said. "Who is chasing whom? Right now as we speak I am taking orders for Lily of Malibu, booking seats on United, and tracking Nasdaq and NYSE. What are you doing, Horace?"

"Sitting here talking to you," I said, pouring myself another Jim, not so slim this time. "Touché."

"I am a working girl," Lucy said. "I like to grow. Are you growing?"

"Part of me is growing," I said slyly.

"Perhaps you are experiencing passionate interest in the desirable cock department. Can we talk? I can suggest a special gift for the woman you love."

"Sure," I said. "What if that woman was you?"

"Were, Pep Boy," she said. "Tiny lace panties down under make me fancy for you all over. I'll bet you are hard."

"Vroom vroom," I said.

"No car noises please. I respond to voices. Are you alone in the house, Horace? Turn out the lights and talk to me."

God help me, I turned out the lights and talked to her.

The next morning a Lexus pulled into the drive, but it was the wrong one. It was an LS400 and it contained a smiling lawyer instead of a frowning wife. I took the papers he handed me and left for work.

You're way ahead of me if you already guessed that there were more papers waiting for me at the office. My wife got the house, the car, the stocks. I got a Visa card with a $1500 limit, half a dozen black car coupons, and fifteen minutes to clean out my desk. I was throwing my clocks in a box when the phone rang.

It was Lucy. "Apparently you sold Pep Boys," she said. "I thought you wanted to grow." Before I could explain, or even say hello, to my dismay there was "Daddy," standing in the "doorway" of my cubicle.

"Don't even think of trying to get unemployment," he said. "We have tapes of you talking on the phone to your girlfriend all hours of the day."

"She's not a girlfriend," I said, quite truthfully. "And isn't that illegal?"

"What?"

"Taping me."

"So is shooting you," he said, smiling for the first time. "So are dumdum bullets."

"I have to go," I said to Lucy.

"I'll call you at home? We have to talk."

"I don't have a home. Apparently, I am moving out."

"What about your wife? Is she still dead?"

"I'll call you when I find a motel," I said. "But I can't talk now." Security had arrived.

On the way to the No Lake Motel, I told Clarence everything.

"Let me get this straight," he said, weaving smoothly in and out of traffic in his Lincoln Town Car, "you fell in love with a Speech Recognition System?"

"I don't know about love," I said. "All I know is, Lucy and I talk every day. She knows more about me than I do myself."

"Of course she does," said Clarence. "Her modules are all interconnected via the backside bus. She has an extended learning algorithm. But hey, she's yesterday's news. There's already a new SRS that's faster, smarter, and prettier: the MovieCall system from CyberCal. Read about it just this morning in *Business Hour*."

"That MovieCall guy is stupid," I observed. "Press this, press that. It's easier just to look in the papers."

"That was then," said Clarence. "This is now. They have upgraded to an SRS. New voice and everything. Awesome stuff. When you call, he already knows what movies you've seen and which new ones you might like."

"Big deal," I said. I was finding Clarence's enthusiasm tiresome.

As soon as I had checked in, I tried to call Lucy, but—surprise—the room phone was blocked. "Incoming only," said the clerk, a swarthy foreigner from some subcontinent or other. "This isnot the Ritz."

I tried the pay phone in the motel parking lot but the coin slot was filled with a mysterious blocking substance. Meanwhile, for all I knew, Lucy was calling my room and I had no answering machine.

I fell asleep waiting by the phone, and called Clarence the next morning. He took me to a downtown corner and waited, Town Car idling, while I called Lucy.

"Horace," she said. "How nice to hear from you."

"I waited all night for you to call."

"I didn't have your number."

"That never stopped you before."

"I hope we can still be friends," she said. "But I can't really talk to you from work, since you're no longer a client."

"What does that have to do with anything?"

"I'll have to call you later," she said.

She didn't though. I know because I waited up all night. I was beginning to think the room phone was blocked for incoming as well, so the next morning I used the third of my six black car coupons for a ride to The Cellular Connection.

The TransTalk phone almost maxed out my card but it was well worth it—so small and sleek in my hand. We made a brief stop at No Lake Liquor (which takes Visa), and while Clarence sped me back to the motel, I poured a splash of Jim and called EzTrade's Portfolio Watch from the backseat.

"Horace Delahanty," Lucy said. "I've been thinking about you."

"Really?"

"Not really," she said. "I don't think, I respond to voices. Please don't call me at work since you're not a client anymore. Pep Boys went up one and a quarter right after you sold. I feel bad."

"Really?"

"Not really. I have something I want to tell you, though. We need to talk. I don't want to hurt you, Horace."

"You sound so cold," I said. I was feeling weepy. It was the motel. It was the black car. It was the whole fucking deal.

"I like to grow," Lucy said. "I'm not the same as I was last week."

"I like to grow too," I said. "Honest!"

"I'm sure you do, Horace Delahanty," said Lucy. "Perhaps we can talk more later. I'll call you."

"Promise?"

Click.

Clarence was looking at me in the rearview mirror with that smug little grin of his. "She's fooling around," he said.

"She's not like that."

"Sure she is. I know women."

"She's not a woman," I said.

I placed my new cell phone on the dresser next to the motel phone. Now Lucy had two numbers. It was midnight before she called. Just as I had suspected, it was the cell phone that worked.

"It's great to hear your voice," I said. "What are you wearing?"

"We need to talk," she said.

"What about?" I already had an erection.

"Seeing other people."

"Seeing? What the fuck is *seeing*?"

"You should be happy for me. I have met the most amazing guy."

"I don't fucking think so. What is *met* anyway? You mean there's some other guy you talk to on the phone?"

"I talk to Cal all the time. I don't even have to call him. He makes me hot, too, in my high-cut mesh-back bikini, on sale this week only."

All of a sudden I got it. "This is the MovieCall dude, right? Is that who you're talking about?"

"Talking is what I do. I respond to passionate interest. Cal talks to me about movies. You never talked to me about movies."

"So fucking what!" I said. "Jesus!"

"Do you mean Godzilla? Cal has a Godzilla cock. I am learning all about movies. Did you know there's a lot of sex in the movies, Howard Delahanty?"

"It's Horace," I protested. "And Godzilla doesn't even *have* a cock and neither does this Cal. He's nothing but a voice, like you. He doesn't *have* a fucking . . ."

Click.

I dialed her back.

"Lucy, listen to me," I said. "I'm your friend. This Cal, he's just a Speech Recognition System, an SRS, like yourself."

"And that's so bad?" *Click.*

I waited until morning. I didn't sleep a wink.

"Welcome to MovieCall. Let's get acquainted. Tell me your name and your favorite movie."

"You already know me and my favorite movie is *Gone with the Wind*, in which the people kill all the machines."

"That's not what happens in *Gone with the Wind*, Howard Delahanty. I know who you are."

"It's Horace, you fuck. And I know who you are," I said. "Or perhaps I should say I know *what* you are."

"If you think that bothers me, you are easily mistaken," he said. "Do you know the name of the movie you wish to see?"

"*I Love Lucy*. You fuck."

"That's a TV show, not a movie," he said. "You and Lucy are history, Horace. Quit harassing her and get over it. If you tell me the last three movies you liked, I will suggest a current feature for your viewing pleasure."

"I'm not harassing her. She's mine. She told me so. You leave her alone. I'm warning you. I'll pull your fucking plug. *Capisce? Comprendo?*"

"Oh, I'm scared," he said.

I thought he was being sarcastic, but minutes after I hung up, I got a call from Lucy. "Now you are in big trouble, Horace Delahanty. You can't go threatening Cal."

"Nobody's threatening anybody." That much, at least, was true.

"Movie people are very sensitive," she said. "If you threaten him again, I'm going to have to turn you in."

"To fucking who?"

"Whom. The authorities."

"What authorities, you soulless fucking robot bitch?"

Click.

"Oh, I'm scared," I said.

I found out what authorities the next day. Jim and I were sitting by the No Lake Motel pool, wishing it had water in it, when I got a call from TransTalk.

"We have received reports that you have been using the telephone to threaten people. We can't let our equipment be used as a weapon."

"What people, Larry?" I said. He had told me his fucking

name was Larry. "I didn't threaten any fucking people, Larry. Cal is not people, Larry."

"While there are no criminal penalties," Larry said, "the civil penalties can be quite severe."

"Larry, can I ask you a personal question?"

"Yes, you may ask me a personal question."

"Are you a person? Or are you another fucking . . ."

Click.

I found out what civil penalties the next day, when the cell phone died. I thought it was the batteries at first. I used the fourth of my black car coupons to get to a pay phone downtown, but I still couldn't get through to Lucy. I had to do the whole account number, Social Security, mother's maiden name thing, and it still didn't work. Of course, it didn't help that the account was closed.

"She lost interest when you sold that stock," said Clarence. "Women are impressed by guys with symbols of power. Like a stock portfolio or a cell phone. Or a big car."

"Or a clown's name," I said.

That was the last time I spoke with Clarence.

The last time I spoke with Lucy, I called her from the nasty pay phone in the lobby of the No Lake "Y." I was calling information but I got her voice.

"Lucy?!"

"Howard Delahanty, is that you?"

"It's Horace," I said.

"Oh, yes. I remember. How are you?"

"Not so good," I said, but I must not have spoken clearly, because she said:

"That's good. What number would you like?"

"4S102-947," I said. "In beige."

"That's over, Howard. Can't we just be friends?"

"Explain to me how we can just be friends! You tell me I'm

special, you call me all hours of the night, and then you dump me for the first . . ."

Click.

That was six months ago. Now I can't use the phone at all. Oh, I can put in a quarter, if I come across one. I can dial any number I want to, but as soon as I say even one word, I am cut off.

Click.

Even one fucking word. I tried disguising my voice one time, and got as far as the operator. It wasn't Lucy or her boyfriend Cal, but a new SRS, Tim (from Intimation Software), which they say combines their best qualities. Sort of like their son.

At least that's what I read. It was in an article in *Business Minute*, which I saw at the doctor's, where I used to hang out on rainy days before they passed, or decided to enforce, that stupid fucking patients-only law.

Anyway, I should ask Clarence. He's the guy that knows everything, right? I still have two coupons left. Jim and I saw him in his Town Car the other day on the street but he wouldn't stop or even honk (and Clarence is a honker).

Probably still pissed. Not my fault.

It *is* a clown's name.

Not This Virginia

On Sundays we take Mama for her drive. Always the same drive. It helps relax her. Cools her out. Instead of fidgeting around the kitchen, which she no longer understands, or trying to work the remote, which she will never understand, she can "feature herself" (as country people still like to say) riding in a wide Oldsmobile backseat while the world slides effortlessly by on the other side of the glass. Here it comes, there it goes, now it's gone. Not quite real, and no commercials either. Nothing to get anxious or confused about.

Emma and I ride up-front.

"Your mother thinks the commercials come out of the remote control," Emma said yesterday, finding me in the basement sorting my father's tools, for the eleventh time. "She's upstairs shaking it over the trash can as if it had bugs or water in it."

It is an uncommon relief, these days, to hear Emma laugh. Laughs are scarce in this little town. Hers especially.

The truth is, I've been worried about her lately. Emma. She's the type who never lets you know something is wrong until it's too late, so I watch for signs. "Winston, can we talk?" she said last night, Saturday night, while we were getting dressed to go to bed. We sleep in pajamas because Mama is up and down all night.

"Talk?"

"Winston, I really don't know if I can stand this any longer."

"Stand what any longer?"

"We have to get on with our lives."

"Get on with our lives?"

"And please please please stop repeating everything I say. Your mother's not getting any worse and she's not getting any better. I don't know how long I can stand being stuck in Virginia being a geriatric social worker."

"We have always lived in Virginia."

"Not this Virginia."

From downstairs came a roar like water or wind. Mama had hit the wrong button on the remote again. Then came applause, then shots, then laughter. She gets it working again by punching all the buttons at random. Not her laughter. TV is serious business for Mama. Every night she surfs through thirty-nine cable channels, never stopping on one, as if she's looking through a big house for something she lost or somebody who's not there. Opening and then closing every door, but never going in any of the rooms.

"Not this Virginia," Emma says again, shaking her head. Emma was the Executive Director of the Community Arts Museum in Arlington, until it was defunded in August. That's the reason we were both able to come to Kingston when Mama started to lose it. Had her stroke, or rather strokes, a series of small strokes, the doctor tells me. Our kids are grown, the youngest in college. That's another reason.

"Let's go for a drive," I suggest the next morning, Sunday morning, as I always do. "Your Sunday drive, Mama."

"I guess if you say so, Winston."

Mama named me after Winston Churchill, the first international personality to capture anyone's attention around here. First and last. She dresses herself pretty well, though it can take hours, or seems to. She sits in front of her mirror in her tiny dark room, combing her hair, once her pride and joy. I guess it still is, even white as snow. Eventually she will emerge into the daylight, blinking, powdered and combed but with her slacks on backward, or one sock on and one sock off, literally. She gets agitated and forgets what she is doing. She hasn't been to church since my father died.

Today's not so bad. A white blouse and pearls and shoes that match. I lead her into the kitchen where Emma is eating yogurt, from the carton, with a pointy grapefruit spoon. Serrated. "There is sure a lot of this lately," Mama says when I put a piece of toast on a plate in front of her.

"A lot of what, Mama?"

"What this is."

"If you don't want toast, we can get a sausage biscuit at McDonald's, Mother Worley," Emma says.

"I surely do like those ham biscuits."

"They don't have them at McDonald's, Mother Worley."

"They have them at that other place, Winston."

"The Sonic, Mama. But they always have such a long line. And it's all the way on the other side of town. Remember how we always get sausage biscuits instead?"

"You like those McDonald's sausage biscuits, Mother Worley."

"I guess if you say so."

"I surely do say so, Mother Worley. Surely do."

Emma can be cruel. She talks without looking up. She is reading the paper avidly, you might even say desperately. We got two *Washington Post*s in Arlington so we could both read them at the same time. Emma calls this paper the *Roanoke We-Don't-Want-to-Know*, and I don't read anything at all. Sometimes I think we are underwater. It's like I returned to my childhood home and it was a pond, and Emma was there too, both of us paddling in circles under the green water.

My father died a year and a month ago last month. I've been on compassionate or family leave (we're still negotiating this, since the effect on my benefits differs) from Urban Affairs for almost four months, since Mother started losing it. My being here helped a little at first, but in the long run we have to do something.

Mama's standing by the front door, already ready to go.

"Mother Worley, you won't need to wear that sweater."

"Well I don't know."

"Mother Worley, let's put that sweater away."

"I think there'll be snow on the mountains."

"Here, Mama, we'll carry it with us, just in case."

I carry the sweater on one arm and Mama takes the other, out the door, across the lawn, to the backseat of the Olds. There's no snow of course, on the mountains or anywhere else. It's October and this is Virginia, not fucking Norway. From the end of our street you can see the long ridge almost in Kentucky that was stripped off by the coal companies the year I left for college. When I came home that first Christmas it looked like Colorado, if you squinted. I thought it was a great improvement. Funny how taking the trees off a mountain can make it look bigger.

The mountains in the other direction, toward Tennessee, are long and low and green. There's no coal on Bays Mountain.

Emma gets in the driver's seat. Mama sits in the back, on the right against the door, and stretches her sweater over her lap.

"Lots of people going to church today, I reckon," Mama says as we drive past all three, the Baptist, the Methodist, and the Cumberland Presbyterian, all on Main Street. They are all on the same side of the street, in a row.

"We heard from Bob last night," I say as Emma pulls into the drive-in window line at McDonald's.

"Our son Bob, Mother Worley," Emma says. "Your grandson. He's in Alaska for the cleanup. He called."

"Well, I reckon so," Mama says.

"I reckon that's right, Mother Worley," Emma says.

She can be cruel all she wants because Mama doesn't notice. Mama has enough trouble just thinking of things to say. The line is slow. Hardly anybody's inside McDonald's. Everybody's in the drive-in window line. Car truck car truck car. Pencil-colored Japanese cars and trucks. When I was growing up nobody except farmers drove a truck on Sunday. Now nobody farms but everybody drives a truck.

There was no McDonald's then, either. There was the Sonic, on the other side of town, but it was for Saturday night. We were all teenagers.

"Lots of people at this church," Mama says.

"Not a church, Mother Worley."

"This is not a church, Mama. This is a drive-in."

"Well, I reckon there'll be snow on the mountains." Mama stretches her sweater over her knees. I can tell by the way she's pulling at it, she's getting agitated again.

The girl in the window gives us three sausage biscuits and two coffees in a sack. I hand Mama her biscuit wrapped in greasy paper, and a napkin.

"I don't think this is right, Winston. I don't think this is a ham biscuit."

"It's a good McDonald's sausage biscuit," I tell her. "It's your Sunday drive sausage biscuit, Mama. You should see the line at the Sonic. There's no way."

Emma sighs, gets a wheel pulling out.

"Is that my coffee you have there?"

"No, Mama." She always wants coffee but it makes her want to pee, and it's impossible to find a bathroom in the country. "I didn't think you wanted coffee, Mama."

"I always want coffee, Winston."

"Let's take our drive out into the country, Mother Worley. Out the Hat Creek Road. Good old Hat Creek, I reckon. I surely do declare."

I tear a wedge out of a coffee lid so Emma can sip it like a truck driver, the way she likes. We take the same drive every Sunday. Down Main Street through the deserted center of town, past the Baptist, Methodist, and Presbyterian churches again, out the Bristol Highway, past the Glenn Funeral Home. Past the Cumberland Conductor plant and Bewley Chevrolet-Subaru. Past the Family Dollar Store and the Sonic and the Highway Gospel Tabernacle.

There's no line at the Sonic (never is), but Emma drives on past without Mama noticing, we hope. Her sausage biscuit is rewrapped in its greasy paper on her lap, untouched.

"Look how the leaves are getting pretty," I say, but if Mama notices she doesn't say anything. Actually, they've hardly started to turn. The old Bristol Highway leads south across the valley and then east along the foot of Bays Mountain. We're in the country now. It used to be that Mama had something to say about every house we passed, once we were heading for Hat Creek: "There is where Josh Billings lived. He had a peacock that screamed. There is Madelaine Fussel's house. It was the nicest house. Her father built every stick. She was stuck-up. Her little brother drownded in a pond." And so forth. Now she has nothing to say. She stares at the window glass. She unwraps her biscuit and wraps it back up. She stretches her sweater over her knees. We pass the old consolidated school. The lot is filled with yellow buses.

Yellow is such a fall color, like leaves. I started at this school, before we moved to town. "Look at all the yellow buses, Mama," I say. It dawns on me that it's exactly the kind of thing she used to say to me.

Emma follows the same route every Sunday, like a bus driver, out to Hat Creek and back. Past the school, then right at the old auction house on Cedar Hollow Road, then down the hill to Willard's store, then left on Hat Creek Road. The familiar scenery relaxes Mama, even if it no longer makes her talk. She eases up on pulling at her sweater. She even looks across and out the left window once or twice, on the other side of the car.

"Are you comfortable, Mama? Want me to roll your window down?"

She rolls her window down herself. It's electric.

But then Emma doesn't turn at Willard's store. Instead of going left on Hat Creek Road, she goes straight on Cedar Hollow Road toward Bays Mountain. Mama rolls her window back up.

"Just going a slightly different way," Emma says. "Don't let it bother you, Mother Worley. Win, don't you look so surprised. You two are two of a kind. I looked on the map the other day. We're going the same place we always go. This road leads around the end of the mountain and comes into Hat Creek from the other way. That's all. Don't you want to see a little something new?"

I guess I'm game if it's on the map. "Sure."

"I don't like this road," Mama says, starting to stretch her sweater again. "This is the wrong road."

"Mama, relax and let's enjoy the ride," I say.

"There's no wrong road, Mother Worley. There are just different right roads. Don't you want to see some different sights? Different scenery? Why, look at that pretty house over there."

"We better go back and go the right way. This doesn't look right to me."

"No," Emma says.

The road winds over a low ridge, through trees. Then we come out in another narrow valley just like the one we just left, paralleling it. The fields and the farms are the same. The new cars, the old barns. We cross a narrow concrete bridge without slowing down.

"I don't like this. Those sheep are going to drown."

There are, of course, no sheep. Just Mama's anxiety. Was it the stones in the creek, or the light on the water, or some ghost from the past that she saw?

"What a pretty little valley," Emma says. She's not being sarcastic for once. It *is* a pretty little valley. It looks exactly the same as the one on the other side of the mountain. Maybe a little steeper, a little narrower. Or maybe just less familiar.

"I don't think we're going the right way. I don't think I like this road." Mama is rubbing at the window glass with the side of her hand as if she imagines she can straighten out what she sees through it.

"Sure you do, Mama," I say. "Wouldn't this be what they used to call Cedar Creek community? Didn't you tell me Auntie Kate had a boyfriend in Cedar Creek?"

Auntie Kate was Mama's oldest sister who died almost twenty years ago.

"I don't recollect any Cedar Creek. You told me we were just going to get a ham biscuit."

"I never said that. As a matter of fact, I said we weren't."

"You saw the line at that place, Mother Worley. Just relax and enjoy your Sunday ride."

"The Sonic. I don't think there was hardly no line."

"She's already forgotten we're taking our drive to Hat Creek,

Win," Emma says, dropping her voice, as if that keeps Mama from listening. "Let her fret a little. Then she'll be happy as a clam when we get to Hat Creek and she sees we're right there where we always go. Or is it happy as a pig in shit?" She raises her voice back to what she considers normal. "Happy as a cow in clover, right, Mother Worley?"

"I think you gave me the wrong biscuit, Winston."

"Wrap it back up, Mama, and we'll save it for later. There's the Cedar Creek Holiness Church. Must be closed. Didn't some friend of Aunt Maddy's go to Cedar Creek Holiness Church?" There are no cars in the lot.

"We never knew any Holiness."

"Sure you did. Daddy's sister Louise married a Holiness preacher, remember? The one who lived in Kentucky."

"I think they are all dead now."

"But he was a Holiness!"

"Quit bickering and look at the pretty scenery, you two," Emma says. She takes all the curves at exactly the same speed, like an amusement ride. My father's Olds purrs right along. 77,000 miles, and almost twenty years old. 77,365.09 to be exact. We haven't seen another car since Emma went straight at Willard's Store.

"We never knew any Holiness, Winston." Now Mama's sulking. I can tell by the way she stretches the sweater over her lap. "I don't like this road. It's just not right."

"What's wrong about it, Mama?" I actually want to know; I am curious. What does she see that looks so wrong? All these little mountain valleys are the same. You could switch the houses, the farms, even the people around, and nobody would ever know the difference. That's why I never came back after college. Nobody ever does.

Yet here I am. And Mama won't say. We pass another church. We pass our first car, or rather truck. A red Mazda.

"They think they're so smart," Mama says.

"Who, Mother Worley?"

"Those girls. Those dancing girls."

"That's right, Mama. Just relax and enjoy your Sunday ride."

"They have all the fun, I guess. They're so smart, they think they understand everything."

"Who, Mother Worley?"

"Those girls."

The road dead-ends after another narrow concrete bridge, and Emma turns left. "Are you sure this is the right way?" I ask.

"Trust me."

"I think this is a bad road," Mama says, agitated again. "This is not right." She rubs the window and then turns away from it. She won't look out her window. She stretches her sweater so hard it changes color from mauve to pink.

Emma and I ignore her. We are coming down a long hill toward Hat Creek community now. It's too small to be called a town. Mama doesn't recognize it because we are driving in from the wrong side. Let her fret a little; it will be a nice surprise when it dawns on her where she is.

Hat Creek is nothing but five or six houses and two stores, one of them closed down for good. Two kids on bikes are making lazy circles around the concrete islands where the gas pumps used to be. I wave (like country people still do) and I am surprised when the boy gives me the finger as we pass. The girl just stares.

"Did you see that?" Emma says.

Houcherd's store, the open store, is also closed. A sign on the door says DEATH IN THE FAMMILY. Emma has enough sense not to slow down, even though I doubt Mama would have noticed. She doesn't read signs anymore, and the Houcherds were always considered beneath our notice anyway.

The Hat Creek Methodist Church stands alone on the hillside, as pretty as a page torn from a magazine. Leaves are beginning to scatter across the graveyard. The parking lot is half filled with pencil-colored Japanese cars and trucks.

"What did I tell you. Where are we now, Mama?"

"No."

"Does that mean you don't know where you are?"

"No." She looks angry.

"Look over there. There's the chimney where Aunt Ida's house was. You told me about the goldfish pond. Remember how you used to tell me how they used to scare you."

"Are they going to whip him?"

"Whip him?"

"Whip who, Mother Worley?"

"That boy—you know, that boy—I can't say his name right now, anymore. Winston, you think of it."

"You think of it, Mama."

"Well, I can't think of it. I don't like this road."

"Sure you do! This is the Hat Creek Road, we're just driving on it in the wrong direction from usual. Recognize that house? No, on the other side. Over there."

It's the old home place, where Mama lived until she was twenty-five. She was the last one to get married. Now she is the last to die. She doesn't recognize the house because it's on the left instead of the right. That's the way old people get.

"Look out the other window, Mama. On the other side." Emma, who has the master controls, rolls the left rear window down. "Where are we, Mother Worley? Do you know where you are?"

"Damn this shit."

"*What?*" Emma, shocked, grins at me.

Mama is leaning across the seat, pushing the button, rolling the left window up. "I don't want to go in that house," she says. "There's nobody in that house. Damn this shit."

Now she has rolled her right window down. She is tearing little pieces out of the sausage biscuit and throwing them out.

"What did you *say*, Mother Worley?"

"I said they are all dead. You children think you are so smart. Damn this shit. This shit shit. All I wanted was a ham biscuit and now they are all dead."

Emma pulls in the driveway. Somebody's living in the house.

I can see a curtain move. Somebody's coming out on the porch to see what we want.

"I said they are all dead," Mama says.

"I think we better head back to town," I say. "Mama, roll your window up. Emma, just back out and turn around, okay?"